He's not going to make it, I thought.

The T-28 was now headed straight for the ground at much too high an airspeed to pull it through. There simply wasn't enough room to pull out before hitting the ground. The aircraft entered a high-speed stall. With its nose slightly above level, it contacted the ground tail-first. The dragging tail threw up a huge spume of dust, then the prop started hitting the dirt as the nose pitched down. The plane thumped into the ground, bounced twenty feet into the air, rolling partially on its side as it fell back. With ripping and crashing noises it cartwheeled off the runway. A wing tore off under the stress and flew crazily into the air as the fuselage flopped over on its back, crushing the canopies.

Khadija held her hands to her face. Nils was sprinting toward the cloud of dust and dirt that had been thrown into the air by the crashing plane. He knelt on the ground beside the wreckage and looked at me and shook his head.

The fun was over.

Also by Berent Sandberg in Sphere Books:

BRASS DIAMONDS

The Honeycomb Bid

BERENT SANDBERG

SPHERE BOOKS LIMITED
London and Sydney

First published in Great Britain by
Sphere Books Ltd 1984
30–32 Gray's Inn Road, London WC1X 8JL
Copyright © 1981 by Peter Lars Sandberg and Berent &
Woods, Inc.
First published in the United States of America by Signet,
part of The New American Library, Inc., 1981

Publisher's Note

This novel is a work of fiction. Names,
characters, places, and incidents are either the
product of the author's imagination or are used
fictitiously, and any resemblance to actual
persons, living or dead, events, or locales is
entirely coincidental.

TRADE
MARK

Set in 9/11pt Compugraphic Cheltenham

Printed and bound in Great Britain by
Cox & Wyman Ltd, Reading

To the Good Guys who never came back,
And the Flag for which they died.

Chapter One

I knew something had gone wrong as the minutes ticked past midnight and Campbell didn't show up. It was mid-July and oppressively humid in the seaport of Piraeus, Greece. I stood waiting by the old Manis wharf, gazing idly up at the moon-splashed hulk of a dead Greek freighter. Her name, *Lygarius*, was still legible across her rusting bow. She had been designed as a bulk carrier, maybe three hundred feet long, with two sets of kingposts forward and a five-deck superstructure aft.

Campbell hadn't mentioned the freighter. Only the pier.

I activated my watch, shielding it with one hand. The green digits glowed brightly in the dark, 12:21. In all the years I have known him, my father-in-law has never been late. Like the trains in the days of his youth, he runs on time and is proud of his punctuality. The message he had sent to my hotel room earlier this evening had been typically brief:

> **Matt. Welcome to Greece. Rendezvous Manis wharf midnight sharp.**
>
> **Campbell**

There had been no explanation, but then Campbell has worked for the CIA most of his life and, aside from the usual reports, has a powerful aversion to writing things down.

Worried, I decided to check the wharf itself.

According to the manager of my hotel, a seamen's strike had been going on in Piraeus for the last couple of months. I hoped I was wrong, but it made sense that a sailor short on cash could have come across Campbell out here and jumped him for his.

I had just started to pick my way gingerly along the decaying planks when I caught the flare of a match from the wheelhouse high

1

on the freighter's superstructure. Instinctively, I slipped into a rib of shadow cast by the rusty hull. Seconds later, a man came out of the wheelhouse to stand at the rail of the flying bridge.

Not Campbell.

Somebody else.

I cupped my hands around my eyes, omitting peripheral objects, centering him in my line of sight. He had long hair, bib overalls with no shirt, a pair of glasses that reflected oddly in the light of the moon. As I watched him smoke a cigarette, I began to think there was something vaguely and disturbingly familiar about him, as if we had met in bad circumstances in the not so distant past, Laos, maybe, or Cambodia, or Vietnam.

He worked for the other side, I thought. Maybe we didn't meet. Maybe I just remember his picture from the DIA files. But I remember him.

When he finally went back into the wheelhouse, I took a slow deep breath. The air around this remote corner of the seaport smelled like the rivers in Thailand: of diesel fumes and excrement and rotting fish.

I picked my way farther along the wharf, past abandoned spools of cable and piles of decaying cargo net, until I was amidships of the freighter.

'Campbell?' I said softly. There was no reply.

I peered up again at the flaring rust-orange hull of the *Lygarius*. She lay ominously silent, rising out of the harbor scum as if forever emptied of all life; but I knew at least one man was up there, and I had the growing and uneasy feeling my father-in-law might be up there too.

There was no gangplank, no obvious way on board except for a springline of three-inch hawser that diagonaled down from the bow to a large cleat on the pier. Tentatively, I took hold of the hawser. It was black with tar, chafed, and slimy to touch.

Be smart, Eberhart, I told myself. You're a retired fighter pilot, not Errol Flynn. Go get the Greek harbor police. Let them check it out.

Then, as I was turning away, I heard a muffled scream from somewhere aft on the freighter. It was a familiar type of scream to me, as if slivers of bamboo were being driven under a man's nails. I snatched for the hawser again and began to go up.

2

I went up hand-over-hand toward a rat shield high on the line. I weighed 190 pounds and the line sagged under me as I went. There were times I thought the lower end would pull free, cleat and all, from the cheesy wood of the pier. The heels of my hands quickly cramped into spasms. When I tried to ease the stress by using my feet against the hull, the hull reverberated as noisily as a hollow steel drum.

'*Christ*,' I grunted. If I was going to get caught, I didn't want it to happen here.

I had reached the rat shield, twenty vertical feet above the pier. The shield was made of galvanized metal and showed no rust. It was conical in shape, about the size of a large megaphone, with the wide end of the cone facing the ship to keep rats on the ship from reaching the pier.

I hung from one hand, tried to reach around the shield with the other, but the flange was too wide, so I began pushing the shield in front of me, shoving it along the hawser, first with one hand and then the other. I was breathing hard, dungarees and jersey sweat-soaked.

When the collar of the shield finally jammed on a splice, I was close enough to the deck to go for a rail stanchion. I went quickly, using what was left of my strength, swinging out and letting go of the line, snatching for the pipe, feeling it wobble in its socket and bend back toward me as I pulled myself up and onto the moon-bright deck.

I moved quickly then, keeping to a half-crouch, dodging and weaving around obstacles and debris, hatch coamings and mooring bitts and a piece of dunnage the size of a short bat which I picked up as I went by; heading aft past the kingposts and cargo hatches, following the steam exit pipes toward the superstructure where I had seen the man in overalls and from where I had heard the scream and where I heard it again now, sudden and louder and more terrible than before.

Campbell.

The two scars on my back were aflame, the blood pumping in my neck. I darted through the door to the ship's mess, where there was a stench of garbage, and a shuffled patter of rats, and circles of moon-light on the floor; finding a companionway to the second deck and

3

then one to the third, never realizing the girl was behind me until one deck below the wheelhouse the screaming stopped suddenly, and I stopped too, and heard on the metal stair below me the quick tread of her boot.

I ducked and wheeled, ready to use the chunk of wood I had picked up on my way in.

'*Don't try it,*' she said.

She had a sharp, thin face, like the blade of a trowel. Her hair was straight, and dark; the tips of her ears showed through. Everything she wore was black: pants, boots, and jersey. The jersey was damp with sweat, as if she had had to run to catch up with me. Through it her breasts showed high and pointed like the gun she was holding in her left hand. It was a chopped .45 caliber automatic. She held it cocked, with the muzzle aimed steadily and precisely at my heart.

'Mess with me one time, baby,' she said, 'and you're dead as a hammer.'

Chapter Two

For half a second, I thought I could take her. I was crouched, well balanced, my left foot solidly supporting my weight, the other ready to push off from the riser of the next step. I held the chunk of wood low in my right hand, arm cocked in the backswing of a bowler. The girl was close to me, closer than she needed to be, and I think if I had made my move in that instant, if I had flipped the wood up under her gun and gone in low, I could have taken her.

But too many years had passed since I had been tuned up for this kind of thing, too many years since I had been in the combat mode in Vietnam with all my senses honed under fire toward the mission and survival. There, lives had been measured in seconds and a man's actions and reactions to danger became, of necessity, more instinctive than logical.

Here, I had hesitated, just long enough to figure the move I was going to make, and she had seen my wheels turning, had backed down another step, and the moment was lost.

'That,' she said, pointing her gun at the chunk of dunnage I held. 'Put it down.'

Her voice was raspy and low, accent American with traces of Southcentral and Midwest, as if she might have grown up in Arkansas and gone to school in Chicago. Her style was commanding. I had no idea if she had ever shot anyone, nor any doubt she was prepared to. I put down the club.

'Turn around,' she said. 'Go up the stairs, one at a time.'

At the top of the companionway, a narrow passage ran the width of the top deck. The overhead was low, less than six feet. I had to duck forward as we went in. The air in the companionways had been stuffy, but here it was worse: sultry, and sweet with the odor of vomit. I swallowed, held my breath. Behind me I could hear the crunching sound of flaked paint under the girl's light tread.

5

As we went, I tried to commit the details of the passage to memory: how long it was, how at its far end there appeared to be another companionway like the one we had just come up, how the moonlight was bright where it came through the portholes but dimmed toward the center of the passage, how there was nothing I could see on the walls or floor that might serve as a weapon.

I tried not to think about Campbell: whether he was in fact on this derelict ship; whether he was alive or dead. It seemed a long time since I had last heard the sound of the screams that had brought me here.

Midway down the passage, at its most shadowy point, the girl told me to stop. She rapped twice on a steel door, then twice again. A male voice asked her to identify herself. 'Dixie,' she said, and we went in.

We went through the chartroom, into the wheelhouse. She stayed close behind me: I could feel the hard muzzle of her gun against the small of my back.

The wheelhouse was a spacious, rectangular room running the width of the ship's superstructure. At either end, a door led out to a flying bridge. The room was softly lighted by two kerosene lanterns that hung from the ceiling. Except for the starboard side, which faced away from the port of Piraeus, all the windows had been covered by blankets.

The man I had first seen smoking the cigarette on the flying bridge stood now by the ship's telegraph, staring at me as I came in. He wore bib overalls, stained around the cuffs and crotch, no shirt, a pair of tan leather work shoes, ankle-high. He was big, at least my height and maybe twenty pounds heavier, but seemed to have no articulated muscle. His pale flesh looked as if it rose in one soft deep layer from the bone. He had wire-rimmed glasses with small round lenses that greatly magnified his eyes. His hair was orangy in color, straight and stringy, and damp where it touched his shoulders.

There were other people in the room – three men playing cards at a round table to my left, and a regal-looking black woman in a leotard, sharpening the blade of a machete with a small Carborundum, to my right.

But it was the man in the bib overalls who dominated the scene. When he spoke, his voice was sharp and strong.

'Where the hell did you come from?' he said.

There are usually two ways to go in a situation like this. One is to be humble, and the other is not. This guy struck me as the sort who might dine on humility.

'Wolf Point, Montana,' I said. 'I spent a happy childhood there, probably before you were born.'

He nodded once, and I felt a stunning blow to my left kidney and a bright flash of pain. I arched back and almost went down. When I tried to breathe it was like trying to breathe with half a lung. I grunted and gasped. The man with the overalls came to me and began going through my pockets. Up close, he smelled like old fat in a can by a stove.

He spun me around. As he did, I caught a glimpse of the trowel-faced girl. She held the gun by its muzzle, had hit me with the butt. The men playing cards hadn't skipped a beat. Somewhere behind me I could hear the gritty scrape of the Carborundum against the machete, and somewhere a long way behind that the sound of a ship's horn in the harbor.

'There's a thousand-drachma note in a money pocket at the front of my belt,' I grunted. 'That's all I'm carrying. My passport and wallet are in the safe at my hotel.'

'Which hotel?'

'The Makeiros.'

'When we come on board this tub we bring the gangplank with us. How did you get from the wharf to the deck?'

'I went hand-over-hand up one of the mooring lines.'

'No shit?'

'No shit,' I said.

'Are you CIA?'

I shook my head.

'No,' I said. 'I'm retired Air Force.'

He seemed interested in that.

'Combat?' he said.

'Some,' I said.

'When did you get out?'

''74.'

'Did the war mess up your head?'

'You could say that. I stayed drunk for a year after I got out.'

He smiled. I saw no reason not to tell him the truth, and I thought

7

for as long as I did tell him the truth I might be able to stay alive. He paused for a moment, as if he was thinking, trying to remember something that had gotten vague.

'I was in Nam in '68,' he said finally.

'I know,' I said. 'Your name's Art Farmer. You were on Radio Hanoi during Tet.'

Now he did look pleased. His mouth opened like a small pocket under his nose.

'You heard me do that?' he said.

'No, but I heard about you. A couple of years later, I was tapped to be air attaché in Phnom Penh. When they briefed me for the job, they showed me photographs and vita sheets on the important militants. Jane Fonda was one. You were another.'

'No shit?' he said.

'No shit,' I said.

I knew we were going to get around to why I was here, and I knew he wasn't going to be happy when I told him I didn't know. 'Welcome to Greece,' Campbell's message had said. 'Rendezvous Manis wharf midnight sharp.' No explanation for that. I had been visiting my son at the clinic in Switzerland when my father-in-law had summoned me to Greece. He had said there was a job he wanted me to do. No explanation of that either.

Farmer walked back to the ship's telegraph and began moving the handle of the annunciator slowly fore and aft, from full ahead to full astern, as if he were trying to decide the direction our relationship was going to take. The brass handle was pitted with corrosion, and grimy like the fingers of his hand.

'What did you do after you got drunk?' he said. 'After you got out.'

'I worked as a mercenary for a while.'

'Like doing what?'

'I could tell you,' I said, 'but you wouldn't learn anything from it. If the wrong people found out I'd told you, I could lose my chance for doing that kind of work again.'

He smiled.

'Try me,' he said.

I looked at him, judging the consequence.

'All right,' I said. 'I took a team into Cambodia after the country fell to the Khmer Rouge. We grabbed a pouch of diamonds out of an abandoned hotel by Kampong Som.'

'Sihanouk's place?'

'That's the one.'

'Who paid you to do that?'

'There might be a way you could force me to tell you,' I said. 'But you'd have to work at it.'

He laughed. The men at the table had stopped playing cards and were listening to us. They were quiet men in their early thirties. One looked like an Arab, the other two might have been Greek. I couldn't tell if they understood what Farmer and I were saying, but one way or another we had attracted their interest. Maybe Farmer didn't usually talk to people for as long as he had been talking to me. I could sense his curiosity as if it were something tangible that moved under his pale flesh and behind the thumb-stained lenses of his glasses.

'What did you do with the money you made?' he said.

'I bought a beat-up farm in Virginia.'

'You married?'

'I was.'

'Got kids?'

'Your questions are getting personal,' I said. I pressed my hand against my left kidney where the trowel-faced girl had whacked me with the gun. She smiled. 'I should have taken you when I had the chance, Dixie,' I said. 'Next time, I will.'

Farmer laughed.

'You've got yourself a set of balls,' he said.

'Not really,' I said. 'In combat on a scale of one to ten I might come in around seven.'

'Tonight,' he said, 'you're going to come in dead.'

I felt the scars on my back begin to pulse again, the way they do whenever somebody gets my beak up.

'People who kill people usually don't talk about it,' I said. 'They just do it.'

'Oh, we'll do it all right,' Farmer said. 'We're going to take a little walk first. I've got somebody downstairs I want you to meet.'

9

Chapter Three

He told me to follow him. Dixie backed him up with her automatic, looking as if she hoped I'd make some kind of move. As we left, the three cardplayers went back to their game, and the black woman went on improving the edge of her machete.

I thought I had sensed among those four an aura of lassitude. They seemed to have been waiting too long for something to happen. Their interest in me, which had risen briefly during my exchange with Farmer, had already faded. Not one of them bothered to watch as the three of us went out the door.

We went to the next deck below, using the companion-way opposite the one Dixie and I had come up. Through the portholes on this side of the freighter, I could see the flat, moon-bright water of the harbor, and the distant lights of the waterfront cafés I had passed on my walk from the hotel. It had been a long walk, three, maybe four miles, the last mile taking me into an area of abandoned warehouses and wharves, making me wonder finally whether the people I had asked directions of had understood what I had said, and whether Campbell had gotten the name of the wharf right – though I never really doubted that.

We went into the captain's quarters, directly below the wheelhouse. Another man who looked like an Arab let us in.

There were two small rooms. The first was a sitting room with a built-in desk, a torn vinyl sofa, a washbasin with a single tap. Pieces of cardboard had been taped over the portholes. On one wall there was a chart of the Aegean Sea with several small islands circled in black; the other a large poster of a pretty girl in a red print dress, advertising Coca-Cola in Greek.

A lantern burned on the desk. From its light, I could see into the second room, which was smaller than the first. There was a bunk bed, a chest of drawers, and a single straight-backed chair. A man sat

10

slumped forward on the chair. His ankles had been wired to its front legs, his arms tied behind him. He was naked. On the floor next to him, in what looked to be a handmade cage of bamboo, a rat the size of a mongoose crouched as if ready to spring.

'It doesn't take much to make a man spill his guts,' Farmer said. 'All we have to do is set that cage on Timmie's lap, and Timmie tells us what we want to know.'

'Like the VC,' I said.

'That's right,' Farmer said.

He was standing close to me. The Arab had gone into the other room and was teasing the rat with the hook of a coat hanger. Dixie stood just behind me and to my left. I could feel the heat of the lantern where it burned steadily on the desk by my right side. I gave no indication of that, or of the relief I felt that it was not Campbell strapped to the chair, or of the sense of rage and helplessness I felt for the man who was.

'Wake him up,' Farmer said.

The Arab stood up and slapped the man in the chair twice, hard on each side of his face. The man cried out. He looked to be in his late twenties, had prematurely thin hair and wispy sideburns, delicate features, and an expression just now of abject terror. Farmer stared at him.

'You screwed up again, Timmie,' he said.

Timmie shook his head. He was perspiring.

'You told us you were dealing with one guy,' Farmer said.

'I was. Honest to God, Artie.'

'Then how come this one shows up?'

Farmer jerked his thumb in my direction. Timmie looked up at me through his frightened eyes.

'I don't know,' he said. 'I don't know who he is. I never saw him before.'

'You told us the guy we set up on the wharf tonight was your connection. You said he was the only one.'

'He was. Honest to god, Artie. I've never seen this guy before.'

'He's telling the truth,' I said. 'I came out here to meet a friend. He didn't show. I was about to leave when I heard somebody in trouble on board this ship – Timmie here, most likely, when the Arab put the rat on his lap.'

11

'So you just hauled ass up that mooring line,' Farmer said.

'That's right.'

'Because you thought maybe it was your friend who was in trouble?'

'That's right.'

'Let me tell you what this friend of yours looks like,' Farmer said. 'He's lean, tall, maybe fifty-five years old, with blue eyes and black hair – looks sort of like Abraham Lincoln without the beard.'

I was silent. Farmer had just given a perfect description of Campbell.

He stared at me for a moment through the oily lenses of his glasses, then went into the smaller room and stood next to Timmie's chair.

'I told you there were two ways you could die,' he said. 'One was fast and the other was slow.'

'Don't kill me, Artie,' Timmie said.

'We've got a deal going down tonight. You almost screwed it up for us.'

'I didn't mean to. I just wanted to go home, that's all.'

'So you copped to the CIA.'

'I didn't tell them anything, nothing they could use. The other guy told you that. I didn't even make my deal yet.'

'But you were going to.'

Timmie began to sob. Farmer looked disgusted. He stepped to one side and nodded at Dixie. She had been pointing the gun at me, but now she pointed it at Timmie.

'Waste him,' Farmer said. He sounded annoyed.

She was six feet away. Timmie never had a chance to scream. She held the gun with two hands and squeezed off the shot. The slug hit him heart-high, just to the left of the sternum. Its force and the reflex action of his legs tipped the chair over backward. I heard and saw these things in the same few instants it took for me to react, not hesitating this time, snatching the lantern by its wire hoop and swinging it full bore in an arc that caught Dixie flat against the side of her head, the glass globe of the lantern shattering, the metal frame folding inward from the force of the blow, the light winking out.

Then the room was plunged in blackness, and stank of kerosene. I could hear the chittering of the rat, the startled cries of the Arab, the

12

piglike sound of Farmer grunting as he tried to orient himself in the dark.

I was across the room in three strides. I knew exactly where the door was. I snatched it open, bolted through, slammed it behind me. I took the left option down the passage. When I reached the first companionway, I shot a glance behind me and saw the Arab dart out of the captain's quarters and head the other way. He hadn't seen me. Not yet.

I took the stairs four and six at a time, hanging onto the metal railing to keep from falling, spilling and skittering out onto the main deck where the moonlight seemed as bright as the sun. I ran along the starboard rail, looking down at the wharf, which seemed a long way down, and wished now I'd bolted for the port side of the ship where I could have taken one long dive into the oily waters of the harbor.

But it was too late for that. Figures had already emerged from the superstructure and were running along the opposite rail. I could hear voices shouting and the sound of feet pounding on metal.

I ducked into the shadow of one of the two aft king-posts. They rose over thirty feet in the air from either side of a low masthouse, and were joined near the top by a twenty-foot spanner. I could see the door of the masthouse about eight feet away, toward the center of the ship. It looked like the door of a meat locker and hung slightly ajar.

Crouching below the raised coaming of one of the cargo hatches, I crabbed my way to it, went in, shut it behind me.

The masthouse was about six by fifteen, with a low ceiling and a single porthole on either side. An open door in the opposite wall led to one of the cargo holds. I looked in. The hold was covered by four big hatches, each about thirty by twenty. The one on the far port side was open. I could see the cargo boom positioned overhead, silhouetted against the night sky. A line ran from the boom into the hold itself.

Voices were coming closer. I could hear footsteps on the roof of the masthouse. At my feet, a metal ladder dropped vertically into the darkness below. Hanging onto the doorframe, I swung around and started down. As I did, I saw a face appear suddenly at the porthole on the starboard side, heard somebody shout they had found me.

13

It was forty feet to the bottom of the hold. I went down the ladder four rungs at a time. When my feet hit the tanktop, I wanted to run to the far bulkhead, where I was sure I'd find another ladder, or a door leading further into the bowels of the freighter. What I needed now was cover and concealment until I could find a way off the ship. I no longer believed Campbell could be alive, not after what Farmer had said, not after what he and his people had done to Timmie.

I wanted to run, but it was too dark for that. I had to shuffle along, pawing the air in front of me, trying to pick out obstacles, making my way with agonizing slowness toward the place where the open hatch spilled a rectangle of moonlight onto the floor of the hold.

I stumbled over tin cans, pieces of rope, clots of something that smelled like spoiled fruit. Every sound I made was turned into an echo and amplified by the steel skin of the ship and by the empty ballast tanks below my feet. I could hear Farmer's voice in the masthouse, the sound of feet coming down the ladder.

In the center of the moonlit area below the open hatch, a crate the size of a footlocker was secured to the cargo line that ran up to the overhead boom. I kept to the shadows, darting for the bulkhead, trying to find a way out. There were no doors here, no ladders. I felt a tightening clutch of panic. Farmer's people were coming toward me. I could hear them calling to each other as they came. The hold was a riot of sound now, of echo and clatter and shout.

I slipped into the darkest area of shadow I could find, standing motionless beside one of the transverse vertical frames that supported the skin of the ship. I tried not to breathe, but my breath was coming in gasps. A man tripped and stumbled in the darkness at my left. I heard him swear. Then he was up and moving again, coming my way, using the ship's framing as a guide.

I dropped into a crouch, hoping he'd go by, but he must have sensed my presence, because he started lashing out suddenly with his foot, shouting for the others to come. I caught him by the ankle, pitched him up and back, heard the melony sound when his head hit the deck.

More of Farmer's troops were coming down the ladder from the masthouse. I could see the glow of lanterns bobbing as they came. I ran for the rectangle of moonlight below the open hatch. People passed me on either side, shouting in confusion. I hit the cargo line as high as I could, springing from the crate, snatching the line, going up hand-over-hand, using my feet, knowing it was over, that the bullets would hit me before I heard the sound of the gun, hoping they would hit me as mercifully as they had hit Timmie, and maybe Campbell too.

Then, while I was still going up, with my arm and shoulder muscles coming through my skin and Farmer's troops gathered in a circle below me, screaming obscenities in three languages, I saw her.

She was crouched on the boom above my head, the black woman in the leotard with a short Afro and the features of a Nigerian queen. She held the machete in her right hand. The moonlight glinted from its blade and seemed to gleam from her eyes and the perfect white slice of her smile.

I was a third of the way up the line when she cut it with a single stroke and I dropped like a lamb into the circle of wolves below.

Chapter Four

I went out in distance and back in time. The Cambodian communists were firing 122mm rockets into the west side of Phnom Penh. It was the season of the northeast monsoon. The winds were dry and cool and gusty. The rockets were big. They made a *swish-swish-swish* sound as they came in. Their impact noise depended on what surface they hit: concrete, dirt, hangar, or house. The explosions never sounded the way they do in the movies. When you were close it was a flat, short crack, very loud.

Then the sound of the rockets changed to the concussive sound of the five-hundred-pound bomb that had killed my wife Diana and all but mortally wounded my son Brian. It was the chance-in-a-million freak bomb, dropped from a T-28 propellar aircraft by a defecting Khmer fighter pilot whose name was Tru.

On Tru's flight away from the city, it had been his plan to kill the Cambodian premier; and he would have if he hadn't dialed too many mils into his gunsight so his bomb, instead of landing on the palace, landed a yard and a half from my house. I was monitoring a radio transmission with one of the Marine guards at the embassy, four blocks away, when it happened. I started running toward my house as soon as I heard the blast. I knew. Don't ask me how I knew, but I did.

So in one instant my wife and son had been vibrant and alive, and in the next she was gone and he was locked in a deep coma, where he would remain for over a year. He was recovering now at the famed Franki Clinic in the Alps east of Zurich: out of his coma, sitting in a wheel-chair several hours a day, relearning coordination and speech. Before the bomb had gone off, he had been an honors student at the French lycée in Phnom Penh. Now, at seventeen, he was trying to learn the alphabet again.

I heard the sound of the rockets for a while, and then the sound of the bomb. I was in a dark place and knew I had to get out, but couldn't find a door. My head hurt. The pain started behind my ear and pulsed like a heartbeat in my frontal lobes. I was lying on my back. The surface under me was hard and cold. I wanted to get up, but couldn't.

When I finally opened my eyes, I saw Campbell.

He was sitting on a stool by a workbench, examining some sheets of paper. He had on a pair of gray grease-stained chino pants and a blue polo shirt. He was tanned, familiar-looking: long-boned and sinewy, with strong forearms and hands. I could see his gold wedding band, and the silver ID bracelet his wife Midge had given him for Christmas one year. A carpenter's candle stub burned on the bench. Through its halo effect, his Lincolnesque features had the nebulous quality of a dream. At last, I managed to sit up, my brain splitting in half as I did.

'*Campbell?*' I croaked.

He swung abruptly down from the stool, put an arm across my shoulder, helped me stand. We were in a fairly large triangular room. There were sacks of cement and kegs of sand on the floor; rusty tools, frayed hoses, metal cylinders along one wall; workbench and cabinets along the other. Beyond the bench, an iron ladder led up to an overhead hatch.

'Better take it slow,' he said.

'What is this place?'

'As far as I can tell from the ship's blueprint, we're in an area called the boatswain's store. It's located at the extreme bow of the freighter. There aren't any portholes or inspection panels. The door in the wall behind you leads to the chain locker. It's full of rats, and the only egress is through the chain slot, which is suitable for the rats, but much too small, I'm afraid, for us. The only way out is through the hatch.'

'Locked?'

'Yes.'

'Are the bad guys still on board?'

'Yes. They come out on deck from time to time. You'll hear them.'

'What have we got for a weapon?'

'There's a pinch bar on the bench.'

'My God, it's good to see you,' I said.

17

He shook his head, blue eyes intense. 'I made a damn fool of myself this time. Farmer set me up and I fell for it.'

I sat on the bench and told my father-in-law what had happened to me since I had arrived at the wharf. He sat on a stool. The candle burned softly between us, flickering now and then in a draft that came under the door to the chain locker.

'I can go part of the way toward feeling sorry for a man like Timmie,' he said when I was through. 'He started out as a USAF dental technician at Hellenikon Air Base in Athens. Then, during Vietnam, he became radicalized and went AWOL. We don't know how or when he joined up with Farmer, but several weeks ago he apparently decided he had had enough and wanted to go home.

'He established contact with the embassy. He said he had important information about Farmer that he would be willing to trade if the Air Force would drop prosecution and give him a satisfactory discharge.

'I've been trying to get a line on Farmer, regarding another matter, since I came to Greece. When the agent data came through, I said I'd handle Timmie myself. Tonight would have been our second meeting. Everything was still preliminary. Timmie was skittish. One minute he'd say yes, he was going to make his deal, and the next he'd back off. Our phone contacts had been the same. He'd say he was going to call me at one place, change his mind and call me at another.

'Originally, our rendezvous tonight was to have been at the seaman's hall in Piraeus. At the last minute, he changed it to the old Manis wharf. It was so typical of his *modus operandi*, I scarcely gave it a thought. I wanted you to meet him, tell him you were Air Force, verify the channels we were going through to upgrade his situation.'

Here, again, Campbell shook his head.

'I'm sorry, Matt,' he said. 'I think I was a pretty good field man once.'

'You still are,' I said. 'You've been shuffling too much paper is all. You're out of the mode. I felt that way tonight when I got waxed just about three minutes after I came on board.'

He nodded. 'Was it the one with the automatic? Or the one with the machete?'

'Automatic first,' I said. 'Machete later. I think I like combat better when it was just between us guys.'

He started to laugh, then cautioned me to be quiet.

'Listen,' he said.

18

I could hear banging noises on the deck overhead, and the muffled sound of voices; then a small boat engine idling up along the port side of the freighter and stopping somewhere amidships. Campbell went and pressed his ear to the bulkhead. He stood that way for several minutes, then came back to the bench.

'They're offloading something,' he said quietly. 'They're hand-cranking the boom winch.'

I told him about the crate I had seen under the open hatch on that side. He seemed interested.

'Notice any details?' he asked.

'It was painted gray. The corners had been reinforced and there was some pretty solid strapping around it. The top was stenciled with what might have been a U.S. government code. I couldn't be sure about that.'

'Farmer's been into everything,' Campbell said. 'He's run guns and dope, smuggled stolen paintings from one country to another, transported mercenaries, committed piracy on the high seas. We've tracked him for years. So has Interpol. He seems to lead a charmed life. He started off as a radical at Berkeley back in the days when their *cause célébre* was the four-letter word. He helped the North Vietnamese during the war by putting out some very foul but effective propaganda. He's worked with the Cubans, the IRA, the PLO; just about any terrorist group you can name. He's got a pathological hatred for the establishment.'

'We had a talk in the wheelhouse,' I said. 'There were a few minutes there when he seemed civilized enough. He even asked me if I had any kids. I think that came just before he said he was going to kill me.'

'You were lucky. I was told if I said one word, the woman with the machete would be ordered to cut out my tongue. There was a vague reference to the *Koran*. I kept very quiet while they brought me here.'

'Did Farmer give you any idea what his long-range plans are for us?'

'No. But I think we're about to find out.'

Heavy steps were coming along the deck just above our heads. I picked up the pinch bar, jumped off the bench, took up a position alongside the ladder that led up to the hatch. Campbell waited until I was ready, then extinguished the candle flame with the palm of his hand. I heard the sound of a chain being dragged through the hasp of a lock. Then Farmer was peering down, his pale face framed in a circle of moonlight, his glasses opaque.

'Comfortable?' he said.

We didn't answer. His voice reverberated through the room; the small pocket of his mouth lifted toward a smile.

'Die slow,' he said.

I was making pretty good time up the ladder when he slammed the hatch shut.

Chapter Five

'Didn't Diana tell me once about a stunt you and a friend pulled when you were taking metal shop in high school?' Campbell asked. He had the candle going again and had resumed his study of the construction details of the ship. After Farmer had left, there had been a flurry of activity on deck. Then the small boat had started up and pulled away, and now, except for the two of us, the freighter was silent.

'We welded the shop teacher's car to a parking meter,' I said. 'Diana always liked that one.'

My father-in-law laughed. He has one of the finest laughs of any man I know. It rises up from somewhere deep inside him and carries with it qualities of integrity and joy. That he could laugh in these circumstances may have indicated nothing more than his relief that we were alive, and his knowledge that we were resourceful and had materials at hand. Whereas earlier he had looked chagrined at having gotten us into this jam, he now looked positively eager at the prospect of getting us out.

'I took an inventory when I first got here,' he said. 'We don't have much in the way of serviceable tools. We do have acetylene and oxygen: six cylinders in all; two empty, two partially full, two full. We've got a pair of hoses with brass fittings –'

'Then Farmer's not as smart as he thinks,' I said.

'Don't underestimate him,' Campbell said. 'Take a look at the cylinders.'

I got down from my seat on the bench and went to the wall where they were racked. All six were dirty and battered; the three acetylene tanks were marked with red paint, the three oxygen tanks with green. The regulator gauge on top of each tank had been smashed.

'Which ones are the full ones?' I asked.

'Judging by weight, the two on your right.'

I tried the knurled valves. There was a healthy hiss from each tank.

'We can manage without the gauges,' I said. 'Have we got a torch?'

'We had two,' Campbell said. 'They were hanging on the wall just above the tanks. Farmer took them. He waited until he was sure I had noticed them. I think he enjoyed it.'

'I'm hoping we're going to meet him again somewhere,' I said. 'I thought I had this part of my life behind me, but he's gotten me ginned up.'

'Maybe you will meet him again,' Campbell replied. He said it as if he had not intended to. I looked at him.

'Why did you ask me to come to Greece?' I said. 'Was he part of it?'

'I'd rather not go into that right now.'

'I'd like to know. You said there was a job. You didn't say what it was, or who I'd be working for.'

'It's a covert operation with CIA involvement.'

'Why me?'

'It calls for a pilot.'

'There are lots of pilots,' I said.

'One of the principals is familiar with your background,' he said. 'He made a special request. If we're going to go into that matter now it's going to use up a lot of time we could put to better use by getting ourselves out of here. Can we wire the two hoses side by side and start burning?'

'No,' I said. 'They're half-inch-diameter. Openings that big would diffuse the mixture and bleed off the pressure too fast. We'll have to jerry-rig a torch. Who made the special request?'

'Later,' he said. 'I've got my reasons. When the time's right, I'll tell you what they are.'

'You sound like a Company man,' I said.

'I *am* a Company man,' he said. 'I always have been. Your father was too before he got killed. Now will you let us get on with it, please?'

I found a two-foot section of curved copper tubing in one of the cabinets over the bench. We broke it at the middle by bending it back and forth. Then we slid about five inches of tube into each hose and tightened them with a couple of screw-and-ratchet clamps Campbell found in one of the sand kegs. We wired the exposed tube

22

ends, crimped apertures to an even smaller diameter, and wrapped the tube-to-hose connection as tightly as we could with pieces of rag.

'What do you think?' Campbell asked when we were through.

'I don't see any reason why it shouldn't work,' I said. 'You're going to have to manipulate the valves for me. If I remember right, we'll need about a three-to-one mixture of oxygen to acetylene. Without the gauges, you'll have to guess at it. Where do you want to start cutting?'

'We can't cut indefinitely, can we?' he said.

'No,' I said. 'This rig is going to be pretty inefficient.'

'Do you see any practical way to operate from the top of the ladder?'

'You mean can we cut through the hatch?'

'Yes.'

I squinted up. The ladder was narrow and rose vertically from the floor. The hoses were too short, the tanks too heavy. Even if we managed to lug everything up there, it would be an impossible position to work in.

I shook my head. Campbell glanced at his blueprints again, picked up a piece of chalk, marked out about a two-foot square on a bulge in the wall to the right of the bench.

'We'll be gambling,' he said. 'But as far as I can tell it's the best chance we have. If I'm right, we'll be cutting into a hollow tubular forging. The thickness of the steel should be five eighths of an inch.'

With anyone else, I would have asked questions. With Campbell, I didn't.

I brought the two full cylinders over. He handed me a pair of welder's goggles.

'We'll have to play it by ear,' I said. 'Try three turns on the oxygen valve and one on the acetylene.'

We blew out the candle twice, filling the air with acetylene soot, before we got the mixture right. When we finally did, I held the point of the blue flame about an inch from the target steel, then onto it. The yellow surrounding flame splashed in a three-inch circle around the contact point. A spot about the size of a quarter glowed dull red, turned to a bright cherry, then yellow, then white.

'Excellent,' Campbell said.

'Try using the pinch bar,' I said. 'See if you can beat through the white spots as I trace the outline. We're probably running better than three thousand degrees centigrade here. Watch your hands.'

Ordinarily it would have been quick work. This time it was slow. Campbell banged away with the pinch bar. I cut up, then across, then down. Pressure was bleeding out the back end of the makeshift torch, and twice we had to shut everything down and retie the rags. When the convex chunk of plate finally clanged to the floor, my ears were ringing from the noise we had made.

'We're about out of business,' I said. 'These tanks are almost empty.'

'How long are we going to have to wait for the edges to cool?'

'Half an hour, maybe. Like a hot stove.'

I sat down, resting my back against the bench. While we had been working, I had forgotten how much my head hurt. Now I was remembering again.

'Are you going to be all right?' Campbell asked. He sounded worried.

'Fine,' I said. 'A little dizzy is all.'

He brought me a soggy strip of burlap from a pile near the chain locker. I pressed it against my forehead.

'Better?' he said.

'Yes,' I said.

As soon as the edges of the cut we had made were cool enough, Campbell padded them with pieces of the burlap and poked his head in the hole.

'See anything?' I asked.

'Nothing much,' he said.

'What's the next step?'

'I go into the tube. If my calculations are right, you'll hear nothing for a few seconds, and then a splash.'

'What if your calculations are wrong?' I said.

'Then you will have inherited the mantle of responsibility,' he said. 'I'm going feet first. Give me a hand.'

There wasn't going to be any talking him out of it. He wriggled into the tube until all I could see were his hands where they gripped the burlap at the bottom of the cut. The tube appeared to angle down to the right.

'Tallyho,' he said.

24

There were a few seconds of silence, and then a splash. When I poked my head in the hole, I could see him bobbing in a moonlit circle of water beyond the end of the tube.

Well I'll de damned, I thought.

Tallyho.

Chapter Six

Campbell had a room over the Pericles Taverna on the waterfront in Piraeus. We arrived there with seaweed in our shoes in the last hour of that oppressive night, both happy to be alive.

'Help yourself to the bath,' Campbell said. 'I'll arrange to have your things sent over from the Makeiros. I've got some calls to make. Don't shave.'

He said we had been lucky on the *Lygarius*, that the freighter had been designed with an extra hawsepipe to pick up a special mooring at one of its original ports of call. He had seen similar arrangements before, but, he said, they were not common. Most freighters had two pipes, one port, one starboard. The *Lygarius* had three.

'Of course,' he said cheerfully, 'if it hadn't been there, we'd have found something else. This place is secure, by the way. I've known the family for years. Their name is Xenoupolos. I'll be back in an hour. Enjoy yourself.'

The bath was in a cubicle across the hall from his room. There was a sink and commode, and a square tub that looked about four feet deep. I used the water massage to soap up, rinse off, then soap up and rinse off again. Then I cleaned the sludge out of the tub, filled it with cool water, and settled in. I was still there when Campbell came back. He had found his own place to clean up. He looked relaxed and fresh in a pair of dark slacks and a white shirt and tie.

'I think I know how that brain of yours works,' he said. 'You've probably been going over everything since I asked you to come to Greece; point by point, item by item.'

'You're right,' I said.

'And you've guessed by now who the principal is.'

'Coyle?' I said.

'Yes.'

I got out of the tub and toweled off. My suitcase and personal effects were in Campbell's room. My head was still throbbing. I popped a couple of aspirins, pulled on a clean pair of pants and a shirt.

'I gave up wearing neckties,' I said. 'I had a friend once who got strangled with his. It happened in an alley in Kuala Lumpur. A couple of thieves ran the knot up so tight on him the tie disappeared in the meat of his neck.'

'With me it's a habit,' Campbell said. 'Unless I'm in the field.'

'I gave up working for Coyle too,' I said.

'Let's talk about it over some coffee.'

We went downstairs. The taverna had just been closing when we arrived. Now it was empty except for the Xenoupolos family, who were busy cleaning it up from the night's activity. Four enormous wine kegs were racked along one wall. The other walls were off-white stucco, the floor a pink-and-white mosaic of octagonal one-inch tiles. There were small round tables with wire-backed chairs, and except for the kegs and a lingering scent of retsina, the atmosphere was like that of an ice-cream parlor. We took a table away from the oval window that looked across the main street to the harbor. Campbell introduced me to Gregori Xenoupolos, a gentle, proud-looking Greek in a peppermint-striped apron.

'I have three months in your country,' he said, 'to visit last year my uncle in New York. You will be pleased to stay now in Piraeus. Here, you will know where you go. Athens is too close, too many people, too many buildings. You are welcome to me as a friend of Mr. Cooke.'

He and Campbell spoke to each other in Greek. It's a language that has always interested me, but one I've never been able to master. With my mind fixed on another subject, I only pretended to listen. I was thinking about R.J. Coyle.

He was a Virginia fat cat who, since the death of Howard Hughes, was said to be the richest man in the United States. He and Campbell had served in the OSS under my father during the Second World War. They had been on the same mission when my father was killed after parachuting into the Alps in '44. Campbell had stayed in government service after the war was over; Coyle had peddled his personal fortune and influence into Coyle Enterprises, a vast international conglomerate in import-export that had its tentacles into most of the major capitals of the world. White Oaks, his estate in Virginia, was so big it had its own Zip Code. When Diana and I were married, we had the reception there: a gift to us from Coyle which meant more to Diana than to me.

I had never liked Coyle. He had always struck me as the kind of man who would put power ahead of principle, who judged people by the size of their bank accounts and the length of their pedigrees.

It had been Coyle who had hired me as a mercenary to go into communist-held Cambodia and retrieve a pouch of diamonds one of his agents had hidden in Sihanouk's hotel at Kampong Som. He had persuaded me to undertake the mission by offering to pay for a year's treatment at the Franki Clinic for my son. The going rate there at the time had been nine thousand dollars a month. That had been a year and a half ago. The fees were even higher now. I had carried them for the last six months with my percentage of the diamonds. But since I had bought my farm, Cedar Run, that money, as I am sure Coyle knew very well, was running out.

'I think you've always been too hard on him,' Campbell said, after our coffee arrived. It was made in the Turkish manner, and he had ordered it *pikrón*, black and unsweetened.

'There were things he told me about the Cambodian mission that turned out not to be true,' I said.

'I grant you that. Nevertheless he did live up to his end of the bargain. Without the clinic and Dr. Franki's innovative treatment, Brian would still be at Walter Reed, buried in the oblivion of a coma no one except Franki believed could be reversed.'

'I know that.'

'Do you also know that Bob has kept in constant touch with the clinic? That he has visited Brian there on several occasions, once as recently as a month ago?'

'Yes.'

'There's nothing in your original contract with him that requires him to do that. I happen to think he's doing it because he cares.'

'Sorry,' I said. 'I've never believed Coyle cared about anything but himself. I still don't.'

Campbell sighed.

'Then we'll have to approach this from another tack,' he said.

'There's a job that needs doing. It involves Coyle Enterprises and the CIA. Bob's one of the principals, and I'm the other. Your background is tailor-made for the work. If you accept, the pay will be excellent. Enough to take care of Brian for another year.'

I finished my coffee, careful to stop before I got to the dregs. Through the distant window I could see the big ships in the harbor, lying at anchor in water tinged pink by the early morning light.

'I don't know how many times I almost got killed in Southeast Asia,' I said. 'I stopped counting after a while. The war went sour, and I went sour with it. I remember the first time I stood by Brian's bedside at the clinic – long before he came out of the coma. I told him I was going to buy a farm in Virginia one day, something solid but rundown so I'd have plenty of work to do bringing it back. It was a pipe dream then. Now it's a reality. I've felt better these last six months than I have in years. I've got two hundred and fifty acres of land with a brick house and some beat-up outbuildings and a lot of broken fence. I get up early, work all day, go to bed before prime time starts on the tube. I don't drink half what I used to; I smoke maybe six cigarettes a week, usually on Saturday night. The next part of the dream is to have Brian join me there.'

'He will,' Campbell said. 'It's a matter of time. That's all.'

I shook my head.

'Maybe when he's finally well enough to come to Cedar Run, he'll decide he doesn't want to,' I said.

My father-in-law was silent. I wanted him to reassure me, but he didn't. He looked sad, as if our talking about Brian had led him to some deeply personal and touching memory of his daughter, Diana. When Gregori Xenoupolos came to clear our empty cups from the table, he spoke briefly to Campbell in Greek before walking away.

'The authorities have removed Timmie's body from the freighter,' Campbell said. 'There was no one else on board. As we suspected, the crate you saw was gone.'

'Where is Coyle?' I said. 'Here or at White Oaks?'

'He's here, on board a yacht lying off Piraeus. The tender's waiting for us.'

'If I were a smart fly,' I said, 'I'd stay away from the web.'
Campbell smiled.

'Give Bob a chance to tell you about this,' he said. 'I think you'll find it interesting.'

Chapter Seven

We were apprehensive as we picked up our luggage and crossed the street to the harbor. There was no telling where Art Farmer's people had gone once they had left the *Lygarius*. It was possible some of them were still in the seaport. They knew what we looked like and who we were, and they had made it clear they wanted us dead.

The waterfront was already crowded with Greek seamen who had been idled by the strike. There were times when we had to make our way through knots of them, passing close enough to catch the odor of sweat from their clothes, hearing them shout '*Malaka!*' and '*Skata!*' and seeing the pent-up anger and frustration in their faces that nothing short of some hard work and a paycheck was going to cure. Campbell and I were out of place here, too well dressed, too American, too obviously well fixed. The atmosphere as we passed was layered with tension. When I finally spotted Coyle's man Maul waiting for us at a small docking float, I felt a tangible sense of relief.

Maul was a retired Green Beret master sergeant, with combat experience in Korea and Vietnam. I carried a special fondness for him: A couple of years ago when I had gotten into a jam in Switzerland, he had saved my life.

He was a short, broad-shouldered, large-knuckled man, with a salt-and-pepper crewcut and a face like a stone quarry. Today he had on tennis shoes, chinos, an open-throat shirt. The docking float was about the size of a boxing ring. Maul stood warily in one corner, as if waiting for an opponent to show up.

'How you been keeping yourself, Eberhart?' he growled.

'Fine,' I said.

'I hear you got a farm.'

I said that was right, that my place wasn't far from White Oaks and I hoped he would pay me a visit sometime. Before he could reply, Campbell interrupted.

31

'Let's save the small talk for later,' he said. 'We had some trouble here. We don't want any more. I take it you and Jean-Paul are armed?'

'I've got a .38 in an oilcloth in the boat,' Maul said. 'He's got an automatic tucked in his shirt. I don't know if he's any good with it.'

'Jean-Paul is Algerian,' Campbell said. 'He fought with the Pied Noirs. He'll be fine.'

'Maybe so,' Maul said. 'But he can't drive a boat for sour apples.'

A fifteen-foot tender with fresh paint and an outboard motor was tied between two skiffs alongside the float. Jean-Paul stood in the stern. He was a shy-looking, slender man in his thirties, who wore clean working whites and a French sailor's hat with a pompom. He smiled warmly as we took our places. Campbell and I sat amid-ships, sliding our suitcases under the seat. Maul sat facing us in the bow. He looked quite miserable as we pulled away.

'I tried to tell him you can't stand up when you're driving this small a boat,' he said. He gestured behind us, toward Jean-Paul. 'It screws up the center of gravity. All he can do is speak French. When I try to tell him the problem, he keeps pointing to his eye like if he sits down he won't be able to see. There he goes. You can feel him doing it. He keeps shifting his weight. First one foot and then the other, back and forth. He did it all the way in from Pasalimani.'

Maul was a man of few words; this was one of the longest speeches I had ever heard him make. Though we were still in the inner harbour, putt-putting through water as smooth as an oil spill, he looked decidedly green.

'Bob's been cruising since the middle of June,' Campbell explained. 'Maul's been with him from the start. I think he'll be glad when it's time to go back to White Oaks. Am I right, Maul?'

'I'm no good in a boat,' Maul growled. 'Between tours in Nam I got sent to squid school in Key West. That's what they told me there. "You're good in the water, Sergeant Maul, but you're no good in a boat." '

He was holding the gunwales, glowering back toward Jean-Paul.

'Look at the raghead,' he said. 'He's smiling. Can you feel how he's rocking us back and forth?'

It was true. The boat was wobbling slightly from side to side. Jean-Paul seemed to steer – at least in part – by shifting the balance of his feet as we wove our way through a maze of moored liners, freighters, and tugs. Gulls shrieked in the polluted air, horns blew, engines throbbed. A patrol boat passed, leaving us to bob dangerously in its wake. Maul gripped the gunwales and sighed. When I turned to look at Jean-Paul, he was standing serenely at the helm, the black ribbons at the back of his hat fluttering in the breeze.

It was then that I first saw the launch two-hundred yards off our stern; but there was nothing about it at the time that struck me as suspicious. It was a working launch painted battleship gray with a hull like a Boston Whaler – twenty feet long, raised center console with a ship's wheel, braided hemp fenders hanging over the sides. I had seen a dozen similar boats tied up along one of the wharves near the docking float where Maul had met us and a half-dozen more chugging around the port.

As we came into the outer harbor, the water began to turn red from the effluent of the sulfur and potassium factories that had been built along the coast. Ahead of us, a series of small uninhabited islands rose like boulders out of the sea.

'We'll be turning south now,' Campbell said. 'Pasalimani is the name of the harbor where we'll rendezvous with Bob. I was with him there at the yacht basin the other night. He showed me around. It's all very plush.'

'They've got tap beer in the club,' Maul said.

The boat lifted on one small wave, wobbled in the air, smacked down on another. Maul, whose chin had been resting on his chest, straightened on his seat and frowned aft.

'I think we're picking up a tail,' he said.

Campbell and I swung around on our seat. The launch I had seen a few minutes earlier had closed to 150 yards. We were in open water. There were no other boats within hailing distance. Whoever was behind us was bearing down fast.

Campbell spoke sharply in French to Jean-Paul. He told the Algerian to head for the islands, to go at full throttle, and to give me his automatic. Jean-Paul looked puzzled, as if this many instructions had overloaded his circuits.

'*Depêchez-vous!*' Campbell snapped. '*Plus vite que ça!*'

Maul was unwrapping his revolver from the oilskin. I swung my legs over the gunwale, reversing my position on the seat. Jean-Paul

33

advanced the throttle, and we were skimming along through a light chop. He was reaching inside his shirt to hand me his gun when I heard him grunt and saw him start to pitch toward me. As he did, the boat swerved to the right.

I tried to grab him to keep him from toppling overboard, but I was too late. He went over the left side an instant after I heard the report of the first shot, a flat, cracking sound that was closely followed by another.

I shouted to the others to get down. Maul had his .38 in hand, but at this range we all knew it wasn't going to do us much good.

I crouched behind the motor, pouring on the throttle, straightening us out again, zigzagging toward the first of the islands. I could see a figure kneeling in the bow of the gray launch, smoke clearing from his rifle as he squeezed off another shot. A slug tore through the upper left corner of our transom, splintering wood. I banked to the right in a sheet of spray, veered back left. The gray launch bobbed in our wake; bullets whipped the air.

'Watch it!' Campbell warned. 'You've got islands up front!'

I rounded the first one, cut between two others, pointed for a third. The pursuit boat was out of sight, but still coming on. We could hear the pulse of its engine, echoing behind us. I glanced ahead. The island we were approaching was larger than the others, a steep, treeless hump of rock, with the marble columns of a ruined temple rising starkly from its summit.

A stone beach appeared to circle the base of the island. Steps had been cut out of the rock, winding up from a narrow inlet that broke the eastern shore. Behind us, the sound of the gray launch grew closer.

Campbell leaned toward me over the center seat. His hair was damp from spray; he had loosened his tie. To be heard over the noise of our motor, he had to shout.

'We're not going to outrun them!'

'No way!'

'How many did you count in the other boat!?'

'Two! One in the bow! One at the helm!'

'Put ashore on the island! We'll find cover and take them with Maul's gun as they come in!'

I had the tender wide open. I was trying to look behind me and ahead at the same time. The inlet was a cul-de-sac formed by the island and a series of low ledges that curved toward us like the blade of a sickle. Maul was kneeling, with elbows braced on the center seat, looking over my shoulder, back in the direction of our pursuers. He had his revolver gripped firmly with both hands; there still had been no good chance for him to fire. Campbell was crouched in the bow, facing the island. As we raced into the inlet, I heard him shout a warning and saw him gesture with his arm, indicating there was an obstacle in the water dead ahead.

I swerved sharply to the right. As I did, the bow rose suddenly and there was a tearing, ripping crash. The boat kept heeling up and over. I could hear the snarl of the exhaust as the prop came out of the water and the engine wound up. Maul and Campbell came tumbling toward me. I hung suspended for an instant, then slammed backward into the bay.

I twisted, went as deep as I could, and swam underwater away from the boat. When I came to the surface, the first thing I saw was the gray launch speeding toward the entrance of the inlet. I shouted for Campbell and Maul. There was no sign of either of them, no answering call. The tender was floating belly up, low in the water, fifty feet behind me. Its hull was gashed. The launch was closing fast.

I swam for the beach, churning the water with my kick, fighting the leaden pull of my clothes and shoes. By the time I stumbled out and ran for the stairs, my breath was coming in gasps.

The two men in the launch had sped at full throttle past the upturned tender and were heading straight for me. The shooter was still in the bow. He sent a bullet ricocheting off a rock to my left. I heard the close explosion of the rifle, the crunching sound of the launch as it came into the beach; then there was a sudden ominous quiet when the helmsman cut the engine.

I reached the summit of the island and looked back. I recognized the two men as they sprang over the gunwales of the launch and sprinted for the stairs. They were the Arabs who had been with Art Farmer on the *Lygarius*. They both wore olive-drab clothing and carried rifles with shoulder slings. One was the card player. The other was the one who had tortured Timmie with the rat.

I ran between the marble columns of the ruined temple. There was nowhere to hide. The whole top of the island was not much bigger than a village square. It ended in cliffs that dropped sixty feet to the sea. I stopped at the edge, looking back, forcing air into my lungs, stripping off my shirt and shoes. The cliff below looked negotiable, but I knew I was out of time.

As soon as the Arabs appeared, they saw me and began to shoot. They fired erratically as they came. They had bolt-action rifles and were so ginned up with the idea of killing me they were having trouble working the bolts.

I turned away from them and dove.

I dove toward a suck and surge of water that was salmon-colored and opaque. It seemed to take a long time before I hit the surface. When I did, I hit it hard, trying to shallow out my dive, praying there was enough depth here to take me.

The water was cool and stung my eyes. I plummeted down past a bed of kelp toward a reeflike dune of sand. Schools of small fish darted away from me. By the time I reached bottom, I could feel the pressure building in my ears. When I looked up, the lighter water at the surface shimmered a long way over my head.

I had taken a deep breath just before I hit the water. I forced myself to hold it, peeled off my slacks, and began to swim. With nothing on but a pair of briefs, the swimming was easier than it had been when the tender capsized. I was sure Campbell and Maul had survived the accident. It was inconceivable to me that either one of them had drowned.

I made my way underwater to the place where the island began its sharp rise up from the bottom, then swam laterally along the rock, holding to a depth of fifteen feet. I kept going until my head began to throb and my chest clamped shut as if someone was squeezing the life out of me with a rope and a turnbuckle. When I couldn't stand it anymore, I rose to the surface.

The Arab who had used the rat on Timmie had picked his way down the cliff and was waiting to finish me off. He was standing on a low outcropping of rock near the point where I had gone in. He had his rifle trained on the water and was moving it back and forth, trying to anticipate the place where I would reappear. I filled my lungs and slipped below the surface again.

I stayed close under the overhang, pulling myself along, coming up quietly when I estimated I was directly below the Arab's position.

36

The distance between the water and the underside of the rock where he stood was very narrow. The only way I could breathe was to hold my head sideways, with one side of my face pressed against the stone.

There were times when a wave would fill the space and I would have to hold my breath until it receded. Fish pecked at my toes. As the moments passed and I didn't appear, the Arab began to get restless. I could hear him shouting toward the summit, telling his partner in Arabic that something had gone wrong. There was no answer from above. When he finally crouched down to have a look at the place where I was, I reached up, grabbed him by the shirt, and pulled him in.

He wasn't a large man, but he was wiry and very strong for his size. We went under in a thrashing tangle of arms and legs. His rifle sank like a stone. We fought until he ran out of air. Then he fell away from me, drifting like a spacewalker, down toward the underwater dune.

I broke the surface, sobbing for breath, still close in to the cliff. I thought there was a good chance the other Arab would come down from the summit to investigate the sudden disappearance of his partner, but I was sure if he did he would be very careful not to disappear in the same way. I thought if I was lucky, I might be able to outflank him by swimming around the north side of the island and taking him from behind.

I settled on this as a plan, and began making my way in that direction. I hadn't gone far when I heard the sound of the launch.

It was coming at a high rate of speed, rounding the south shore. For the first time since the incident had begun, I felt I was trapped. I still had good cover from above, but nothing at all to keep from being spotted from the water except the water itself.

In desperation I began to hyperventilate, waiting for the launch to come into view before I went below. When it finally did, I saw Campbell standing at the wheel.

His clothes were sopping wet, his tie askew, his dark hair plastered to his skull. With my adrenaline still pumping, I waved him over. He helped pull me in, obviously relieved to have found me alive.

'Where's Maul?' I asked.

37

'Maul has the high ground,' Campbell said, pointing to the summit of the cliff, where the grizzled master sergeant had appeared, standing in his undershorts, holding a rifle. 'He tells me at this range he can knock the eye out of a newt. Is your man dead?'

'Yes,' I said.

'We took the other one alive. Maul stunned him with an oar as he was coming down the stairs. We've got him tied up with the anchor line.'

On our way back to the beach, Campbell filled me in on the rest. He said when the tender had capsized, he and Maul had surfaced under it. Maul, who had lost his revolver in the accident, had told him this was the place to stay until they were free to move out.

Our luggage had washed up on the beach. I got out a pair of soggy slacks and pulled them on. Then Maul and I stowed the bags in the launch, along with the motor from the tender. The hull of the tender itself was too badly ripped to be worth salvaging. While Maul and I did our work, Campbell questioned the surviving Arab.

'He's says they saw us come out of the taverna. They had just brought the launch back from somewhere south of Glifada, where they dropped off the others. He says they knew Farmer would reward them well if they showed him our heads. He doesn't know what the locker contained, or where it was going to be delivered. We'll turn him over to the authorities at Pasalimani and tell them what happened. I know the officer in charge. There won't be any trouble.'

Maul, still in his undershorts, was inspecting the launch.

'I like this boat better,' he said. 'The other one was too small.'

Chapter Eight

Coyle stood waiting for us on the afterdeck of the *Cri de Coeur*, a seventy-eight-foot Fleur de Lys Ambassador class cruiser tied up in the Zea marina at Pasalimani. She carried a French flag and was exactly the kind of yacht I would have expected him to have.

He was a short, slender man with delicate features and gray, penetrating eyes. He wore a dark-blue blazer with a light-blue ascot; his slacks and his hair were white.

'Welcome aboard, Matthew,' he said. We shook hands. His grip was powerful. I had always suspected as a younger man he might have developed it through exercise to offset the slightness of his build.

'Nice boat,' I said.

'You're looking fit.'

'I've been doing a lot of brush-hogging and fence-mending lately,' I said. 'I've got a feeling this boat's worth more than my farm.'

He smiled.

'She was built to order in England in 1973,' he said. 'The purchase price then was seventy-five thousand pounds. When Campbell called to explain what had happened and why you were late, I put in an order for a new tender. They'll be delivering it within an hour. It's larger and more powerful than the old one.'

Maul expressed his approval of this, excused himself, and went below. Coyle asked if Campbell and I wanted to change. We said no; we had dried off well enough on the trip in.

'We could have breakfast first,' he said.

'No thanks,' I said.

'Campbell?'

'I agree with Matt,' Campbell said. 'Let's get on with it.'

We went into the salon. I had expected a lot of dark wood and brass, but the room had decidedly feminine decor; ivory paneling,

39

white wicker furniture upholstered in soft yellows and greens. A dozen fresh tulips were arranged in a crystal vase on a glass-topped table in the center of the room.

Campbell and I sat on a large sofa, facing Coyle, who sat on a chair. The windows to the salon were open. The sea air was fresh. Gulls cried and wheeled in a perfect morning sky.

'The sum of the situation is this,' Coyle said. 'During the last two years, one of my divisions has been exporting sophisticated electronics systems to the Turkish air force. The terms of the contract are CIF. We manufacture the systems, insure them, and freight them to a bonded warehouse at Esenboga Airport. After they arrive, a Turkish procurement officer from Ankara goes to the warehouse to inspect the goods and check the purchase order against the bill of lading. When he is satisfied a proper delivery has been made, he authorizes payment.'

'I'm familiar with the routine,' I said. 'What's the problem?'

'Someone's been diverting the systems after they arrive at Esenboga – not all of them, but enough so our insurance people are up in arms and the Turks are threatening to cancel an additional thirty million dollars' worth of orders. We've worked hard to establish our export position in this industry. We have a reputation for being one hundred percent dependable. Until we get on top of this Turkish problem, that reputation is in jeopardy.'

'What's the CIA interest?' I said.

'There's classified material involved,' Campbell said. 'Inertial navigation systems that are on the Munitions Control list.'

'That means your Turkish buyer had to sign an end-user certificate.'

'Correct,' Coyle said. 'Once the systems arrive in Turkey, the Turks are required under the control section of the contract to keep them there. They can't turn around and export them to somebody else without U.S.G. approval.'

'We assume the man who's stealing these systems is doing it in order to sell them to one or more of the countries on our embargo list,' Campbell said.

He asked me if I had heard the name Mahmet Pazar.

'Isn't he the Turk who brokers deals for the PLO?' I said.

'The PLO and others,' Campbell said. 'He helped Colonel Qaddafi

40

supply the insurgents last July in the raid on Khartoum. We're quite sure he's the one responsible for diverting the systems. What we don't know is who's getting them and why.'

'Where do I come in?'

'Last week, Pazar started advertising through the mercenary underground for a blue-ribbon pilot-mechanic team, certified in the C-47 and jet fighters.'

'What's the mission?'

'We don't know. We think it might be tied in with the missing navigation systems. Pazar is willing to pay top dollar for the right people. Apparently he intends to put the candidates through some sort of competition before he makes up his mind who he's going to hire. A half-dozen teams have already showed up at Esenboga Airport.'

'And you want me to show up there too.'

'Yes. You'd be traveling as a mercenary, of course. The Agency will provide you with the necessary credentials and backup.'

'Is there some link between Pazar and Art Farmer?'

I thought Campbell hesitated before he replied.

'We're still not sure about that,' he said. 'There could well be. Farmer and his people are wanted on drug charges by the Turkish authorities, so I don't think you'll have to worry about their coming into the country while you're there.'

'Who have you got for a mechanic?' I said.

Coyle, who had been listening carefully to our conversation, broke into a smile.

'I think you're going to be pleased,' he said. 'We've hired your old friend Bock Vanderwald. He's waiting for you in Turkey.'

'I thought Bock had gotten out of the mercenary game,' I said. 'The last time I heard from him he and his wife Colette were running their own brasserie on the Normandy coast.'

'We were able to make Vanderwald an attractive offer,' Coyle said. 'He's like you, I believe. He requires action.'

'You mean we can't be happy unless someone's shooting at us?'

'Do you agree?'

'No,' I said. 'I don't.'

'But you are interested in the money.'

'How much?'

41

'A thousand a day and expenses. Double that if you land the job with Pazar, plus whatever he pays.'

'I always have the feeling with you there's a hidden agenda,' I said. 'What is it this time?'

'That's uncalled for,' Campbell said. 'Bob's told you what he wants and why. He's working with the Agency on this one. It's important. You'll have to take my word for that.'

'Which means you've got information you haven't told me about.'

'Nothing firm. I've given you everything you need to start. If anything breaks, we'll be in touch, and I'll let you know.'

I rubbed my eyes. I was tired. I trusted Campbell implicitly, but there was something about this I still didn't like.

'Run it by me one more time,' I said.

'It's simple enough,' Coyle said. 'We want you and Vanderwald to go undercover to Esenboga Airport in Turkey. We want you to do whatever it takes to get the job with Pazar. Once you're in, find out how he's taking my navigation systems, who's buying them from him, and why.'

Campbell nodded.

'Does that clear it up?' he said.

'It clears up the business in Turkey,' I said. 'What bothers me is the business with Farmer. Since midnight, his people have tried twice to kill us. You seem to be passing over that fact as if it wasn't important. I'd like to know why.'

'You were in the Air Force long enough to be able to operate on a need-to-know basis,' Campbell said. 'That's the situation we have here. If you pick up any information establishing a link between Farmer and Pazar, of course we'll want to know what it is. That's all I can say. If you're not comfortable taking the contract under these conditions, we'll have to find somebody else.'

So, there it was. Take it or leave it. As usual, my father-in-law had been tough but fair. I looked at him.

'Okay, Campbell,' I said. 'The fly's in the web.'

Coyle stood up.

'We're two hundred nautical miles from Turkey,' he said. 'I'd like to have the captain get us underway. Are the financial arrangements satisfactory?'

'They'll do,' I said.

42

'Good. The cook is in the galley. I'll send up one of the crew to take your orders for breakfast. You'll each have a stateroom. I meant what I said when I welcomed you on board, Matthew.'

I didn't reply. Once he was gone, Campbell looked annoyed.

'All right,' I said, 'I'm tired and my head hurts. I'll apologize later.'

While the *Cri de Coeur* got underway, we had the kind of breakfast I like: eggs and bacon, toast and coffee. I even had a glass of milk. Campbell continued to look peeved, and as soon as he was through eating he excused himself and went below to take a nap. I had gotten past the point of being able to sleep. When I heard piano music coming from somewhere forward, I decided to track it down.

Though Coyle loathed publicity, he was a prominent figure and drew occasional ink in the gossip columns around the world. He had never married, but in recent years his name had been linked with that of Dominique Fabray, the widow of Henri Fabray, who had been active in the French underground during World War II. After the war Henri had made a fortune from a string of fashion boutiques, which Dominique inherited and now ran.

I had never met Dominique, but I had seen her picture, and I recognized her at once as I walked into a smaller salon toward the bow of the cruiser. She was a trim, sparkling woman in her late forties with auburn hair and green eyes. She wore a white silk blouse with the sleeves rolled back, and white toreador pants with a sash that matched the color of her hair. She was seated at a baby grand, playing one of Chopin's nocturnes.

'*Bonjour!*' she said brightly.

'*Bonjour, madame,*' I said.

We introduced ourselves. She said she had known my father during the war.

'You have the same strong features,' she said, in the way French women have of pleasing a man. 'Your hair is a lighter brown, but the rest is very similar, especially the set of the jaw.'

'I've been told that's a sign of stubbornness,' I said. 'I think it ran in the family.'

She laughed.

'Your eyes are also the same as your father's,' she said. 'They change with the light: now gray, like Robert's; now blue, like Monsieur Cooke's. It is a quality I like.'

43

'Did you know my father well?'

'I was only fifteen when I met him. It was before I married Henri. But I remember him well. Henri always said of your father that he was very brave. Robert says the same.'

'I'm surprised to see Bob this far from White Oaks,' I said.

'There was a period of time when he would not travel at all. It was his interest in your son that changed him. He never had children of his own. Now, when he speaks of Brian, he speaks as a father. It is good for both of them. I think. Brian always seems happy to see Robert.'

I didn't respond to this.

'Have you visited the clinic?' I asked.

'*Mais oui!* I have met Brian. He too is handsome, but his features are not the same. They are, how should I say it, more delicate?'

'Not as rough,' I said.

'Yes. I have also met Brian's nurse, the marvelous one who Maul has been writing all the postcards to.'

'Nurse Major Wilma "Whiskey" O'Neil,' I said.

'Yes! That is the one! She is quite superb!'

We chatted for a while. I liked Dominique. She struck me as a good match for Coyle, bright and independent.

The yacht, as it turned out, belonged to her.

Later, I went out on the afterdeck to get some air. I found Maul there, leaning on the rail. The new tender hung from davits near the place where he stood.

'Mr. Cooke wants to meet with you for a briefing at sixteen hundred in the lounge,' he said.

'Fine,' I said. 'That will give me some time to sleep.'

'I hear you're going to Turkey.'

'That's right. I'll be hooking up with a friend of mine in the seaport of Izmir. Campbell tells me it's the birthplace of Homer.'

'Homer who?' Maul said.

Chapter Nine

I found Bock Vanderwald in the Legionnaire's Café on the water-front at Izmir. He was laughing. His laugh came in great booming yelps that all but shattered the long gilt mirror over the bar. The café was jammed.

'Hey, pilot!' he shouted when he saw me. 'Hey, Mateus!'

He stood, six and a half feet tall, his back to the bar. It was Bastille Day and he was surrounded by ex-Legionnaires, Turks, expatriate French, transients from a dozen countries who had come here to celebrate. His blond hair had thinned since I had seen him last, and his weight looked as if it had come down some from the 240 pounds I remembered him carrying. Though he was a Dutchman by birth, his features resembled those of a benign Charles de Gaulle: small eyes beaming over a truly heroic nose. He wore a white collarless shirt buttoned at the throat; his face had taken on the ruddy glow of wine.

'Hey, Mateus!' he shouted, over the heads of the crowd. 'Come and we will drink together! For us, and for France!'

I made my way toward him through a minefield of heavily occupied tables bristling with chairs, past clots of ebullient men who were blocking access to the bar. The atmosphere was chaotic. It was late afternoon; most of the patrons looked as if they had been drinking since dawn. The café reeked of alcohol and smoke. The Turks, with abominable accents, were practicing their French in honor of the day. The French were shouting out songs of the Legion, their voices loud and charged with emotion. When I finally reached Bock, I had to step over the body of a man who lay on his side, unconscious, below the footrail of the bar.

'Eh, Mateus,' Bock said. 'Too long, eh? Too long!'

He clapped his arms around me in a bear hug, almost lifting me off my feet, then banged a kiss off each of my cheeks. I stand six-two and carry a fair amount of weight, but around the Dutchman, I've always felt small.

He shoved a tumbler of red wine into my hand, raised his glass, and bellowed a toast in French that said we were the best of friends, that though I had not served with the Legion, I had the heart of a Legionnaire. The crowd cheered happily at this. Their affection for Bock was clear. The man who lay at our feet continued to lie there. He hadn't moved.

'What's the matter with him?' I asked.

'It is of no importance,' Bock said. 'He had too much to drink. That's all.'

'His shoulder looks funny,' I said.

'He slipped off his stool,' Bock said. 'Soon they will come and take him away.'

'Has anyone checked his pulse?'

'He is Slavic,' one of the Turks said who stood nearby. 'You cannot find the pulse of a Slav.'

I squatted down. The Slav was about Bock's size, but younger, with long curly hair and a round, pugnacious chin. His deltoids and biceps bulged out from his sleeveless jersey; his forearms were corded with muscle and marked with tattoos. He could have been a dock worker, a weightlifter, a stoker in a steel mill. His hands were padded with calluses and grease-stained. There was a gold ring in the lobe of his right ear. He lay on his left side, with his left arm extended in front of him. His right arm was broken at the shoulder. His jaw was dislocated. His front teeth were split. His pulse, when I found it, was shallow and quick.

'He must have taken quite a tumble from that stool,' I said.

Bock looked uncomfortable.

'Someone will come and take him away,' he said. 'The authorities have been called.'

'Do you know him?'

'Not well. Hardly at all. Now listen, Mateus. You and I and the others will sing. First "Pauvre Soldat." Then "Le Boudin." Do you need more wine? Do you prefer the rosé? It is from Portugal. Not the best you and I have drunk together – certainly not the worst. Your voice will add to the singing. Let us begin, *mon ami*. Let us begin!'

He led off. The rest of us followed. We sang the two songs he had

46

mentioned, and then a couple more. The Turks joined in with their terrible accents and irrepressible joy. Nobody came for the Slav. He groaned once, and blew small bubbles out of one corner of his mouth. Bock never looked at him while we sang. His own voice was louder than all the rest. He had joined the Legion in his teens because, as he told me once, it had been the best way he knew at the time to go and fight the Nazis. Since then he had become a devoted Francophile and considered himself more French than Dutch.

He was having a splendid time right now, and I could see how much he wanted to stay.

'Come on, old friend,' I said, finally. 'We've got a plane to catch.'

We went out of the café onto the Kordon, the boulevard that skirted the harbor. We were in the *gümrük* area between the Konak clock tower and the statue of Attaturk. The sea air was humid, but still refreshing after the smog in the bar. We turned up a back alley, heading into one of the seedier parts of town.

'You had no trouble finding my room?' Bock asked.

'No trouble,' I said. 'Campbell gave his usual good directions. I left my flight bag there. The hotel manager told me where you'd be. When did you get in?'

'Last night.'

'Any problems?'

'No. None,' he said. 'And you?'

I glanced at my watch.

'That's a long story,' I said. 'And we're running late. I'll fill you in once we're on the plane. Tell me about the big guy on the floor back there. When was it you knew him?'

'Six, maybe seven years ago. We were on a job together for Air France. He pretends to be a mechanic, but he has neither brains nor skill – only strength. They used him once in place of a hoist to lower an engine into a truck.'

'When did he show up at the café?'

'An hour before you.'

'What happened?'

Bock looked embarrassed. He walked with his hands in his pockets, striding along, head down.

'Please, Mateus,' he said. 'It was of no significance.'

'Was he on his way to Esenboga?'

47

'Yes. He had heard of the competition.'

'Did he brace you about it?'

'Yes.'

'What did he say?'

'He said I was too old to compete.'

'You told him he was wrong, of course.'

'No! I told him he was right! I am not one who looks for trouble, Mateus!'

'That's true,' I said.

'I told him he was right about everything. I said we would drink to his own country, and then to the honor of France.'

'Did he agree to drink with you?'

'No. He said France was the cesspool of all nations.'

'Oh oh,' I said.

'He left me no choice. We had to fight.'

'I understand.'

'It was only a small fight.'

'His arm was broken at the shoulder.'

Bock winced.

'I think his jaw was broken too,' I said. 'You could tell he'd been in a tussle.'

'I am ashamed of myself,' Bock said. 'You must never tell Colette. I have convinced her I am a gentle man.'

'You are,' I said. 'But you did a terrible job on his teeth.'

'He insulted the honor of France!'

I laughed. Bock looked at me, grinning.

'Well, that's what he did, the filthy *cochon*! Eh, Mateus,' he said. 'You look fit! Not like the last time, when your stomach hung over your belt. It is grand to see you, *mon ami*!'

We went to his room, picked up his tool kit and the rest of our luggage, caught a taxi to the airport. Campbell had provided us with 6,300 Turkish liras apiece, passports, round-trip airline tickets from Paris to Esenboga, and the coded number of a bank in Brussels. Bock's passport was French, mine was American.

Inasmuch as we had both worked as mercenaries in the past, we would be traveling under our own names. In my case Campbell, through the CIA and his own connections in Thailand, had put together an impressive string of backup numbers and references. Bock, whose exploits with the Legion in Africa and Indochina were well known among mercenaries, was at little risk of being challenged.

He was fifty-five years old now. I had first met him in Tripoli in 1956. He had been working for Air France then. I had been flying gunnery out of Wheelus, in the third year of my service. Since then our paths had crossed in Laos, Singapore, Portugal, and France. The last time I had seen him was a couple of years ago in his brasserie in the seaport of Honfleur on the Normandy coast. I had been on the skids then. Bock had done what he could to pull me up.

We arrived in front of the terminal at Cumàovasi Airport behind a cream-and-red *otobus* designed to hold twenty passengers and carrying forty. In spite of the heat, the women in the bus wore long coats and the men jackets and ties, upcountry hill folk on their way to Ankara, I guessed, to buy items for the late-summer trade fair in Izmir.

We shouldered our way through the crowd and went to the Turk Hava Yollari counter, where Bock checked in his tool kit. It was over two feet long and a foot high, constructed of a stipled gray metal with a leather-bound handle. Even Bock had not carried it easily.

'How much does that thing weigh?' I asked, as he reluctantly surrendered it to the attendant.

'Thirty-five kilos,' he said. 'It is not a full complement, but what I have brought will serve for field maintenance. My tools are my children.'

There was time for a quick beer at the small refreshments bar before our flight was called and we had to line up to pass through security control. I felt a slight click of apprehension as two Turkish soldiers in dark-green uniforms, holding Heckler and Koch G3 rifles, directed women one way, men the other. Bock and I went individually into curtained booths that separated the main terminal from the loading gates. A genial Turk who seemed to know a dozen words in a dozen languages patted me down while a grim-looking secret service man checked my face against the pictures in a large tattered photobook. As he bent forward, I could see the Turkish MKE pistol in his shoulder holster. He glanced from the book to my face several times. Then, as if disappointed, he nodded to the other, who said, 'Okay now, mister. Good flight, mister.'

I joined Bock in the waiting room. In moments the gate was opened and we were led onto the ramp and to the airplane. Lined up near the baggage compartment were all the suitcases and boxes the passengers had checked in. Each owner had to identify his luggage before it could be loaded. In this way no explosive device could be placed on board with its owner remaining behind. Bock identified his tool kit. The bags we were carrying were small enough to fit under our seats.

We sat as far aft as possible. I noted the locations and operating procedures of the escape doors as we passed them. Usually, I take the aisle seat. This time, as a concession to Bock's age and size, I gave it to him. The passenger configuration for the THY 727 is about as cramped as the British Airways Tridents that haul people like cattle between London and Paris at exorbitant fares. State-owned airlines have never been much given to passenger comfort or competitive pricing. I was hoping Freddy Laker would soon change all that.

The flight attendants made the appropriate announcements in Turkish, French, and English. Then we were airborne, climbing out directly on course, east to Ankara. As soon as the No Smoking sign went off, eighty percent of the passengers lit up. The smoke from Turkish cigarettes is heavy and smells like old dust. Even the cabin air conditioning couldn't do much with it.

During the flight, I quietly gave Bock the details of what had happened to Campbell and me in Piraeus, and the nature of our mission as Coyle had spelled it out for me on board the *Cri du Coeur*.

'Pretty melancholy name for a yacht,' I said when I had finished.

'It is from the song sung by Piaf,' Bock said. 'It speaks of voices tormented with sadness and joy; and how, without pity, the singer has walked over her tears.'

He was silent then, gazing somberly into the middle distance, through the pall of cigarette smoke that filled the plane.

Chapter Ten

We touched down at Esenboga Airport, thirty kilometers north of Ankara, at dusk. The field elevation was 3,100 feet, the air unusually clear. In the distance, I could see the gnarled and aging hills of Turkey under a purpling sky and yellow moon.

'What is our destination here?' Bock asked as we filed with the other passengers toward the concrete terminal building.

'A place called the Merhaba Hotel,' I said. 'Campbell wasn't sure where it was. We'll have to get directions.'

My father-in-law had disembarked the *Cri du Coeur* in Izmir and had flown from there to Istanbul. He had not explained why, nor had I asked. The history he had put together for me was that of a USAF fighter pilot gone bad: an officer with a distinguished career who had become embittered by what the war had done to him and his family, and who had finally resigned his commission to become a mercenary. As I told him when he briefed me on it, there was more truth to that history than I liked to admit.

He said I could contact him anytime by using a blind number he had set up through NATO South headquartered in Izmir. The CIA would monitor that, and the UHF guard channel on all airborne radio communications. My code name would be Papa Wolf, the call sign I had used when I had been a squadron commander flying FAC missions out of Ubon, Thailand. Campbell's name would be Delta One. As an operations chief for the Agency, with a high-priority charter, he assured me I would be able to reach him quickly, day or night, wherever he happened to be.

We had said our goodbyes, standing at the seawall in Izmir, watching the *Cri du Coeur* as she cruised slowly out of the harbor, flying the Turkish courtesy flag. Coyle and Dominique had waved casually to us from the afterdeck. I had not apologized to Coyle for my bluntness during our meeting. I had thanked him and

51

Dominique for their hospitality.

The airport bar at Esenboga was crowded. Bock and I shouldered our way in. The bartender, a stout Turk with a mustache that looked as if it had been trimmed off the back of a St. Bernard, welcomed us as we ordered our drinks.

'*Hos geldiniz,*' he said. 'You will please have what?'

'Whiskey,' I said. 'Cognac for my friend.'

I told him we were looking for the Merhaba Hotel. If the name meant anything to him, he did not let on. He said the Merhaba was west of the airport on the road to Sirkeli.

'How far?' I said.

'Twenty-two kilometers,' he said. 'It is a distance which in a taxi will leave you poor. If you like better to rent a car, I tell you it is easy. I have a fine *oto* like you have never seen. It performs like the wind in an olive tree and has the comfort of many cushions.'

'*Ne kadar odemeliyim?*' Bock said slowly. He had hooked on a pair of spectacles and was studying a small phrasebook which he had pulled from his shirt pocket.

'For you,' the bartender said, 'one thousand liras per day.'

'*Ucyuz!*' Bock shot back.

'Eight hundred,' the bartender said, rolling his eyes.

'*Besyuz, besyuz,*' Bock said. His expression was one of indifference.

'This now is taking bread from the mouths of my children!' the bartender said.

'*Besyuz,*' Bock said, suppressing a yawn.

'Okay, misters. Five hundred, then, per day. But it is you who must pay for the gas.'

Bock nodded, then looked at me solemnly.

'I have practiced my Turkish,' he said. 'It is good.'

As Bock was concluding his deal for the car, a freckled man in his early thirties jostled up next to us. He wore tan pants and a blue denim shirt, had curly red hair, wash-blue eyes, and a thin line of grease under his nails, down near the quick where it's hard to get out. I had noticed him earlier on our walk in from the plane. He had been wearing a pair of coveralls then and had been closing the inspection panel on one of the engines of a Lockheed Jetstar with American NC markings. It had been conspicuous as the most impressive aircraft on the civilian flight line.

'That's a nice piece of machinery you've got out there,' I said.

'I'm her crew chief is all,' he said. He spoke with a slight drawl. 'She belongs to Diebolt Forge out of Erie. They've got me hung up here a week waiting for a spare.'

'What's the problem?'

'We can't get full power on number four. Those J-60s can be antsy sometimes. You fellas here on business or pleasure?'

'Little of both,' I said.

We introduced ourselves. He said his name was George Wyatt. The three of us were standing close together at the bar. Wyatt was drinking a beer. Bock was peering down at him through the spectacles he had put on to read his phrasebook.

'This engine of yours,' he said. 'Is it a matter of low RPM?'

'No,' Wyatt said. 'Low EPR. She's got a broken bleed strap.'

'That's all?'

'Far as I can tell it is. I've been over it with a comb.'

'I am familiar with this engine,' Bock said. 'If everything else is sound, it should perform as high as seventy-five percent power. There is no need to wait for a new strap.'

Wyatt grinned.

'I wish I'd had you with me when I told my boss that,' he said. 'If there'd been two of us, could be he'd have listened better. Are you both mechanics?'

'Bock's the mechanic,' I said. 'I'm a pilot.'

'Civilian?'

'That's right.'

We talked back and forth for a while. I found myself liking Wyatt, but not quite trusting him. There seemed to be a subtle persistence to his questions that went beyond the requirements of bar chat. Neither Bock nor I gave much away, but we didn't get much either. Bock drank cognac steadily, without noticeable effect. I tried to take it easier than usual on the whiskey. Wyatt nursed his beer. He had a way of looking at us and past us at the same time, as if he were expecting someone he knew to come into the bar. The room was still crowded, loud with multilingual conversation and filled with a curtain of smoke that was nearly impenetrable at the ceiling and thinned out as it got toward the

53

floor. My eyes stung the way they had when I had been underwater in Piraeus.

'There were a couple of Swedes in here earlier today, asking directions to the Merhaba,' Wyatt said. 'A pilot and a mechanic, same as you. They'd just finished a contract for SAAB in Zambia.'

He said the two Swedes had been hired to convert six SAAB-built Safari airplanes into the military version known as the Supporter. Sweden's neutrality act prevented their selling the planes with a military configuration. SAAB did, however, install hard points under the wings and allow room for electrical plumbing before the planes left the factory at Linkoping.

'These boys did the conversions in the field and cross-trained the Zambian pilots and mechanics,' Wyatt said. 'Then things got slow, so they came up here. They told me one of the local Turks was hiring out of the Merhaba. They asked me if I knew what the job was, but I couldn't help them.'

'You were in the Air Force,' I said. 'Where did you do your tour?'

He looked up in surprise.

'How'd you know that?' he said.

'Just a guess,' I said. 'I was in for a while. When you called the engine on your Jetstar a J-60, I figured you might be military. The civilian designation is JT-12.'

'I did one tour as a chopper mechanic in Nam,' he said. 'I got out in '67 and never looked back. It was a bullshit war.'

'Roger that,' I said.

A short while later, Wyatt excused himself and sidled down the bar to talk with someone else. I watched him for several minutes, decided finally he was probably just what he appeared to be: a man who had gotten stuck in a foreign place, who was lonely, who had come in here at the end of a long day to taper off.

When Bock and I left, we went into the trinket shop, where Bock bought a hubbly-bubbly pipe to send home to Colette. He used his spectacles and phrasebook again, but here, the prices of the merchandise were firm. We were about to leave when I grabbed his arm and turned him back toward the counter.

'*Qu'y a-t-il?*' he said quietly.

'One of Art Farmer's men is just outside the store,' I said. 'He was on that freighter I told you about.'

It was one of the Greeks who had been playing cards in the wheelhouse when Dixie had first brought me in to have my talk with Farmer. He was standing with his hands in his pockets, examining the contents of the display window.

Chapter Eleven

The Greek studied the window for a while, then walked off in the direction of the bar. He walked absently, as if he were waiting to make connections. As far as I could tell, he hadn't recognized me. I was wearing a loose-fitting flowered shirt and had a stubble of whisker. The lights in the shop were bright fluorescent, the lights on the freighter had been dim. Most important, the Greek had no reason to suspect I might be here. He would assume I was dying of rat bite or thirst, with my father-in-law, in the boatswain's store of the *Lygarius*.

I found the pay telephone booth inside the main terminal building and put in a call to the blind number Campbell had given me. I left a message, telling him when Farmer's people had split up from the freighter, one of them had showed up at Esenboga. I also gave him George Wyatt's name to run through his computers on the off chance something might develop there.

I said I thought if we had to, Bock and I could handle the Greek.

The car Bock had rented for us was an aging Volkswagen sedan: a black, sand-scoured Beetle with a plastic rose wired to the aerial. The top of the car was dented, as if someone had jumped onto it from the roof of a garage. Rainwater had collected and gone scummy in the dent. There was no rear seat. The front buckets bloomed with exposed stuffing. Bock looked dismayed. I clapped him on the shoulder.

'It's okay,' I said.

'But, Mateus, for this we will pay five hundred liras per day?'

'He started at a thousand.'

'Plus gas!'

'The engine could be fine,' I said.

We loaded our gear into the front luggage compartment. When

the lid wouldn't close over Bock's tool kit, he kept applying pressure, gradually molding the lid like tinfoil over the kit. I had never before seen him treat a vehicle with anything but reverence. When the latch finally clicked shut, he slapped his hands together, then gave me the keys. I got in behind the wheel and cranked the engine on. We idled out of the airport lot, enveloped in a cloud of blue smoke and backfire.

'How it is?' Bock said.

I smiled.

'Like the wind in an olive tree,' I said.

'Sacriste,' he muttered.

We drove north, first on asphalt, then on gravel chippings. The headlights of the Volkswagen were dim. Several times I had to gear down to avoid black-robed shepherds who, with their flocks safely bedded for the night, were walking to the nearest *kahvehane* to sip coffee and play *tavla*, the national game of backgammon. Even with the passenger bucket pushed all the way back on its rails, Bock's knees still touched the dash. Our talk centered on airplanes, and the places we had known. He had memorized many fine passages from Saint-Exupéry, the great French aviator who, with his pilot friend Mermoz, was one of Bock's special heroes.

'And do you remember the words of Mermoz,' Bock asked, 'as he contemplated his death, having elected to live a life of danger?'

I did, but I shook my head so I could hear Bock recite them. He raised his hand and said with feeling:

' "It is worth it. It is worth the final smashup." '

'Not bad,' I said.

'Magnifique!' Bock said.

We ran twenty kilometers on the gravel road, then fifty meters up a dirt road to the Merhaba. It stood three stories high, an aging brick-and-wood structure that had been designated H-4, the least favorable rating on the Turkish scale that started at one. A dozen nondescript cars and one motorcycle – a Moto Morini 500 Sport – were parked haphazardly around the dusty courtyard in front of the door. The downstairs lights were on. Through the open windows on the ground floor, we could hear an uproar of profane laughter and shouts, whistles and applause.

'Sounds like the mercs have taken over the bar,' I said.

'I have only three desires,' Bock said. 'To eat a meal, to drink a bottle of wine, and then to sleep.'

'In the old days,' I reminded him, 'you were the last to fold.'

'Ah, but Mateus,' he said sadly, 'that was then. This is now.'

We carried our gear inside and checked into one of the few remaining rooms at the Merhaba. It was a small cubicle on the third floor with two bunk beds, two casement windows overlooking a vegetable garden, and a pink washbasin on a round table below an unframed shard of mirror.

The room was hot, and my beard had started to itch. When I looked in the mirror, I saw a face that definitely would not have been used on a recruiting poster. I wanted to shave, but Campbell had told me not to – advice that had paid off once, and might again.

We went downstairs to the area that served as dining room and bar. The walls were plaster and had been painted the shade of yellow one finds in municipal buildings in the States. A ceiling fan, set at half speed, did what it could to stir the heat and smoke. The room was crowded with mercenaries who had come here to fight for the job that had been advertised by the broker, Pazar. There were a half-dozen pilot-mechanic teams from as many countries, men who if the financial incentives were right would happily operate outside the laws of any nation, at great risk to their lives. Some, like Bock, would hold to a personal ethic that ruled out trafficking in drugs, white slavery, genocide, or military adventures against civilian populations. Others – and these usually constituted the majority – would undertake missions of any kind, assuming the pay was right.

As Bock and I came into the room, a contest was underway. One of the Swedish mercs, a tall, platinum-haired pilot, had bet the crowd he could empty a half-liter stein of beer in two swallows. The money had been collected and the stein was waiting on the bar. There was now disagreement as to how the contest should be judged.

'Hey, Bogan!' one of the American mercs shouted. 'How the fuck are we supposed to tell how many swallows you took?'

Bogan explained in halting English that if his Adam's apple bobbed more than twice before he finished the beer, he would lose. As he was explaining this, a younger man with dark hair and a handsome face walked past Bock and me. He slipped up behind

58

Bogan and, from a bowl on the bar, ladled a spoonful of powdered red pepper into the stein.

The younger man's name was Lutz. He wore tight pants and a macho shirt, a tiger's tooth on a necklace, and a heavy gold Air America-type bracelet with the double elephant clasp and his name and pilot's wings embossed. I recognized the design of the bracelet as that of Vilay-Phone's out of Vientienne, Laos; and it was my guess Lutz had at one time or another hired out to René Enjalbal and the opium dealers in the Golden Triangle.

It was too late for either Bock or me to warn Bogan about his doctored drink. With a confident flourish, the Swede took half of it in a single swallow, dropped the stein, clutched at his throat, and ran, bulging-eyed, from the room.

Lutz howled with laughter. His laugh was high-pitched and nasty. The rest of the mercs, as soon as they realized what had happened, began to laugh with him: Americans, Germans, Italians, many of them sadistically amused over the fate of the Swede. Bock muttered something to Lutz as we passed him on our way to an empty table.

'What did you say?' I asked, as we took our seats.

'I told him it is cowardly to trick a man behind his back,' Bock said. He put on his spectacles and got out his phrasebook. 'Now, Mateus,' he said, 'do you trust me to order?'

'The waiter *could* speak English,' I said.

'*C'est à savoir!*' he said. 'But as guests of his country, we will show our respect by speaking his tongue!'

'Okay, fine,' I said. 'This is what I have in mind: soup to start, then some meat and vegetables, then some fruit. All that, and a bottle of red.'

'*Très bien,*' Bock said. 'To make it simple, I will specify the same thing twice.'

When the waiter came, Bock ordered *corba, kebap, pilav, meyva,* and a bottle of *kirmizi sarap*. When the waiter complimented him on his pronunciation, the old Dutchman beamed; and it would have been a very pleasant evening if it hadn't been for Lutz.

He had taken offense at Bock's remark and began needling him. While we were having our soup, he did it from the bar. While we were having our vegetables and meat, he did it from a position halfway between the bar and where we sat. By the time we got to our fruit, he was standing just behind Bock, ridiculing the way Bock held his spoon.

'You keep that up, my friend,' I said, 'and one of us is going to pinch off your head.'

Lutz reddened.

'Is he such a coward that you must speak for him?' he said. He spoke his English with a Belgian accent.

I started to get up, but Bock waved me down. He had been eating a bowl of cherries with great relish, in spite of Lutz's yapping at his heels. Now he finished his wine, patted his lips with a napkin, folded it neatly, took his spectacles off. Then he stood up. It seemed to take him a long time to reach his full height. Wringing wet, Lutz might have qualified as a welterweight. Other things being equal, Bock could have picked him up with one hand and thrown him through a wall.

'I have called this man a coward,' Bock said, loudly enough for the other mercs to hear. 'And now he has called me a coward in return. I challenge him in your presence to a contest of reflex and nerve which will settle this matter between us.'

The mercs were silent for a moment, then shouted appoval. As they crowded around, Bock strode to the bar and turned the speed switch to high on the overhead Casablanca fan. Then he pointed up.

'I will stop the blades with my head,' he said. 'And you, Lutz, if you are truly brave, will answer my challenge by doing the same.'

I had seen Bock perform this stunt years ago in Tripoli. He was the only man I ever knew who could make it work.

He glanced at the fan to determine the speed of its rotation and the pitch of its blades. Then he stood on a chair and quickly raised his head into the blur of its motion. There was a barely audible ticking sound, and a half second later the fan had stopped, one of its blades resting against the back of his skull.

The crowd cheered him wildly as he stepped down. Lutz, his pride now at stake, watched nervously as the fan resumed its speed.

'And now my friend, it is your turn,' Bock said.

No one except Bock had ever gotten it right.

When Lutz stood on the chair and finally poked his head up into the blur, the leading edge of one of the blades caught him *Whap!* behind the head and knocked him flat. He hit the floor spread-eagled, spilling the chair into the crowd.

Bock towered over the place where he lay.

'*Voulez-vous danser, Monsieur Lutz?*' he said.

Would you care to dance?

Chapter Twelve

Khadija Al Hakim arrived at the hotel at seven-thirty the next morning. She arrived with her Arab bodyguard in a battered three-quarter-ton Dodge truck that carried camouflage paint and no cab. The bodyguard sat on the passenger seat. Khadija drove.

I had come downstairs early and was sitting at one of the window tables in the bar-dining room, having breakfast with Bogan, the Swede. The room was bright with morning sunshine, the breeze through the open window fresh. Bogan seemed to have shrugged off the incident with the red pepper, though he did occasionally glance in Lutz's direction with an expression of vague contempt.

Lutz sat with his back to us at a table across the room. He struck me as the kind who would need to get even for the humiliation he had suffered the night before; but if this was true, he gave no sign. He was having coffee and rolls with his mechanic, an evil-looking one-eyed man with a scar on his cheek and a badly dropped shoulder. Bogan said the man's name was DeBoor. He and Lutz were both Belgian. The rumor was that DeBoor had been injured in the crash of a C-47 off a runway, fighting in the Congo for Moise Tshombe.

Bock had decided to sleep late, as had Bogan's man Nils, who was suffering dysentery. Most of the other mercenaries were up and about, their mood subdued from the night before, and wary. There was a murmur of recognition when, with her bodyguard at her side, Khadija walked into the room.

She was in her late twenties, the daughter of the Syrian Dr. Zahida Al Hakim who had gained prominence as a militant Islamic nationalist. His name had been linked for years with those of Arafat and Qaddafi, and, more recently, with that of the terrorist Abu Daoud. From what Campbell had told me on board the *Cri du Coeur*, Hakim fit well into the pattern of Pazar's known clientele.

Two years ago, *Der Spiegel* had published an interview with

Khadija. I was living in Wiesbaden at the time, drinking myself silly; but I remembered reading her story with interest. She held degrees in economics and data processing from Cal Tech, and had taught both subjects at the American University in Beirut. Articulate and attractive, she had, since the *Der Spiegel* piece, become popular with journalists and had appeared several times on U.S. television via satellite transmissions from Damascus. When responding to political questions, she usually stayed close to her father's fanatical line; but I sensed that the years she had spent in California had widened her perspective enough to allow her to look at more than one side of an issue, and I suspected – though I had no proof – she might in fact be more loyal to her father than to his cause.

Her features were Arabic; aquiline nose, dusky skin, dark eyes. Her hair was brown with tints of red, quite long and full, but pulled back from her face now in a less feminine style than I remembered from the photographs and TV films. She wore khaki pants and shirt, a pair of Wellington boots, no jewelry, and, as far as I could tell, no makeup of any kind. Her bodyguard was an Arab about Bock's age and size: a somber, intelligent-looking man with a graying beard, who wore khakis darker in color than Khadija's, and a white muslin headpiece. He carried no visible weapons. He stood behind her with his arms folded across his chest as she took her seat at a table by the bar. The room, which had gotten noisy, quickly became silent.

'My name is Khadija,' she said. 'As some of you may know, I am the daughter of Zahida Al Hakim.' Her voice was steady, business-like in tone, her English pronunciation formal and scarcely touched by accent. The only indication she might be nervous was a slight tremor in her hand. She said it was her father who – acting through Pazar – had been responsible for bringing us here. Then she gestured behind her.

'This is my uncle,' she said. 'His name is Sabah. He will give you sheets of paper on which to record your name and experience. If you are a pilot, please list the airplanes you have flown and the total time in each. If you are a mechanic, please list your airframe and engine qualifications. We are not interested in seeing licenses. We are interested in references that may be confirmed by telex or radio within forty-eight hours. All pilots must have time in the C-47 and in the

F-86. All mechanics must have avionics qualification.'

At this there was a confused stirring among the group while those who had no trouble with English translated what she had said for those who did. Finally, one of the Americans piped up from the back of the room.

'When Pazar put out the word he was hiring,' he said, 'he talked gooney-bird and jet-fighter time. He didn't say squat about the F-86.'

'For security reasons, we didn't tell Mahmet that this and the avionics would be a requirement until this morning,' Khadija replied. 'If any of you have been inconvenienced, it is our fault and not his.'

'Well now, *goddammit*, lady . . .'

'To any of you who have been inconvenienced,' she said coolly, 'we will pay the equivalent of one thousand dollars each in the currency of your choice.'

It was a good ploy. The Americans and two other teams picked up their money from Sabah and went out of the room. They sounded disgruntled, but looked content. That left the Swedes, me and Bock, Lutz and DeBoor. I filled in Bock's qualifications and references as well as my own. Bogan did the same for Nils. Then we handed them in, and Khadija looked them over.

'Good,' she said when she was through.

'We got sidetracked on the questions,' I said. 'I'd like to get back to them.'

She looked at me without expression.

'Yes?' she said.

'According to the word that was passed to me and my mechanic, the job you're hiring for is going to go to the winners of some kind of competition. Is that right?'

'Yes,' she said. 'The competition will be held today, and tomorrow, at Mahmet's private field,' She glanced at my sheet of paper. 'Your background qualifies you to take part.'

'I'm not worried about that,' I said. 'You just paid six men good money for doing nothing more than showing up at this hotel. How much are you going to pay for the competition?'

'The losers will receive the equivalent of five thousand dollars each in the currency of their choice. The winners will receive the equivalent of ten thousand dollars each.'

'Does that come off the top of the mission?'

'No. Payment for the mission will be negotiated directly with my father.'

'What kind of money are we talking about?'

'Not less than the equivalent of half a million dollars.'

Lutz whistled his approval.

Bogan took a deep breath.

Nobody asked what the mission was. We all knew at this point no one would tell us.

Chapter Thirteen

When I went up to our room, I found Bock standing in front of the window, gazing out at the vegetable garden that grew behind the hotel. He had his trousers and suspenders on. A clean white shirt was lying on the bed behind him. He did not turn around as I came in.

'We made the first cut,' I said.

I told him what had happened downstairs. He listened absently, had little to say. The atmosphere in the room was uncomfortable as I picked up my kit and got ready to leave. I used the time to work up a speech.

'It took me a long while to learn what depression was all about,' I said. 'I went through about thirty upbeat years before my roof fell in. When it finally did, I went all the way down. I wouldn't have come back if it hadn't been for some good friends who just flat refused to give up on me even when I'd given up on myself. You were one of those friends, Bock. I never thanked you the way I probably should have, because it would have made me feel awkward, and besides that I figured you knew. I don't know what's eating at you right now. The first time I picked up something might be wrong was on the flight in from Izmir. You seemed depressed then too. Whatever it is, if you want to talk about it, I'm ready to listen.'

He was a tall, proud man who, I suspected, had never bent one inch in his life toward the phony sentiment of self-pity; but now when he turned toward me, I could see he was moved.

'I am sorry, Mateus,' he said. 'It is only a small thing.' He shrugged his shoulders, drawing them back. 'It is Colette. She has attracted another, whom she says she prefers.'

'Then I'm sorry too,' I said. 'I only met her once, but I thought she was a good woman.'

'She is the best of women. It is I who have been unworthy; and here I repeat the offense by burdening you with my complaints.'

He put on his collarless shirt and picked up his enormous tool kit and travel bag.

'Now,' he said, 'let us proceed to the pleasure of our work.'

'No reason why it shouldn't be fun,' I said. 'At least for a while.'

He smiled.

'Mateus,' he said, 'you are one who enjoys competition.'

'I love it,' I said. 'So do you.'

I knew I needed to tell Campbell about the involvement of the Hakims, but there was no secure way to do this from the hotel. I was going to have to wait for an opportunity, and the way things were shaping up, it looked as if that might be a while.

Khadija had given us directions to the airstrip. We were to proceed twenty kilometers further on the gravel road that had brought us to the Merhaba, then turn north through open gates spanned by a grillwork arch carrying the name Pazar. After five kilometers on a dirt track, we would pass Pazar's villa on our right; an additional five kilometers would bring us to the field.

The plastic rose on the aerial of the Volkswagen had attracted a pink butterfly, which hung around in the heat shimmer while we loaded up our gear. Khadija and her uncle had already left in their truck. Earlier, I had seen DeBoor checking the oil of a rented Peugeot that was still parked in the lot. Bogan and Nils had a van which would take them to the competition as soon as Nils was feeling up to it.

The Moto Morini 500 Sport belonged to Lutz. He had come out of the hotel and was warming it up. Motorcycles in recent years had gotten to sounding like sewing machines, but Lutz's sounded good: deep and throaty.

'What are his credentials?' Bock said.

'He told Bogan he was a captain in the Belgian air force. Apparently he got cashiered for running dope out of Amsterdam. He's got time in the F-86 and the F-104. Bogan says he talks as if he's a pretty shit-hot pilot. He's been on the mercenary circuit for about five years.'

Bock snorted.

'He is a child,' he said.

'If that was all there was to it, I wouldn't worry,' I said. 'But I've got a feeling our friend Lutz has a screw loose. I don't care how good a pilot he is; I wouldn't want him on my wing.'

'He is harmless,' Bock said. 'You make too much of him.'

As before, I drove the Volkswagen. Bock's feet were too big to fit comfortably into the space provided for clutch, brake, and gas pedal.

As I turned my circle in the courtyard and headed for the exit, I heard above our own engine noise a loud blatting sound coming toward us. I glanced in the rear-view mirror, saw it was Lutz on his bike. He had on a pair of goggles and was bent low over the handle-bars. As he reached Bock's side of the car, he swerved slightly and gunned his engine, sending up a roostertail of dust that poured onto Bock through the open window. I braked to a stop.

'Merde!' Bock bellowed. Sputtering and coughing, he leaped out of the car, almost tearing the door off the hinges. *'Putain!'* he shouted at the rapidly disappearing figure. *'Imbecile!'*

Shaking his fist, he looked around desperately for something to throw, but it was too late. I think if I hadn't been sitting in the car, he would have picked it up and dashed it to the ground to vent his fury.

'I guess we'll have to credit Lutz with some nerve,' I said. 'He knows damn well you're going to see him again.'

'He thinks I will not fight him because of the discrepancy in our size! *That* is his nerve!'

'Maybe he's a master of the martial arts,' I said.

Bock glowered at me.

'Bah,' he said.

Still muttering, he dusted himself off as best as he could and climbed back into the Beetle. His shirt, which had been clean and white, was now the same brown color as the dust. I tried not to smile, but I couldn't help it. I thought his anger had been superb.

We moved up the gravel road. It was dry and dusty, and we didn't have far enough to travel to worry about the time we made. Bock, whose feathers had been ruffled, stared moodily ahead. There was no traffic. I let my mind wander to events of the recent past.

I thought if Campbell was sitting next to me now, I could tell him the following things: (A) Hakim and his terrorists were putting together some sort of clandestine mission that called for the services of a pilot who had experience in the C-47 and F-86; (B) the avionics requirement for the mechanic suggested a tie-in with Coyle's stolen navigation systems; (C) the payoff for the mission was going to be uncommonly high, which meant the mission was probably going to be uncommonly hazardous.

Unless I had missed something along the way, I was pretty sure you didn't pay mercenary pilots half a million dollars to smuggle contraband, or to strafe or bomb limited targets in an insurgency operation. I was also sure you didn't usually specify the need for a mechanic, or winnow out your applicants by observing how well they performed in competition.

Hakim had something special in mind. He knew what it was. We didn't. The most recent terrorist activity I knew of had been carried out by South Moluccans who had hijacked a passenger train in the Netherlands, taking 161 hostages. That had happened at the end of May, and it had taken until the middle of June before the Royal Dutch Marines had finally cleared them out.

I didn't think Hakim was about to hijack a train.

There were a lot of threads so far, but no ball of yarn. Someone at Esenboga had been stealing classified electronic equipment that had been air-freighted from Coyle Enterprises destined for the Turkish military. Campbell had said there was evidence linking Pazar to the thefts. That meant there could well be a connection between the stolen systems and Hakim; also – now that I had spotted the Greek at the airport – between Hakim and Art Farmer.

But what?

I tried one combination and then another, all with no result. I found myself wishing Khadija were the daughter of somebody else. I liked the way she had handled herself; I liked the way she looked. There was a toughness that rippled through her, like muscle under skin. She reminded me of Jillion Leggett, an old friend of mine and the only other woman I knew who would have come with one body-guard to the Merhaba Hotel and dealt as coolly with the mercenaries as Khadija had.

But she was Hakim's daughter, not somebody else's; and, how-ever mixed her feelings might be about her father's fanatical cause, the fact was she was here in Turkey, doing his recruiting for him.

'Ah, Mateus!' Bock said suddenly. 'I believe the gods have been kind to us!'

We were on a straight, flat ribbon of gravel. Hills stretched away on either side. The landscape was bleak, the sun savage in the morning sky. On the road ahead, I saw a small black dot.

'What is it?' I said. 'A shepherd?'

'No,' Bock said. 'Unless I am mistaken, it is our good friend Monsieur Lutz.'

The dot remained stationary, growing larger as we approached.

'You're right,' I said. 'He must be having trouble with his bike.'

'It would only be courteous for us to stop,' Bock said. He was already opening his door.

As I pulled over, I could see the Belgian frantically working the enrichment lever and start button on the 500. The air around the bike smelled gassy.

'*Bonjour*, Monsieur Lutz!' Bock said cheerfully.

As we walked toward him, Lutz lowered his kickstand, jumped off the 500, and backed away. Bock took a brief look at the bike, then went and got his tools.

'I don't want your help, Dutchman!' Lutz shouted from a safe distance.

'But I insist,' Bock said. 'It is the least I can do. I suspect the difficulty here is very minor, but one can never be sure. Italian machinery is unpredictable.'

While I kept an eye on Lutz, Bock opened his kit.

First, he spread a black rubberized fender apron on the ground. Then, like a surgeon selecting the proper instruments for an operation, he laid out certain tools. There weren't many: three screwdrivers of varying size and type, a ratchet and extension, four or five sockets, two open-end wrenches, and a ball-peen hammer.

Flexing his fingers and humming quietly to himself, he put on his spectacles and walked once around the bike. Then he began.

He disconnected the front wheel cables, dismounted the wheel, unbolted the fender, disassembled the disc brakes and rotors, and removed the valve steam from the tire.

While the air was hissing out, he removed the speedometer and tach, unhooked the throttle and brake cables, removed the headlamp and directional signals, and separated the front fork from the main frame.

Lutz looked mad enough to bite through a hubcap.

Minutes later, the gas tank and seat were lying on the ground

70

while Bock, letting the mufflers and exhaust pipes cool, removed the rear shocks, disconnected the chain drive and hydraulic braking system, and slipped off the rear wheel – removing the valve stem from that tire as well.

After he had dewired the junction box and broken the engine down into its component parts, he finally held up two very small strip filters. They were of a pleated felt, and filthy with road dirt.

'The carburetors have been starved for air,' he said. 'These filters must be cleaned or replaced.'

He laid them carefully on the ground next to the many other parts of the bike, than packed up his tools. When he had finished, he walked over to the Belgian.

'Monsieur Lutz,' he said quietly, 'twice now I have treated you with kindness. If you provoke me again, I will dismantle you just as I have dismantled this machine.'

Lutz had turned white. A single vein bulged at his temple.

'Have a good day, Monsieur Lutz,' Bock said, waving pleasantly as we got back into the Beetle and drove away.

Chapter Fourteen

Pazar's airstrip was a dirt field in a valley surrounded by hills. There were two corrugated tin hangers, an operations shack, and a bunkhouse that looked like a budget motel.

The area behind the hangars was a graveyard of junked airplanes: T-6s, T-33s, some Fouga Magister airframes, two Tiger Moth biplanes, several other skeletons I tried to identify but couldn't. Most of them squatted on flat tires, and had gaping holes and bent tubing and braces where the engines had been mounted.

Three big C-47 transports were parked at the east end of the field. Two of these looked to be in dilapidated condition. One, set somewhat apart from the others, had a fresh coat of camouflage paint and was guarded by two men with rifles.

According to what Khadija had said, the strip itself lay at an elevation of two-thousand feet and on a line that ran roughly east to west. Across from the hangars, a windsock had been attached to a pole. Already, a fresh morning breeze was moving the sock on its swivel. I thought crosswinds on such a strip were liable to be tricky and unpredictable as the sun continued to warm the surrounding hills and the breeze increased.

The three-quarter-ton truck was parked in front of the operations shack. I pulled up behind it, and Bock and I went in. Khadija was there; her uncle was not. She was sitting at the flight planning table, studying an aeronautical chart, and paid no attention to us. I found this irritated me, though there was no particular reason why it should.

A Turkish caretaker, who apparently spoke no English, issued us a room in the bunkhouse. The building was unpainted cinderblock with a flat tar roof. There were eight rooms in all, each with its own entrance. Ours had a couple of cots, a chest, and a chair. There was an outhouse behind the building, with a red rubber hose and plastic shower attachment hooked to one of its outside walls. Bock surveyed these things and announced to me that this was decidedly not the Georges Cinque.

After we had put away our gear and washed the dust out of our eyes, we walked over to see if we could get a look at the hangars. I half expected we would find them guarded, and housing a couple of F-86s. I was wrong on both counts.

There were no guards. The big doors were open. Each hangar contained a T-28, the low-winged, prop-driven plane built for use as a trainer by North America in the early '50s. The 28 is all-metal, has a tricycle gear, and was designed to hold two people, one behind the other. I had flown them years before in pilot training, and more recently in Cambodia, where they had been modified for ground attack. These were the B-model version, each powered by a Wright-Cyclone R-1820 that would turn over fourteen hundred horsepower. Though I knew it was likely Pazar had bought the planes as surplus from the Turkish air force, there were no markings on either to indicate that.

In each hangar there were crates of engine oil and hydraulic fluid and barrels of 110-120-octane Av-gas. Near one of the T-28s, there was a large cart with four big 24-volt batteries hooked to a standard power cable. Bock inspected these materials and each of the planes with a quick, practiced eye.

'What do you think?' I said when he was through. 'Do they look operational?'

He shook his head.

'Perhaps,' he said. 'But according to the indicators, each engine has turned many hours. They are both due for overhauls. If I had to choose between them, without knowing more, I would select the plane in hangar number two.'

'I'll keep that in mind,' I said.

'Do you think these are the planes you and the others will fly in competition?'

'There's not much else around,' I said, 'except for the C-47s.'

Shortly before he was injured in Cambodia, my son, Brian, asked me if it was true that flying airplanes was like driving a car: that if you could drive one model well, you could drive them all well. One of his fellow students at the lycée, the son of an Army major, had told him this. Brian had said it was nonsense.

I remember telling him that in one way his friend was right. Just as the average driver can switch from a Chevy to a Lincoln, the average pilot can switch from, say, a Piper Cub to a Beech Bonanza. When you transition from a light plane like the Bonanza to a prop fighter, you're making a move in the order of going from a Chevy to one of the championship cars at Indianapolis. When you go from prop fighter to jet, you're in the rocket-boosted, land-speed-record class at Bonneville.

Lutz, Bogan, and I had all earned our tickets in that class. There was a good chance both of them, during their training as fighter pilots, had also flown the T-28, or some similar aircraft. If not, they could be expected to pick it up pretty much on the spot.

While Bock and I were still poking around in front of the hangars, DeBoor and Lutz arrived in DeBoor's rented Peugeot. They backed into the shade of a nearby juniper tree and offloaded the parts of the motorcycle, which DeBoor immediately began to reassemble. Lutz stood by, watching him and, at the same time, looking at us. I recognized the look. It said once again that he intended to get even. It said this time the Dutchman would wish he had never been born. It said if we were wise we would not turn our backs on him. I mentioned this, quietly, to Bock. Bock paid no attention.

Khadija came out of the operations shack and walked past us, without comment, on her way to the guarded C-47. She walked with purpose, a clipboard in one hand, arms swinging at her sides. I watched as she boosted herself nimbly up through the cargo door and disappeared inside.

'Does she interest you?' Bock asked. He was smiling his benign smile.

'Yes,' I said.

'In one way? Or in many?'

'Oh,' I said, 'many.'

'Ah,' he said. 'This is good.'

She came back fifteen minutes later with her uncle, Sabah, who had also apparently been in the plane. During the interim, Bogan and Nils had rolled up in their van. Nils was a gap-toothed, stocky man, younger than Bogan, with corn-colored hair and a dark stubble of beard. He looked as if he had beaten back his dysentery

74

mainly by force of will, and was ready now to meet whatever competition this daughter of Hakim might raise. The outside temperature had reached ninety. Dust was swirling around us, stirred by the capricious winds.

'It is my father's wish,' Khadija said, 'first to test the ability of the pilots to fly skillfully at low level.' She glanced at her uncle, who had taken a worn leather notebook from his shirt pocket and was studying it. After a moment, he spoke to her in Arabic. She asked him to repeat what he had said. Then she looked at us.

'You will have your choice of either plane in the hangars,' she said. 'You will have time to prepare the plane of your choice. Then, after takeoff, the pilot will fly back down the runway at a level lower than the top of the windsock pole, and will pull up into a loop. He will complete his loop, recovering at the same altitude it was started, below the top of the pole.'

We all turned and looked at the pole. It topped out at about twelve feet.

'Your order of flight will be determined by the number you receive on one of these three slips of paper.' She held them up. We each took one and unfolded it. I had drawn the number three. Lutz would go second, Bogan first.

'Have you flown the 28?' I asked the Swede.

'*Ya, ya,*' he said. 'Many times.'

He and Nils went to inspect the planes. Lutz looked amused, as if he thought he already had this particular part of the competition in his pocket. He cranked on a smile and struck up a conversation with Khadija. At first she was cool toward him, but he persisted, and finally she warmed up some to his charm. He asked her why Pazar was not on hand to watch the fun. She said he was in Istanbul, but expected to be on hand tomorrow. Lutz asked her what tomorrow's competition would involve. She shook her head and nodded toward her uncle.

'When he is ready, he will tell me,' she said, 'and I will tell you.'

The Swedes had selected the plane in hangar number two. Nils had hooked up the battery cart to that T-28 and had opened the gull-wing engine cowlings and every other inspection panel he could find. Bogan sat in the cockpit, moving switches and controls at his mechanic's command. Several empty tins of oil and hydraulic fluid were piled behind the battery cart. I watched as Nils finally pumped the Av-gas into the internal wing tanks. The tanks had a capacity of over eighty gallons each, but he kept them light, putting in just enough to allow Bogan to make his run and loop, with a small margin in reserve. Carrying extra weight would do nothing but hamper the aerobatics.

When everything was ready, they pushed the airplane out of the hangar. Then Nils stood on the wing next to the cockpit while Bogan turned over the engine. It misfired twice, coughed, then roared to life. Bogan smiled and gave us the thumbs-up sign.

We were quiet as we watched him taxi downwind on the dusty strip, his mechanic riding the wing. At the east end of the strip, he turned into the wind and began the engine power checks. He made prolonged high-RPM run-ups. Nils climbed down from the wing and made a couple of last-minute adjustments. Then he stepped back and waved toward the cockpit.

Bogan added power and the plane accelerated down the runway. The dust it stirred up swirled and blew off to the right in the gust of a crosswind. Once airborne, he snapped up the gear, holding the plane low to gain speed. Then he pulled up in a graceful arc and began to climb in wide circles above the field.

Khadija listened for a moment, then asked Lutz if something was wrong. He explained that the T-28 had a split exhaust system, a set of stacks on each side of the engine. If you were to one side as it went over, you heard the snap of only half the cylinders. It sounded as if the engine was about to fail. If you were directly underneath, you would hear a smooth roar. She nodded, looking reassured.

Still maintaining climb power, Bogan leveled off at about five thousand feet. Then he dropped the nose and began to dive. He dove for about three thousand feet before pulling into a neat loop.

'The Swede must practice,' Lutz said, speaking contemptuously.

'I don't blame him,' I replied.

'This trick is not so difficult.'

'I don't blame him at all,' I said.

Apparently satisfied, Bogan climbed back up and flew downwind directly over the runway, still at climb power. He did a few left and right aileron rolls along the way, checking his controls. As he reached the end of the runway, he abruptly rolled inverted and entered into a split-S maneuver. That's where you roll the airplane on its back and pull through what looks like the last half of a loop. It's a good way to lose altitude, gain airspeed, and change your flight direction by 180 degrees. Bogan didn't have to do it this way; he could simply have backed off from the runway and come diving in toward the ground. The extra bit of flair was a neat rejoinder to any possible criticism of the practice loop he had made. I smiled at Lutz, who looked away.

Bogan came down the runway, right on the deck, at tremendous speed. His prop, almost touching the ground, threw up a huge stream of dust that the wingtip vortices sent spiraling off to each side. Opposite us and directly in line with the windsock pole, he pulled up. The plane shot straight into the air, engine roaring now at takeoff power. I watched as the nose of the plane reached the vertical and started around the top side of the loop.

He's not going to make it, I thought.

Now inverted, he pulled the nose through the horizon and started down the back side of the loop at extremely high speed – too high for the maneuver he was trying to perform. I wanted to shout, *Break it off! Break it off!* – knowing he could still throttle back and roll out.

But he didn't.

Nils, who had walked back parallel to the runway, stood alone, watching his friend.

The T-28 was now headed straight for the ground at much too high an airspeed to pull it through. Too late, Bogan started the nose up, aiming for the spot on the runway where he had entered his loop. There simply wasn't enough room to pull out before hitting the ground.

He snatched back on the stick, pulled the throttle to idle. The plane shuddered, the roar of its engine muting, as he did. The aircraft entered a high-speed stall. With its nose slightly above level, it contacted the ground tail-first. Bogan slammed the throttle forward. The engine roared again as he tried to blast his way out of trouble.

The dragging tail threw up a huge spume of dust, then the prop started hitting the dirt as the nose pitched down. The plane thumped into the ground, bounced twenty feet into the air, rolling partially on its side as it fell back. With ripping and crashing noises it cartwheeled off the runway. A wing tore off under the stress and flew crazily into the air as the fuselage flopped over on its back, crushing the canopies. It slid another fifty feet before it finally stopped. There was no fire. Bogan must have turned off the magnetos as soon as he lost control.

Khadija held her hands to her face. Nils was sprinting toward the cloud of dust and dirt that had been thrown into the air by the crashing plane. Bock and I ran behind him.

When we reached the overturned cockpit and looked through the splintered canopy, we saw Bogan hanging motionless in his harness, neck broken, lower body crushed by the engine.

Nils knelt on the ground beside the wreckage. Bock looked at me and shook his head.

The fun was over.

Chapter Fifteen

The ambulance came from Serkeli and took the body away. The attendants rolled it in a tarp first and packed it with ice. It had taken Nils over an hour to cut his friend free from the wreckage. Bock and I offered to help, but he declined. Just before he drove away in the van, Khadija paid him the equivalent of ten thousand dollars in Swiss francs. He said both he and Bogan had family in Skara, and he would notify the appropriate next-of-kin and pay out Bogan's share. When he said goodbye, he shook hands with Bock and me. He did not shake hands with Lutz and DeBoor.

These two had paid little attention to the death of the Swede. The dust hadn't settled on the runway before I had seen them both heading for hangar number one and the remaining T-28. They had been working on it for almost two hours when we finally caught up with them again.

For some reason or other, they had removed the front canopy which would enclose the pilot in the cockpit during flight. It lay rails-down on the floor of the hangar next to one of the Av-gas barrels.

When they were ready, they rolled the plane out into the sun. Lutz climbed into the cockpit and tried the engine. It ran very raggedly at first and sent huge balls of flame and smoke out of the exhaust stacks as it backfired. Then DeBoor made some final adjustments under the cowling and it began to run smoothly.

Lutz grinned at us as he taxied by the hangar, with his mechanic standing on the wing. He had his macho shirt and motorcycle goggles on, the chain with the tiger's tooth, and the big gold bracelet from Villapone's.

'Why do you think he has chosen to fly without the canopy?' Bock asked.

'I guess he's a hot dog,' I said. 'He wants us to see him.'

'It almost always seems to be true,' Bock said, 'that men such as Lutz survive, and men like the Swede do not.'

I wanted to be able to tell him he was wrong, but found that I couldn't.

Pazar's caretaker had taken the three-quarter-ton truck and winched the wrecked plane away from the strip. Lutz did his run-ups at the east end. At one point, I heard the engine sputter and almost quit. Bock attributed the power loss to a bad magneto. He said Lutz would have to rely on the backup magneto to deliver spark to the cylinders.

Soon he was airborne. The gear was slow in retracting. He seemed to hold his airspeed down longer than necessary until the gear was fully up and the gear doors closed. After he had climbed out, he did some rolls and throttle bursts high over the far side of the strip. Then he began his run.

Bock and I stood directly across from the windsock pole. Lutz came down the runway at about the same airspeed as Bogan, and just as low. He held the plane in a slight crab to compensate for the crosswind, kicking it out as he began to pull up. Then I realized why he had come in with excess speed. He did a perfect aileron roll at the top of his loop – starting from the upside-down position, and returning to the upside-down position – before he came down the back side.

It was beautifully done. He throttled back some as he approached the bottom of the loop, holding his left wing low to compensate for the crosswind. As he neared the pullout point, he eased back on the stick, added power, and came across his starting point, right side up, right on the deck, well below the top of the pole.

'I don't like him much,' I said, 'but the son of a bitch can fly.'

'You will do as well,' Bock said.

'If we want the marbles,' I said, 'I'm going to have to do better.'

Lutz landed, picked up DeBoor, taxied back to the hangar, and shut down. His hair had flattened some from the slipstream over the windshield, and except for the circles where his goggles had been, his face was covered with a light film of dust and oil.

He grinned as he climbed out.

'You see, pilot?' he said. 'It is not so difficult. The Swede was incompetent.'

He strolled past the hangar toward the place where Khadija and her uncle were standing. DeBoor limped after him. Khadija's uncle had taken out his notebook and was writing something in it – an evaluation, probably, of Lutz's flight. I was watching them when I heard Bock call me.

He was up on the wing of the T-28, peering into the cockpit. I could see he was angry about something as I climbed up next to him.

'What's up?' I said.

'Merde!' he said. 'Look at this!'

The plane's instrument panel resembled a Swiss cheese. The altimeter and airspeed indicators were missing. So were the gauges for monitoring engine RPM, manifold pressure, fuel, oil, and the electrical system. So were the gear position indicators.

'DeBoor stripped the panel before takeoff,' Bock said. 'The parts are all lying in a pile under the detached canopy. It will take hours to reconnect them. On some, the glass has been broken and the needles bent.'

I called for Khadija and her uncle. When they came over, I showed them the instrument panel, and the pile of gauges in the hangar.

'Who did this?' Khadija wanted to know.

'The Belgians,' I said. 'They did it before Lutz took off, so there's no problem there. I wanted you or your uncle to stand by while we service the plane, so you can verify that I'll be taking it up in exactly the same condition as he.'

Speaking Arabic, she related to her uncle what I had said. Then she turned back to me.

'He does not require this,' she said. 'Your mechanic may replace the instruments if you like.'

'No thanks,' I said. 'We'll do it their way. All I'll need is a pair of goggles.'

Twenty minutes later, we had taxied to the end of the runway. The sun was westering, the wind still erratic. We had to guess at the performance of the engine on the run-up checks. Bock looked grim as he gave me the thumbs-up sign and I moved into takeoff position.

It was clear now why Lutz had removed the canopy. Without flight or engine gauges, everything had to be done by feel: the sound of the engine would indicate power; the sound of the wind, and control response, would indicate airspeed. In performing low-level aerobatics, every nuance would count. If he hadn't removed the canopy. I would have.

I advanced the throttle to near max power and began my takeoff roll. When things felt right, I lifted the nose wheel off the ground and seconds later was airborne. I hadn't used the flaps, so all I had to do was raise the gear. Bock gave me a wave from the ground to indicate they were up.

In removing the instruments, and performing a roll at the top of his loop, Lutz had brought this competition of ours pretty close to the edge. I wanted to beat him, and I thought there was a way I could do that, but I knew it wasn't going to be easy. Every weekend during the spring, I had been flying light planes from a small airport near my farm. Two weeks ago, I had flown the British Hawk out of their test facility at Dunsfold, reviewing that fighter for an international armaments magazine.

So, I was reasonably current, if not razorsharp. The sharpness here was going to be honed out of necessity, and the special sense a man develops when he has flown airplanes most of his life.

I pushed the throttle and pitch to climb power and took the T-28 to about five thousand feet. I did a few tight turns, then left and right aileron rolls. Satisfied with these, I tightened my harness, adjusted my goggles, rolled the plane upside down, and waggled the wings. While I counted to ten, dirt, trash, glass from the broken instruments, and other debris fell past me and out of the cockpit. At the count of ten, I rolled upright.

To beat Lutz, I intended to do a snap roll at the top of my loop, come down the back side, roll inverted, and pass the windsock pole upside down. It was going to be a sweaty maneuver, and I didn't want to do it with glass in my eyes.

I came down the runway at close to red-line speed. I had to crab left about ten degrees to counter the crosswind. I could feel the wings being buffeted by the gusts, and I couldn't hold the plane as low as I would have liked for fear of being wind-gusted into the ground.

I flashed past the pole at about ten feet, then eased back on the stick into a five-G pullup. The engine noise in the slipstream was terrific. My body sank on the seat cushions, my arms felt like lead. I had to force blood into my head to keep my vision from graying out.

As I came to the top of the loop, I eased off on the Gs and tilted my

82

head back to catch the horizon as the airplane came toward level, inverted flight. Then, just before the nose met the horizon, I did my snap roll, doing it pretty well, coming neatly back into the inverted position at the top of my loop.

Okay, I thought. That's the easy part.

I held inverted just long enough to check my position relative to the windsock pole and the runway. Then I started down the back side of my loop, controlling my speed. If I developed too much before I leveled out, I wouldn't be able to pull out in time, and, like Bogan, would hit the ground.

At about fifty feet, I pushed the throttle and pitch to takeoff power and seconds later was streaking down the runway toward the pole. Three hundred feet short of it, I pulled up until I had wing clearance above the deck, rolled inverted, and fought to keep the nose from dropping.

The blood surged to my head as I hung upside down from the lap and shoulder harness. Dust was swirling around me. I had to force my feet against the rudder pedals to keep them from dropping off.

I kept my eyes glued to the far end of the runway to maintain position, strained to crab the airplane against the crosswind that threatened to drive it to the ground. I passed the pole, inverted, at ten feet. A split second later, I was climbing to altitude, rolling upright as I did.

The backup magneto had done just fine. I cruised downwind and prepared to land. I liked flying without the canopy. The engine noise, swirling air, and sound of the slipstream past the cockpit kept my adrenaline up. This, I knew, must have been what it was like to fly Camels and Fokkers in World War I.

I had spent most of my time encapsulated and helmeted in jet fighters, where you just didn't get the old-fashioned, true sense of flying.

'You see, Lutz,' I wanted to say, 'it's not so difficult.'

Chapter Sixteen

I landed the T-28, picked up Bock, taxied to the number-one hanger, and shut down. My knees were shaky, my throat dry. As I climbed out of the cockpit, Khadija smiled at me. It was a brief smile, but I found I was happy to have it. Her uncle was writing in his notebook. Lutz and DeBoor were standing by Lutz's motorcycle, carrying on a private conversation. For the first time since I had known them, DeBoor seemed to be doing most of the talking.

'They have decided they do not like the accommodations here,' Khadija said, 'and will return to the Merhaba. We have told them they must report back to this airfield before seven-thirty in the morning. You may return to the Merhaba as well, if you like.'

'This place is fine,' I said. 'We'll need something to eat.'

'The caretaker will see to it. He keeps a bar as well.'

I smiled.

'I thought the Prophet frowned on whiskey,' I said.

'I am a Sunnite,' she said. 'The original prohibition was of wine. Within the Four Rites of Moslem Law, it is possible to interpret the prohibition as not extending to whiskey or other hard liquors. Are you a religious man?'

'I was once.'

'But no more?'

'No.'

'Then I am sorry for you.'

'A lot of blood has been spilled in this world by people who believed in their gods,' I said.

'And by those who didn't.' She brushed a strand of hair back from her temple. In spite of the heat, her dusky skin was smooth and dry, her Arabic features etched in the oranging light of the late afternoon. I wanted to talk some more; I sensed she did too. I think we shared a hunger for that.

But in the end, neither of us would risk it. I lapsed into silence. She reverted to being the daughter of Hakim.

'We will expect you to be ready in the morning,' she said. 'It is Sabah's wish that we begin early.'

She got behind the wheel of the big Dodge truck, started it up, and drove herself and her uncle away. Moments later, Lutz and DeBoor followed in DeBoor's rented Peugeot. I stood in front of the hangar and watched them go until they were out of sight and the dust had settled over the hill.

'What do you think, *mon ami?*' Bock said. He had been futzing around with the various instruments DeBoor had stripped from the plane.

'I think things got a little rough here today,' I said. 'With a half million at stake, they're liable to get a whole lot rougher tomorrow.'

'How far do you think these Belgians will go to assure their own success?'

'As far as they have to.'

'Yes. At first I might not have agreed. But now I do.'

He had climbed back up on the wing and was leaning into the cockpit of the T-28, examining the sabotaged panel.

'You can't leave it alone, can you?' I said.

'There is only one shower, Mateus!' he said. 'Go and be the first to enjoy it!'

As I left, he was humming and puttering, replacing the instruments, one by one.

That night, there was activity by the guarded C-47. An unmarked troop carrier with Turkish plates backed up to the cargo doors. Four Arabs in combat fatigues spent thirty minutes loading crates and cartons into the plane. They were quiet, well-disciplined men, who worked by the light of the moon. I watched them from the wing shadow of one of the more dilapidated transports.

After we had eaten our supper in the operations shack, Bock had returned to the hangar to work on the T-28. I had taken the opportunity to look around.

The C-47s interested me. They are twin-engined, prop-driven aircraft, with a total length of ninety-five feet and a wing span of about sixty-four and a half. They have two big main wheels, and a much smaller tail wheel. When the plane sits tail-down on the ground, the cockpit rises nearly twelve feet in the air. The overall configuration has a solid but friendly look. The transport was nick-named the Gooney Bird years ago, after the antics of a comical bird in the South Pacific.

Thousands of the planes were built during World War II to carry troops and matériel. Following the war, we had used them in Korea and Vietnam, where they saw duty as gunships and electronic sur-veillance platforms. Hundreds were still in service around the world and could easily be picked up as surplus by brokers such as Pazar. I had been checked out in the C-47 just prior to my tour as air attaché in Cambodia, and had flown one under combat conditions there for a period of nearly two years.

From the start, Pazar had made it clear in advertising for his mercenary pilot that he wanted a man who had time in both the C-47 and jet fighters. It was an unusual if not unique combination, and I was curious to know the motivations that lay behind it. I suspected the answer might be written in some impenetrable Arabic code in the pages of Sabah's leather-bound book.

At the end of a half hour, the guard was changed, and the Arabs drove away in their troop carrier. While they were busy with that activity, I walked back to the hangars, keeping the tail of the older C-47 between me and the men.

'I'm going to take a ride,' I said to Bock.

'Is it necessary for me to go with you?'

'No. I may be late.'

'Take care, Mateus.'

'I will.'

I drove the Volkswagen to Serkeli, where I found a pay telephone and put in a call to my number in Izmir. This time I said I wanted to talk to Campbell himself. It took just over eleven minutes for him to call me back. He did not say where he was.

'The buyer is Syrian,' I said.

'That confirms our information. Do you know the station of import?'

'Negative. But it looks like the goods might be shipped very soon.'

'Have you got your contract?'

'I'm still working on it.'

'This transaction may be even more essential than we thought.

86

We bloody damn well don't want to lose the sale.'

Campbell seldom got that excited about things.

'We'll do our best,' I said.

'We haven't been able to locate a persuasive vita for your man at Diebolt Forge. Have you talked to your broker?'

'Not yet. We're scheduled to meet in the morning.'

'He's a difficult negotiator: smart, very smooth, deadly when he needs to be. Do you copy?'

'That's affirmative.'

'Is our competitor from Esenboga still active?'

'Not as far as we know.'

'I'll be monitoring your progress with interest. Nurse Whiskey sends her regards. Your son wrote his first sentence today.'

Campbell said goodbye and hung up, his last words staying with me a long time after he had. Retired Army Nurse Major Wilma 'Whiskey' O'Neil was an old friend who had taken personal charge of Brian from the moment he had first arrived at Walter Reed. When we moved him to Switzerland, still locked in his coma, Whiskey had insisted on staying at his side. She was a valued member of the staff at the clinic now, working sixteen hours most days – eight for the rest of the patients, and eight for Brian. I owed her more than I could ever repay.

I took the asphalt highway from Serkeli toward Esenboga, then drove on gravel back to Pazar's strip via the Merhaba Hotel. It was late when I stopped in there to pick up a bottle of cognac for Bock, and to take a look at the register.

Neither Lutz nor DeBoor had checked in.

DeBoor's Peugeot was not in the lot.

Chapter Seventeen

At eight-fifteen the next morning, Khadija and her uncle assembled us in the operations shack. The Belgians had just returned from wherever they had gone – forty-five minutes late, and looking red-eyed and disheveled. Lutz sat at the flight planning table, drinking thick Turkish coffee. His hands were steady when he raised the cup. DeBoor stood next to a window, his one good shoulder resting against the frame. He seemed indifferent to what was going on around him, as if he were the only person in the room. Bock and I sat on a couple of folding chairs. There was no sign of Pazar.

The routine was the same as it had been the day before. Uncle Sabah consulted his leather-bound book and spoke at some length in Arabic to Khadija. She asked him to repeat portions of what he said, apparently to be sure she had it right.

Then she turned to us and laid things out. Today, she said, we were to fly the C-47. Two were available for this purpose at the east end of the field. As with the T-28s, our mechanics could inspect the planes and we could choose whichever we liked. Both, she said, had similar records of maintenance and performance, and – like the T-28s, would probably need some touching up before we could get them into the air.

'We will have two lines chalked across the field,' she said. 'These will be two hundred and fifty meters apart. We wish for you to take off within that distance, then come around and land, also within the chalk lines.'

She paused for a moment, and I did a rapid calculation. Two hundred and fifty meters was just over eight hundred feet. Landing an unloaded C-47 within that distance would require coming in at just over stall speed, touching down, and climbing hard on the brakes. If everything worked, I was confident that part of the test could be done.

The takeoff was something else again. At sea level on a concrete runway, assuming it carried no passengers or freight, the C-47 could get off the ground in close to the distance Khadija had specified. But here we would be flying from an uneven dirt strip at an elevation of two thousand feet. Normal takeoff under these conditions would require well over a thousand feet of runway, with both engines putting out max-rated horsepower.

Khadija held up two slips of paper that would determine which order we would fly. At this point, DeBoor suddenly shook his head and said, 'No.' He walked across the room in his drag-footed way. Aware that Bock and I understood French, he spoke rapidly in Flemish to Lutz. Lutz nodded, then turned to Khadija.

'My mechanic feels your slips of paper give one pilot an advantage over the other,' he said. 'Yesterday, because I flew ahead of him, this man was able to observe my flight and better it.'

She looked at the two of them, then at the two of us. She had on fresh khakis. Her boots were dusty. Her hair was clean and pulled back.

'Do you agree,' she asked me, 'that yesterday's order of flight gave you an advantage?'

'Yes,' I said.

'Then,' she said, 'perhaps you would volunteer to go first today.'

'No,' I said. 'I wouldn't.'

Lutz smiled, as if this was exactly what he had expected me to say – exactly what he would have said had he been in my place.

Khadija looked annoyed. Sabah stood next to her, arms folded across his chest. I couldn't tell by his expression if he had any sense of the problem that had developed. There was a moment of silence. Then Bock, who had been eating an apple, looked at Khadija and said calmly:

'Mademoiselle, yesterday, had this Belgian followed your orders, there would have been no difficulty. It was by doing the *routleau* at the top of his loop that he provoked the challenge, about which he now complains.'

'I do not wish to argue about this,' Khadija said sharply. 'You will have to settle it between yourselves.'

'There is no need to argue,' Lutz said. 'We will approach the planes at the same time. Whoever is the first to take off, circle the

89

field and land within your lines will be judged the most successful.' Before Khadija could reply, he looked pointedly at me. 'Do you agree, pilot?' he said.

'It's all right with me,' I said. 'As long as we draw the planes by lot.'

'Of course.'

Khadija related to Sabah what had happened. At first he looked puzzled, then actually quite pleased by the turn of events. Again, he spoke to her at length in Arabic. Finally, she turned to us.

'Before you select your planes, he wishes for Pazar's man to inspect them both,' she said, 'and to alter each of them in a few small ways so that he may observe the proficiency of the mechanics as well. The alterations would be identical in each case. He wishes to know if this is agreeable.'

Lutz immediately said it was fine. I said Bock would have to decide for us. He had finished his apple and had gone to drop the core in a wastebasket.

'If this plan is satisfactory to the Belgians,' he said, 'surely it is satisfactory to me?'

We broke up then. Khadija and her uncle went out to watch Pazar's caretaker mark out the lines on the runway and do his work on the C-47s. Lutz and DeBoor retired to their room in the bunkhouse – where I would have bet a fair share of a week's pay they were both catching up on some sleep. Bock and I went for a walk.

We walked up the dirt road to the top of one of the hills overlooking the strip. The hill was high, and barren of trees. Below us, the sun glinted from the tin roofs of the hangars, and from the wreckage of Bogan's plane that still lay not far from the windsock pole across the field.

I filled Bock in on my conversation with Campbell; also on the fact that, as far as I had been able to determine, the Belgians had not stayed at the Merhaba last night.

'Perhaps they chose another hotel,' Bock said, 'in another town.'

'I guess that's possible,' I said. 'Wherever they went, it must have taken a while to get there. They don't look as if they've had much sleep. I don't know what they're up to, but I'm beginning to think I should have agreed to go first in the C-47.'

'To do that,' Bock replied, 'would have been to give up an advantage.'

'I know. And I've got a feeling they were counting on my seeing it that way. You watched DeBoor work yesterday. How good do you think he is?'

'I would say he lacks finesse, but is knowledgeable and quick.'

'As quick as you?'

Bock shrugged.

'There's not that much difference between Lutz and me,' I said. 'At least not in the T-28. He's good enough to have done what I did yesterday. The only reason he didn't was that he didn't think he had to.'

'Then why do you suppose he has pressed today to approach the planes at the same time?'

'I keep going over that. All I come up with is that he wants to get us in the air at the same time.'

Bock asked me why Lutz would want to do this. I picked up a stone and pegged it down the road.

'Maybe he's figured out a way for the two of us to wind up like Bogan,' I said.

'I believe you are the better pilot, Mateus,' Bock said. 'I do not believe this Belgian can force you to crash. If the planes are equal and the drawing is fair, we will be the first to take off and the first to land.'

'I hope that's a Bock Vanderwald bona-fide guarantee,' I said.

He nodded vigorously.

'*C'est une certitude,*' he said, '*absolue.*'

On our walk back down to the field, we reviewed our combined knowledge of the C-47, its assets and liabilities, quirks and tolerances. We went over our takeoff and landing procedures, rehearsed our emergency drill, agreed on a simple set of hand signals should one of us have to leave the cockpit and go aft during the flight.

We were, I thought, efficient and thorough.

But even then, I had the uneasy feeling we were busily sorting oranges when we should have been shooting ducks.

Chapter Eighteen

Khadija drove us in the Dodge truck up by the east end of the runway where the C-47s were parked. Bock and DeBoor stood in the back with their tool kits. Lutz and I rode on the front seat. Nobody talked.

The two airplanes had olive-drab camouflage paint that was weather-stained and faded. The wings and fuselages were covered with dust; Turkish air force insignias were peeling away from the sides. There was a battery cart next to each, and barrels of fuel and containers of oil and hydraulic fluid. Both planes were parked facing away from the field; both had numbers on their rudders. The number we had drawn was 753. There was no apparent advantage of one over the other. Pazar's man, who had tinkered with the planes, was standing by.

'He will act as an unbiased observer,' Khadija said. 'He believes it should take from one to two hours to ready the aircraft for the flight. My uncle and I will follow your progress from the operations room.'

She told us we could begin, watched for a moment, then drove away.

The first thing Bock and I did was an exterior airframe inspection. As we walked around the big transport, Bock methodically called out what he saw and I wrote down a list of popped rivets, control surfaces out of rig, holes in the fabric, tailwheel skewed, badly worn tread on the main tires, and main gear struts low on hydraulic fluid. We omitted listing nonessential items such as loose antenna mounts, cracked de-icer boots, broken navigation lights, and missing cargo doors.

By the time we had finished, Lutz and DeBoor were already in the cockpit of their plane. A light breeze was blowing dust off the fuselage. I looked at Bock.

'What's your initial impression?' I said.

'There are not enough loose rivets to weaken the aluminum skin,' he replied. 'The holes in the control-surface fabric can be taped over, and we can probably pour in enough oil and hydraulic fluid to fly for a short time. But she's a very old lady, Mateus. From what I have seen so far, I will not be surprised if this is her last flight.'

'I won't take her up if she doesn't check out,' I said.

'When we have finished all that we have to do, that decision will be yours,' he said. 'If you determine we shall fly, then we shall fly.'

We climbed into the fuselage through the cabin door and went up the incline to the cockpit. The plane had been rigged for cargo. The floor was bare except for the tie-down rings; the metal troop seats had been folded up and secured against the side walls.

The cockpit was full of dust, and harbored a nest of bees. Bock quickly took care of this with a shot of engine solvent from his kit. The two leather seats were cracked, with wads of upholstery protruding from them; the air in the plane was stuffy and hot. We opened the small sliding windows on either side of the cockpit, letting a breeze come through.

'Please check all switches off,' Bock said. 'I am going out to swing the props to test for hydraulic lock.'

I got into the left seat and began the check. Moments later, I saw Bock on the ground below my window.

'Switches off?' he called.

I told him they were.

He reached for the closest prop blade and swung it through, grabbing the following blades as they came into reach. He did the same with the other engine, then signaled for me to come down. As I climbed out, the right engine on Lutz's airplane began to turn over. After about five revolutions, it started to pop and spit smoke out the exhaust stacks, firing on only a few of its fourteen cylinders. Lutz nursed the throttle and mixture until the engine ran smoothly. I hurried up to Bock.

'Sounds like we better get a move on,' I said.

'These matters take time,' he said. 'To rush them is to invite delay. Now, you must help me.'

An hour later, we had filled all the hydraulic reservoirs, drained and refilled the engines with fresh oil, drained out quarts of water-contaminated fuel, and pumped in about sixty gallons of

Av-gas – thirty in each wing tank. Lutz had long since shut the one engine down. He and DeBoor were now performing the checks Bock and I had already done. Pazar's caretaker kept a close but unobtrusive watch on the progress of each team, smiling whenever one of the mechanics discovered and repaired a piece of his handiwork. The men who were guarding the third C-47 paid little attention to us.

We climbed up on our right wing, and Bock began to work on the engine. I handed him the various tools. The wing surface was hot. I could feel the sweat pouring off me, could see where Bock's sweat darkened the dust around the place where he worked. When he was finished, we repeated the performance on the left wing. At one point, I heard the old Dutchman give a grunt of surprise and then one of satisfaction.

Lutz had his right engine running again, and was cranking the left. I started to fidget, looking his way.

'You must relax, Mateus,' Bock said. 'Pazar's man disconnected the front wiring harness. Their engine will not start.'

He was right. It didn't.

By the time we were putting duct tape over the holes in the elevator and aileron fabric, I saw Lutz and DeBoor up on their left wing, huddled over the cowling.

Working quickly, we sprayed lubrication on all the control cables and pulleys, both inside the airplane and out. Then, at last, Bock plugged in the battery cart and gave me the signal to start our right engine.

I was in the left seat. He was standing on the ground, ahead of the left wing. I went through the preliminaries, engaged the starter switch, saw the big three-bladed prop begin to revolve.

To clear the engine and ensure oil flow, I counted fifteen blades of revolution before I flicked the mag switch on. I ticked the primer switch a few times, and when the engine popped and finally caught on a few cylinders, I pushed the mixture control to full rich. With a lovely snarl, the engine came in on all fourteen, and I advanced the throttle until I had a thousand RPM and the oil and temperature needles in their proper range.

Bock gave me the thumbs-up sign, and we repeated the routine on the left engine. All went well until the oil pressure showed an increase from zero. I shut the engine down and Bock came into the cockpit. He was hurrying now, said nothing to me, quickly removed four screws from a mounting bracket and let the oil gauge tilt forward. Pazar's man had disconnected the left pressure sensor. In minutes Bock repaired the damage and hurried outside to resume his position ahead of the wing.

As I prepared to crank, Lutz, who had restarted his right engine, recranked his left and brought it up smoothly. I could see him shouting to DeBoor, and DeBoor shouting back. Then DeBoor ran to their power cart, unplugged it, and pulled himself into the plane even as Lutz began to taxi.

'They're not going to bother with that gauge!' I shouted to Bock. He looked unperturbed as he gave me the signal to crank our left engine – which I did. It came right up, with good oil pressure.

I wanted to roll. I wanted to taxi out, nibbling at the skirts of Lutz and DeBoor; but Bock wouldn't have it. He insisted that I lower and raise the flaps. Our hydraulic pressure was low, but in tolerance. He unhooked the power cart, signaled me to taxi a few feet and then stop. I let the Gooney move forward, then pressed the toe brakes. Only the left held; there was no pressure on the right. While I began to swear, Bock ran over and hastily chocked the wheel. Then he signaled me to shut the right-engine down.

I think I actually howled at that point, but I did what he wanted me to do. Lutz and DeBoor had taxied out of sight. Any second now I expected to hear the roar of their engines as they took off.

A couple of long minutes went by before Bock popped out from under the wing and motioned for me to crank up again and run another brake test. I did. Perfect. Bock came into the cockpit, breathing hard and looking pale, as if he might have overexerted himself.

'You okay?' I said.

'Yes. Fine. We are ready now.'

I added throttle, unlocked the tailwheel, and swung out from our parking place. As I came around, I saw Lutz's C-47 cocked at a crazy angle off the runway, one wheel half buried in sand, both engines shut down. He and DeBoor were working frantically in the right wheel well.

'It looks like he was in such a rush he forgot to check his brakes,' I said, aware I might have done the same if it hadn't been for Bock.

Bock nodded solemnly.

'Pazar's man loosened the pucks,' he said.

There wasn't much of a breeze. The windsock barely swung on its pole. The wreckage of Bogan's plane looked flat and old.

Quickly, I swung our C-47 into a westerly heading, and as soon as we were in position I set the parking brake and pulled the yoke into my lap to keep the tail down at high throttle while I ran through my engine checks.

I set the altimeter at zero, bled the manifold valves, checked all gauges in the green, grounded the ignition at low RPM, then ran each engine up separately to check the pitch controls, prop feathering, and magnetos. After a few cycles the pitch changed smoothly; the mag drop wasn't too bad. But neither prop would feather. This meant if we lost power in one of our engines during flight, I would not be able to turn the blades knife-edge into the wind. As a result, the flat blades would create tremendous drag on that side.

Quickly, Bock checked the circuit breakers, the wiring to the feather buttons, and the buttons themselves.

'I cannot find the problem here,' he said. 'It must be in the hydraulics in the hub. This is not something the caretaker has done; nor is it something I can repair.'

He looked at me. It was go or no-go time. We could hear Lutz's engines running at high speed now as he tried to blast his way loose from the sand. I was sure he was going to make it, and I wanted to go. I wanted to take these Belgians, the mission, the money, the whole nine yards.

Bock knew it. He was already strapping himself into the copilot's seat.

'She will fly, Mateus!' he said.

'Okay!' I said. 'Let's roll!'

I rammed the power to the big transport, swung it down the runway toward the first while line. I got by the other plane just as Lutz finally blasted loose. He came up quickly, but the runway was narrow, with soft shoulders, and I kept him behind me.

I stopped at the first white line, with our wheels on the chalk. Khadija and her uncle had come out of the operations shack and were standing just to one side of the runway at the second line. They were eight hundred feet away, but they didn't look anywhere near that far.

I held the brakes, pulled the control column into my lap again, ran up to full power. While I watched the gauges stabilize, I told Bock to drop one-quarter flaps when our airspeed reached forty knots. I had to shout so he could hear me over the noise. He yelled to me that he had understood, and I released the brakes.

The screaming engines yanked the plane forward. Bock lowered the flaps at forty, and I lifted off at fifty-two in a very tail-low attitude. We cleared the second white line by inches. I held the plane low to gain climb speed, careful not to skip off the ground. As our airspeed mounted, I milked the flaps up and started to climb. Lutz took off immediately after me, clouds of dust swirling behind his plane.

'If they're going to make a move,' I shouted, 'they're going to have to do it now! Keep an eye on them!'

Bock twisted in his seat and peered out his window, back along the fuselage.

'They are comfortably behind!' he said.

'They may try to crowd us, even chew up our rudder with one of their props!' I said. 'Let me know if they start to close!'

I leveled at five hundred feet, planning to start a lefthand landing pattern short of the hills to the west. Since the flight would be short, and I was worried about the hydraulic system, I didn't raise the gear. I was holding our airspeed at a hundred knots. The big plane was performing well enough, but, as Bock had said, she was an old lady, and I wanted to get her down as soon as possible, before something crucial in her plumbing let go.

As I banked left short of the hills, I saw the other C-47 at our ten-o'clock position, heading toward us. Lutz had broken left immediately after takeoff, then turned right to intercept. We were swinging toward each other, coming from nearly opposite directions now, still five hundred feet in the air, the distance between us closing fast. I could see Lutz at the controls, but no sign of DeBoor.

Then, as we were about to pass each other, he appeared at the cargo door opening.

I caught just a glimpse of him, crouched on one knee, bracing a small submachine gun against the frame.

Chapter Nineteen

I screamed a warning to Bock half a second before the first slugs started slamming into the fuselage. I had pulled into a tight right turn with the throttles jammed as far as they would go. We were losing altitude, had our gear down, and were way low on airspeed for this much angle of bank. Unless both engines could develop and maintain max power, we were seconds away from a fatal stall.

Bock yelled his own warning back, gesturing at the gauges. I shouted for him to bring up the gear. The altimeter had fallen to three hundred feet. I had the nose down, and let the airspeed build to 130 knots. We were heading straight for one of the hills that rimmed the west end of the field.

'Gear's up!' Bock shouted.

'How much damage from the gun?'

'Nothing essential I can see! No fuel spray from the wings! Critical gauges satisfactory – *but, Mateus!*' He was pointing through he windshield, dead ahead.

I could see our ground shadow flicking up the side of the barren hill. As I rolled to the right, it looked close enough to touch. Then Lutz was coming up on us again, this time traveling in the same direction and with a thirty-knot advantage in speed. He had us neatly pinned between him and the hills. As DeBoor's slugs started walking from wingtip to engine on Bock's side, I horsed back on the yoke and began a climbing right turn over the other plane.

The C-47 had never been designed for a dogfight. It was controlled by upper-body muscle power conveyed through the yoke, via pulleys and cables, to the elevators and ailerons – and by leg power, through foot pedals, to the rudder. There was slack and slap in the lines, and the control surfaces were slow to respond. In combat, I was used to flying highly maneuverable jet fighters, flying at speeds of up to Mach 1 plus. Here all I could do was hold us in a slow, ponderous, climbing right turn, as Lutz slid by below.

We were trapped in the bowl of hills that surrounded Pazar's strip. To get over them, I needed much more speed and fuel than I had. We were way off our heading to land, and I knew if I tried to belly in we'd be at the mercy of DeBoor and his gun. I was glancing in three directions at once, through both wing windows and the windshield, trying to pick up the other transport, relying on Bock to read me the gauges.

'What's our altitude?'

'Four-five-zero.'

'Airspeed?'

'Eighty-eight knots.'

'We're damn near at stall. I'm going to have to take her down to get our speed up.'

It was a trade-off – altitude for airspeed – but I knew Lutz was going to make another pass, and without speed, there was no way I could maneuver. As the big plane began to shudder toward a stall, I put the nose down and held it down until we had dropped 250 feet.

I yelled at Bock to tell me where the Belgians were.

'They are coming from the right,' he said.

When I glanced through the window on that side, I saw Lutz heading toward us, coming in from a much higher altitude and at a much faster speed. I knew when he passed overhead, he would drop his left wing, and this time DeBoor would be able to fire directly down into our cockpit with his gun. If he missed the first time, he could try again; Lutz could stay on top of us for as long as it took. There was no way to evade this time. All I could think of to do was pull up and turn into them.

I already had the throttles at takeoff power. Now I jammed them into the emergency range. The decibel roar of the engines rose to a shriek. In less than five minutes under this much stress, they'd begin to disintegrate.

'Cylinder-head temperature,' Bock warned. 'In the red and rising.'

'Nothing for it. They'll have to take it.'

I turned toward Lutz, banking and climbing at the same time, then rolled wings level and climbed straight for him. I judged we were now about two thousand feet apart, and were closing at over two hundred knots, or about three hundred feet per second. If I was right, that would give me just over five seconds to see what Lutz would do. He was coming down; we were going up. I could already see clearly the outline of his head through his forward windshield. He showed no sign of wavering. I held in enough back pressure on my control column to climb straight up his descent path.

Two seconds passed.

Three.

Four . . .

'Merde!' Bock shouted. *'He's going to ram!'*

I don't think Lutz had a picture in his mind of a midair collision, with fifty thousand pounds of flaming junk raining down on the runway below, and maybe an autopsy report where all they would find would be his teeth. I think we had simply one-upped him once too often, and this time he wasn't going to yield. We were playing a deadly game of chicken, and Lutz was coming toward us with the mindless tenacity of a Surface-to-Air missile. At the last possible second, hands slippery and sweat in my eyes, I dropped the flaps, pulled the control column into my lap, and pitched up over him.

At a bare four hundred feet above the ground, it was a desperate, last-ditch maneuver. I never for an instant imagined Lutz would try to follow me. But he did.

As he was about to pass under us, with no time at all to make a conscious decision, but operating on pure instinct and reflex, he abruptly pitched up after us, banking sharply, as if trying to take one of our elevators with his prop.

Traveling at a high rate of speed, and without flaps, his plane snap-rolled right and began to spin.

He must have tried to recover, throttling back the outboard engine, sticking full power to the inboard to counter the rotation; but he was much too close to the ground to pull out. The C-47 spun to earth, impacting right wing low, with terrific force. That wing broke off just beyond its engine and folded back against the fuselage. The plane twisted another quarter turn, the prop tearing off and shooting like shrapnel across the field. The engines, scorching hot, tore into the wing fuel tanks and ignited the high-octane gas. A fireball ballooned from the still-tumbling wreckage, followed by a steady column of black, greasy smoke.

Bock saw these things happen and reported them to me. He didn't have to say much. We had both seen them too many times before: spin, crash, burn.

Meanwhile, I was trying to unload all the stress and G-forces off number 753. I had to roll her level while pushing the nose down and keeping power in the emergency range. The aging transport couldn't take it. I had just gotten the wings level and the nose lowered when the engines quit.

All the roaring had stopped. All we could hear was the rush of air past our open wing windows. We were a hundred feet above the ground, still off the west end of the field. We were gliding about two knots above stall, with no runway in the direction of our line of flight, and I had absolutely nothing to trade for a turn to the place where the runway was.

'Shoulder harness!' I shouted to Bock. 'Tight!'

In the few remaining seconds we had, he shut off the fuel valves, closed the throttles and mixture, cut the electrical switches, tightened and locked his harness and lap belt. When I glanced at him one last time, just before we hit the ground, I could have sworn he was smiling.

We came in on our belly, with a ripping, tearing thud. The tail broke off, then both engines tore loose, pulled savagely under the wings by the prop blades. The noise was terrific. I clutched the yoke in a dead man's grip as we slid and thumped and finally skidded to a very sudden halt.

We were both thrown hard against our harnesses, much too close to the instrument panel shroud, but not so close that we hit.

There was no fire.

Huge clouds of dust had billowed up and were being blown back by the wind. The late-morning sky was deep blue, the nearby hills stark and gradual against it.

We unsnapped without saying a word. Bock opened the escape hatch in the cockpit roof, and we climbed through and sat down wearily on top of the battered fuselage. The sun bore down on us. My throat was parched, my pulse rate still in the red zone. I stared blankly at the black smoke rising from the wreckage of Lutz's plane. A vehicle was approaching from somewhere behind us. I didn't bother to look. I didn't care. I had thought we were dead when we had to pitch up so close to the ground.

For several moments, Bock was as silent as I. Then, very quietly, he began to laugh.

'Eh, Mateus,' he said, slapping the fuselage. 'The old lady. She won, eh? She brought us down!'

Ten minutes later, Khadija and her uncle pulled up next to us in the big Dodge truck. They had dropped off Pazar's caretaker by the wreckage of Lutz's plane. There were no survivors. DeBoor had been thrown clear. The caretaker had found his body and what was left of his gun, which he had given to Sabah. From where I was sitting, it looked like an Uzi: a light machine gun with a straight magazine and a folding stock. It was a weapon that could be picked up easily on the black market in any major Turkish city, and it would have fit very nicely into DeBoor's tool kit.

We slid down from the intact fuselage of number 753. Bock picked up his tools, and we got into the back of the truck. Khadija had kept the engine running. Her hands were white-knuckled on the wheel. She was angry. So was I.

'Tell your uncle the price just went up,' I said.

'We knew nothing about this,' she retorted.

'That's not the issue,' I said. 'When I get shot at, I get expensive.'

'You will have the Belgians' share in addition to your own.'

'That comes to fifteen thousand. I'll need twenty. So will Bock. You work it out. We'll want it credited to our accounts – the full amount – before we move on to step two.'

She shot some Arabic at her uncle. He nodded gravely, then spoke at some length in return. When he was through, Khadija's translation to us was short and sweet.

'He says he has been pleased with your work. He says you are men of honor. The other two were dogs. He will pay the amount you ask.'

'Good,' I said.

'It is his wish that you and your mechanic join us for supper at Mahmet's villa this evening. There will be facilities there for you to spend the night.'

'Too bad Mahmet missed the show,' I said. 'We could have sold tickets.'

'He did not miss it,' she said. She gestured past the hangars to the hill where Bock and I had taken our walk. A silver limousine was parked at the top; a man stood with his elbows resting on the hood, steadying a pair of binoculars. I could not see his face, only the glint of sunlight from the lenses.

'He called while you were preparing the planes,' Khadija said. 'He was delayed this morning by something unforeseen. He arrived there on the hill just after the planes were in the air.'

'Good seat,' I said.

When I looked that way again, the limousine was gone.

Chapter Twenty

By the time Khadija dropped us off at the bunkhouse, it was just after noon. She said she and her uncle were on their way to Pazar's villa and that they would expect to see us there by eight.

I was tired, but too keyed up to sleep. I stripped down to my shorts and eased myself back on my cot. Bock opened the cognac I had bought him at the Merhaba. He poured a cupful for each of us. It was not very good cognac. We drank the first one quickly, and nursed the second. The room was warm. Flies buzzed lazily around the unscreened window and door.

'We did well today, Mateus,' Bock said.

'We were lucky.'

'Of course. That is also true.'

'Khadija wants no part of the casualty list. She was upset when Bogan augered in, and just plain backed by what happened today.'

'Does this surprise you?'

'It doesn't exactly track with the terrorist image.'

Bock smiled.

'Khadija is like Colette,' he said. 'She becomes more beautiful in her anger. I have many times for this reason deliberately provoked Colette into a rage. Then she beats me on the head with her crêpe pan until my ears ring.'

I laughed. It felt good to let some of the tension go.

'The Colette I remember was much too short to reach the top of your head with a crêpe pan,' I said.

'Ah, *oui!*' Bock said. 'First she must stand on a table. I submit willingly. When she is through, I put my arms around her and carry her off to bed.'

'Where you make her ears ring?'

'But of course!'

I sipped some cognac, stretched my legs until they began to quiver.

'I'm going to have to find a Colette of my own one of these days,' I said.

'What happened to your newspaper correspondent? The *voluptueuse* Australian, whose photograph you showed us when you visited Honfleur?'

'Jillion Leggett?'

'Yes.'

'The last time I saw her was two years ago in Bangkok, just before Christmas, She's on assignment in Singapore now. Neither one of us likes to write. We keep the overseas operator busy.'

'But Mademoiselle Leggett will not come to live with you in the United States?'

'We haven't gotten quite that far. Both of us are skittish. Whenever the subject starts to come up, one of us backs away.'

'Because, as I remember, you believe you are too much alike.'

'She says that. She may be right.'

'Are you reminded of her by this daughter of Hakim?'

'Yes. Some.'

'Ah,' Bock said.

I looked at him.

' "Ah" what?' I said.

He tapped the side of his head.

'If you will pass me your cup,' he said, 'I will fill it.'

The meat wagon came in again from Sirkeli. It stayed longer this time, and then it left. By the time it did, Bock had finished the cognac and had fallen asleep on his cot. I went out and took a shower, standing under the plastic attachment at the end of the red rubber hose. I used a lot of soap, and most of what was left in my tube of shampoo. The water was warm for a long time but finally turned cold, as if the hose had been buried just under the surface of the ground and ran that way for about a mile before it dipped finally into a deep well.

Just before the water turned cold, I lathered my face with shampoo, and shaved. The itch of my whiskers had gotten unbearable. You always hear the first couple of weeks are the worst. They are. Especially if they happen to fall into the middle of a Turkish summer. I knew Campbell might not approve; but then he wasn't the one who had been growing the beard.

I put on my finest pair of slacks, a short-sleeved sport shirt, a pair of crepe-soled shoes.

Bock looked at me on his way to the shower.

'*Elégant*, Mateus,' he said. '*Elégant.*'

We drove the VW to Pazar's villa, arriving there at dusk. The approach was up a half mile of graveled drive, flanked on either side by rows of chestnut trees. The villa was a large, two-story structure of pink marble, with a central portico and symmetrical single-story wings. Tall, narrow windows crossed the façade. Those on the lower floor were barred. The grounds adjacent to and behind the building were enclosed by a high stone wall covered with honeysuckle and topped by glass shards.

We were met by three members of Pazar's domestic staff, a hard-looking trio of Turks in white tunics, who took our luggage and showed us to our quarters in the east wing. We had two rooms with a connecting bath. The majordomo assured us the fixtures in the bath were made of Etruscan gold.

'Okay, you misters,' he said. 'I will tell the Arab lady you are here. She will send her man to get you. Okay, misters?'

'Okay,' I said, shutting the door behind him as he went out.

On our drive to the villa, Bock and I had agreed not to risk talking freely once we arrived. According to Campbell, Pazar conducted most of his black-market business from this place, and it was easy to assume he might wire the facilities used by his guests. Our rooms were lavishly furnished – full of vases, velvet, and velour – and without electronic detecting equipment, it could have taken us a week to dig out a bug.

Khadija and her uncle had been given an even more opulent suite of rooms in the same wing. Our supper was served to us there by more of Pazar's staff. Bock and I were hungry enough to eat the rug. Turkish food can be as good as any in the world.

We began with pink-and-white slices of smoked sturgeon, garnished with cucumber and quartered tomatoes. Next came a dish of bell peppers stuffed with spiced rice, pine nuts, and liver. This was followed by a plate of fried squash and *manti*. The entrée was baked sea bass in a butter sauce containing black pepper and

106

buffalo cream. The dessert was a pudding made of ground chicken meat and sugar.

We drank tamarind water with the meal, and coffee with the dessert. The cook knew his business. I felt better with each course.

The four Arabs I had seen the night before, loading crates and cartons into the guarded C-47, ate with us. They wore fresh combat fatigues and were, according to Khadija, among her father's most trusted men. Quiet and reserved, they seemed neither to accept nor reject Bock and me as new additions to their group.

There was still no sign of Pazar. Sabah sat at the head of the table. He ate heartily. Using Khadija as his interpreter, he informed us that the money we had earned had already been transferred to the numbered accounts we had given him, and that we would have bank confirmation of the fact via telex no later than the morning.

He said his brother, Zahida, had charged him to discover the best of available pilots; and he believed – having witnessed the day's events – that he had not only managed to do this, but had discovered the best of mechanics as well.

We received these compliments politely, and told him we were ready to go to work. He replied that we would be doing that very soon.

Khadija had worn a simple white gown. She had also taken down her hair. It fell below her shoulders and framed her face in thick chestnut-colored waves.

She wore no makeup. There was no need.

She was stunning.

Bock turned in early. I picked up a pack of Samsun's from Pazar's majordomo and went onto the grounds at the rear of the villa to walk for a while and to smoke. Within the walled enclosure there were two acres of formal gardens symmetrically laid out with intersecting paths of crushed white stone, trimmed hedges, columns, and statuary. Beds of jasmine, corn poppy, tulips, and karanfil trembled in a light breeze that slanted my smoke to the east.

The tulips reminded me of R.J. Coyle. He raised them commercially in his greenhouse at White Oaks, and had bred at least one variety that carried his name. Whenever he visited my son at the clinic, he would leave a dozen of them in a crystal vase. According to Nurse Whiskey, Brian had taken an early interest in these flowers. In the first weeks out of his coma, he had somehow made it understood that he wanted to have a flat of them to grow in his room. They flourished there now, under his window; planters provided by Whiskey, bulbs provided by Coyle.

'He smiles whenever he looks at them,' Whiskey said. 'It's like him and those flowers are connected somehow.'

I had not been close to Brian before he and his mother had joined me in Phnom Penh. I had been on active duty during most of his early years, moving from one station of assignment to another, never landing in one place long enough to settle down. He had grown up with my picture on his wall, and whatever cachet there was in being able to say his father flew fighters. He was Diana's child. She had raised him, and had raised him well. Then the bomb had exploded and she was gone; and when the nightmare was finally over and I could dream again, I dreamed of a time when I would have a place of my own, and Brian would be well enough to come live with me there.

I had started telling him this even before he had come out of his long sleep. I had gone on saying it long-distance from Cedar Run. A week ago, I had stood by his wheel-chair with an armload of pictures, showing him the house, the outbuildings, the fences and terrain. I told him we would buy some horses, have some cats and dogs, put a couple of acres in vegetables and corn. I told him there was a stream on the property where we could fish for trout, a pond where we could swim, a decent high school in the next town. I laid it all out with a deeply felt sense of enthusiasm and joy. Brian listened and watched without expression.

He looked much younger than seventeen. His hair was blond, eyes blue, features delicate and still very pale – although he now spent some time each day on one of the sunroofs of the clinic. He could not yet operate his wheel-chair alone. His speech was erratic, and I had more trouble understanding him than did the staff who were with him every day. Usually when he said something to me, I would have to ask him to repeat it; and this would make him sullen or angry. There were times when I wanted to hold him in my arms, times when I wanted to lash out at him to vent the frustration I felt at our apparent inability to connect.

108

'He's blaming me for what happened,' I said in despair to Whiskey.

'He got hurt bad,' she growled. 'He's coming back, but he's still got a ways to go. Don't bully him, tiger. He'll sort it out. He needs time is all.'

'He smiles at you, Coyle, and his flowers – never at me. Not once.'

'How much did you smile at *your* old man when you were seventeen?'

'When I was seventeen,' I said, 'my old man was dead.'

Whiskey whacked me on the arm. She had driven me to Zurich. I was on my way to Piraeus to rendezvous with Campbell.

'How much room have you got on that farm?' she said.

'Lots.'

'Enough for me to move in too, when the kid's ready?'

'Damn right,' I said.

'I'll tell him that. It could make a difference. Me and him are pretty tight.'

'You're on,' I said. 'You may have to take a cut in pay.'

'You try to pay me anything.' she said, 'and I'll pull your asshole out through your ear.'

There was a raised marble pavilion at the southeast corner of Pazar's grounds. Khadija was sitting there on a wrought-iron bench, gazing into the moonlit distance beyond the wall. I had seen her go into the garden after supper. Now she heard me approach, my shoes crunching on the graveled path.

'You should come up here, Colonel Eberhart,' she said. 'There is a splendid view of the lights of Ankara.'

A narrow staircase wound from the path to the pavilion. I went up. The air here was sweet with the odor of honeysuckle.

'It's been a while since anybody called me "Colonel," ' I said.

'Today Mahmet received the reports of your background. He showed them to me. I was impressed; so was my uncle. Please feel free to sit, if you like.'

'I'd rather stand,' I said. 'Do you mind if I smoke?'

'Not at all.'

I popped a Samsun out of the pack and lit up. It irritated me that

I couldn't leave them alone.

'Do you agree the view is splendid?' Khadija said.

'Yes,' I said.

'Damascus lies beyond Ankara in the same direction, and Mecca beyond that.'

'Is Damascus your home?'

'Yes, now it is. Have you been there?'

'Once. A long time ago.'

'Was that when you risked dying for your beliefs, instead of for money?'

I finished my cigarette without replying.

'I did not mean to offend you,' she said.

'I'm not offended.'

'How familiar are you with my father's cause?'

'Not very.'

'Does it matter to you that he is deeply opposed to the Western influences in the Islamic world?'

'No.'

'His family used to be large. Now only Sabah and I are left. The rest were killed by Zionists in a reprisal raid on the border village in the Golan, where I was born. Before this happened – although to this day he would not admit it – my father was inclined to accept the moderating influence of my mother. At her urging, he agreed to let me receive my education in the United States and later to teach at the University in Beirut. Since then . . .'

She paused, perhaps thinking she had told me too much.

'Since then, your father's become radicalized,' I said.

'Yes.'

She stood up to leave. As she did, her hair and gown were stirred by the breeze. Bats whisked past the pavilion in the silky air.

'You and your mechanic may sleep for as long as you wish in the morning,' she said. 'We will not be leaving here before twilight tomorrow.'

'Fine,' I said. 'I'll walk back with you.'

'If you like.'

The stairs were narrow, and dark toward the rear of the pavilion. I went down first, then reached up and offered her my hand. She hesitated for a moment, then took it. Her grip was strong and warm.

'Thank you,' she said.

'You're welcome,' I said.

The chemistry was there. For me, and I think for her.

It was the world that was out of joint.

Chapter Twenty-One

A group of men were lounging on the piazza behind the villa as Khadija and I passed on our way to the east wing. The piazza was lighted by a chandelier that hung in front of a pair of open French doors. When we walked through the pool of this light, the men stopped talking and did not resume until we were inside. I thought I had recognized Pazar's majordomo and one or two of the staff. The other figures had been lost in shadow. When their conversation resumed, it appeared to be in Turkish. When one of the voices sounded vaguely familiar, I glanced back.

'Is something the matter?' Khadija said.

'No,' I said.' Everything's fine.'

I saw her to her door and told her goodnight. I locked my own door behind me. Bock was snoring in the next room. His snores were loud, and there were times when they would stop abruptly and he would sigh as if he slept under a burden of pain. He had left a wrench on the chair next to my bed. It was a yard long and heavy enough to stun an ox. The old Dutchman had moved into the combat mode.

I checked to see if my luggage had been searched. As far as I could tell, it hadn't. I balanced a water tumbler on my doorknob so if the doorknob turned, the tumbler would fall and shatter on the floor. The barred windows in the room were open. Through them I could see the enclosing wall of the villa and a glinting of moonlight along its glass shards. I moved my bed away from the windows.

I decided finally that I had not recognized the voice of the man on the piazza, only the voice of someone speaking Turkish who was not a Turk: one of Khadija's Arabs, perhaps, trying out the tongue.

I got into bed and switched off the light.

Before my hand had traveled back from the lamp, I was asleep.

*　　*　　*

It was late the next afternoon when I had my first meeting with Pazar. He summoned me to his library in the west wing.

'Be careful, Mateus,' Bock warned, just before I left our rooms.

'Don't worry,' I said. 'I will.'

Pazar was an attractive man in his late forties with a closely cropped mustache and brilliantined hair. He wore a lightweight pinstripe suit with a button-down shirt and conservative tie. The lenses of his gold-framed glasses were tinted – just enough to make it difficult to see his eyes. His skin was smooth, with a slightly olive cast; he wore a diamond ring in a platinum setting on the small finger of his left hand.

I knew as soon as we were face to face that something had gone wrong. His majordomo, who had brought me into the room, made no effort to leave. Pazar told me to take a seat, which I did. He remained standing, looking out on his gardens through one of the tall, narrow windows that flanked his desk. Several moments passed before he spoke. When he did, his English was perfect.

'How long have you been a mercenary?' he said.

'Since I resigned my commission in '74.'

'Then you are new to the business.'

'I've been in the business for over twenty years,' I said. 'I used to be particular about who paid me. Now I'm not.'

He nodded, as if this was something he understood.

'When you were with your embassy in Phnom Penh,' he said, 'were you in reality working for Central Intelligence?'

'No,' I said. 'As air attaché, I was expected to keep an eye out for aviation information that might interest my government. It was standard procedure. There was no direct connection.'

'When did you work for Mr. Adune of Bangkok?'

'In November of '75.'

'He paid you to enter Cambodia and retrieve a pouch of diamonds from an abandoned hotel. Is that correct?'

'No,' I said. 'I was paid by others. Mr. Adune brokered the deal.'

'Who were the principals?'

'If you want the answer to that, you'll have to ask him.'

Pazar lit a cigarette. I wanted to light one too, but didn't. Instead, I sat quietly and watched him smoke. He seemed annoyed.

'My negotiating on behalf of these Arabs has been long and

113

difficult,' he said. 'I have had to use agents from many countries. Three days ago, one of these agents arrived here from Greece to conclude his part of the transactions. He happened to see you last night when you were walking on the grounds. He claims he has seen you before, in the seaport of Piraeus. He says you are with the CIA.'

'He's mistaken,' I said.

'Let me be more specific. He says you were captured by his people five days ago on board the freighter *Lygarius* by the old Manis wharf. He says you were in the company of a known agent. He says you were imprisoned and left aboard the freighter, but managed somehow to escape. He is very persuasive in his detail.'

'He's mistaken,' I said. 'The Dutchman and I flew directly from Paris to Ankara. We have our ticket receipts and passport stamps. I haven't been in Greece in many years.'

Pazar sighed.

'I will speak frankly, Colonel,' he said. 'This Greek has proved to be unreliable in the past. I would not have used him, but in the negotiations at hand I had no choice. He had contacts with people I needed to reach, but could not contact directly. Your own credentials seem to be impeccable. Mr. Adune, whose reputation is well known to me, speaks highly of you. Yesterday your performance as a pilot spoke for itself.'

He tapped his cigarette out in a brass ashtray on his desk. I said nothing. He had made the case for me, and I wanted it to rest.

'I have put all this to Hakim's brother,' he said. 'In the end, he is the one who must decide.'

'Fine,' I said. To keep my hands from shaking, I folded them on my lap.

'Unfortunately,' Pazar continued, 'there is another matter that will also have to be dealt with. Perhaps we can settle them both. Please come with me.'

He slid one of his bookshelves back. Behind it was an open cage elevator. As we got in, the cage wobbled on its cables. The majordomo slid the bookcase closed and took us down.

The trip was slow. There was an odor of garlic in the cage, and a lot of whine and hum in the shaft. We passed a wine cellar, shuddered to a halt finally at the start of an arched corridor that looked as if it had been molded out of plaster of paris. Single fluorescent fixtures hung from the low ceiling. I had to stoop to keep from bumping my head. Pazar led the way. The majordomo followed.

We walked by one room and into another. It was not very large. The walls and ceiling were a dirty white, the floor a red tile. There were no windows. The inside of the door had been padded with a mattress to deaden sound. There were two straight-back chairs against the far wall, and a couple of directional floor lamps without shades. The Greek sat in one of the chairs. He started to get up as we came in. Pazar motioned him down. They talked briefly in Turkish. The Greek was obviously upset. He pointed at me and began talking faster. Pazar silenced him.

Sabah stood with his back resting against the wall just to the left of the door, going in. He had on his head kerchief and khakis; his arms were folded across his chest. Two of Pazar's men were also in the room. So was George Wyatt.

He had been tied to the chair next to the Greek. There was dried blood on his shirt and pants, and a lot of blood in his hair. His lower lip was shredded, as if it had been bitten through, not once, but many times.

'Have you seen this man before?' Pazar asked.

'Yes,' I said. 'Bock and I bumped into him in the airport bar the day we arrived. He's crew chief for a private jet out of Pennsylvania. I can't remember the name of the company.'

'The name of the company is immaterial,' Pazar said. 'He's an undercover agent for the United States Air Force intelligence service.'

I gazed steadily into the violet lenses that screened the Turk's eyes. His words had closed on me like a trap.

Oh, Christ, I thought.

When Campbell had said he hadn't been able to locate a persuasive vita on Wyatt, it had been his way of telling me something in Wyatt's background hadn't checked out. The Diebolt Forge cover story probably would have withstood any ordinary inquiry, but Campbell wasn't ordinary. The USAF Office of Special Investigations worked independently of the CIA. Like the CIA, it would have an interest in finding out who was stealing Coyle's classified navigation systems.

'Two nights ago, this man was apprehended going through the

files in one of my warehouses,' Pazar said. 'He was brought here by my men and persuaded to confess. It took many hours. If we had not caught him, the transactions with the Arabs would have been jeopardized.'

Wyatt spat blood on the floor, then looked at me. His suffering was evident in his eyes, but his expression was still defiant. I closed my fist. I felt the same kind of helpless rage I had felt on board the *Lygarius* when I had seen Farmer's man Timmie, also tied to a chair, the Arab squatting next to him, the rat in its cage. I would have done anything I could to help Wyatt right then, but it was already too late. Pazar's two men had drawn automatics. One was leveled at Wyatt, the other at me.

Pazar was perspiring. He wiped his forehead with his handkerchief. I could hear somebody's watch tick. I started to talk.

'You've got a problem,' I said. 'If you shoot him, the Air Force is going to send six more to take his place. I know how they work. They'll jack up the priority and they won't lay off until they've got the answers they want. I don't know what your alternatives are, but if I were you, I'd start thinking about them. If you shoot me, you're fresh out of pilots. I've got a feeling these Arabs wouldn't like that. They've gone to a lot of trouble to put this deal together. They burned up three of your airplanes, and you've got to be a long way out on expenses. If they haven't paid you and their deal goes sour, you're not bloody likely to get paid at all.'

'The Air Force agent is a dead man,' Pazar said. 'Your concern for him is wasted. As for the rest, the Greek insists he saw you in Piraeus. He's perfectly capable of lying, but why, in this case, would he do so?'

'He's not lying,' I said. 'He's mistaken. He's mixed me up with somebody else. What's more, he's trying to tell his story in a language that isn't his own. He may be saying one thing and intending another. I have a passport and travel receipts that prove I wasn't in Greece when he insists I was. You've had access to my credentials and time to check them out. You admit you're impressed, and at the same time you tell me this Greek has a reputation for being unreliable. Where I come from, that's bullshit, mister.'

I could feel the blood pounding through my neck. I was opening and closing my fists, and whatever Pazar read in my expression

116

caused him to back off a couple of steps. His men gestured with their automatics. I paid no attention to them.

'I've told you my side,' I said to Pazar. 'Now you tell the Arab.'

'He's already aware of what you have said.'

'Tell him!' I said.

Pazar repeated it. Sabah listened, and nodded. His arms were still folded across his chest. His expression was impassive above his beard, as if he had already made up his mind and nothing I could say would change it. He waited until Pazar had finished. Then, motioning for the Turk to step aside, he reached behind his neck, just below his head kerchief, and produced a knife.

It was a double-edged dagger with a jeweled handle. He took it by the blade and cocked his arm. Instinctively, I gathered myself to try to spring clear. His wrist snapped forward before I could. The knife flashed by my right side. It missed me by inches, burying itself to the hilt in George Wyatt's chest. He gave a single, grunting exhalation. Then he sighed once, quivered, and it was over.

I felt as if I were trapped inside a vacuum jar. I wanted to scream out the rage I felt, but I couldn't scream. My focus was gone, the room was a blur. I kept swallowing something back that was trying to rise in my throat.

On Sabah's command, Pazar handed me an automatic. He removed the magazine first, leaving a single bullet in the chamber. His men had tied the Greek to his chair. Sabah was looking at me. He had retrieved his dagger. I had seen him pull it gently out of Wyatt's chest and wipe it clean on Wyatt's shirt. The Greek was sobbing. He was trying to talk through his sobs, but he wasn't getting anything out.

I had the automatic in my right hand, and that hand was shaking so badly I had to steady it with my left. Pazar was talking to me and I was answering, but I couldn't hear what I said.

I leveled the gun at the Greek and squeezed the trigger. The gun bucked back sharply. The sound of the explosion was deafening. There had been only one other explosion in my life that had sounded that loud. When it was over, I handed the gun back to Pazar.

'The Arab wishes you to know,' he said, 'that it has been an honor to share with you the ending of the lives of these two men who had set themselves against you.'

I looked at the Greek. My slug had taken him just below the eye.

He was one of Farmer's people, I thought.

I had to keep saying that to myself until it took.

He was one of Farmer's people.

They shot their man Timmie like that, tied to a chair. First they tortured him with a rat.

'We'll go up now, Colonel,' Pazar said.

He wasn't perspiring any more. He had had a problem, and now it was solved.

Chapter Twenty-Two

We took the VW to the airstrip at dusk. Bock drove. The Arabs followed us in the troop carrier. We followed Pazar. He had told us his caretaker would see to it the rental car was returned to Esenboga. Behind the wheel of his silver limousine, he looked like any other very respectable, very successful Turk.

As we drove, I told Bock what had happened in the subcellar at the villa. I found it helped me to talk. Bock listened with care, and when I was through, he told me that I had been without options, that in my place he would have killed the Greek without hesitation. I rode the rest of the way with my chin in my hand, looking and feeling morose.

Our small convoy pulled up finally in front of the guarded C-47. Khadija told us we would be taking off as soon as Bock and I had done our preflight inspections and had familiarized ourselves with the layout of the plane. She was in her khakis again, with her hair pulled back and her clipboard under her arm. I was certain she knew nothing about the deaths of George Wyatt and the Greek.

'What's our destination?' I asked.

'We will fly to the southwest,' she said. 'We have not logged the trip with the Turkish authorities and will fly without navigation lights. You are to maintain an altitude of one thousand feet, and a heading of . . .' Here she consulted her clipboard. 'A heading of two hundred and twenty-seven degrees.'

'I'll need a map of the overland route,' I said. 'I'll also need to know the weather forecast and the wind direction and speed.'

'My uncle will provide all this necessary information once we are in the air. He wishes to leave as quickly as possible.' She turned on her heel and walked away. Last night, on the moonlit pavilion, we had begun to deal with each other as equals. Now she was establishing distance again; and though I felt a certain sense of regret, I knew it was better that she did. In my role as a mercenary, there was no way I could be honest with her.

The interior of the C-47 had been rigged for a long-distance flight. In the main cargo area, six cylindrical fuel bladders had been mounted on wooden cradles, three to a side. The bladders were made of rubber, with a fabric coating. Each one held a hundred gallons of Av-gas. Bock, who had gone into the plane before me, stood in the doorway that led to the flight deck.

'Have you checked the plumbing on this?' I asked.

'Yes. It is all well connected. We will feed the gas directly into the intake side of the fuel strainers.'

Long crates had been strapped inboard of the fuel bladders, leaving a narrow walkway to the flight deck. There were more crates tied to cargo rings aft of the bladders, and four pull-down seats, two on a side, forward of the cargo doors.

'She's really going to be loaded,' I said 'What's your estimate on the gross takeoff weight?'

'Close to thirty thousand pounds,' Bock said. 'Counting what's in the wing tanks, we'll be carrying over eight thousand pounds of fuel alone – enough for a sixteen-hour flight.'

'Going southwest, that would put us somewhere in North Africa,' I said, 'unless they change course once we're in the air. Let's get ready to roll.'

During our run-ups, the engines performed beautifully. The mag drop was negligible, the pitch cycled well, both props feathered on command. Sabah's men sat on the four troop seats aft. Bock had the copilot's seat. Khadija and her uncle sat in the radio and navigation section just behind us. Our two areas were partitioned off, but the folding door in the center of the partition was open. Bock and I would have some privacy, but not much. The control panel for our radio transceiver was located in the ceiling of the cockpit above the windshield. The headsets were plugged into the jack boxes by our seats. The microphones had been removed.

'Everyone is ready,' Khadija called over the noise of the engines. I knew the transport was heavy for a shortfield takeoff, but nobody was going to have to kick my ass off the ground. I was ready to go. There was nothing I could do to change what had happened in this place. All I could do was leave it. Pazar was standing next to his limousine, smiling, as I taxied away.

I ran the engines up to 2,700 RPM, got airborne with about ten feet of runway to spare. I had to make one large circle over the field before I had enough altitude to clear the hills. When the radar altimeter showed a thousand feet above ground level, I rolled out on course and throttled back to cruise. Bock had taken care of the gear and flaps. The night was clear, winds calm, no reports of adverse conditions. Just before takeoff, Sabah had handed me these weather particulars, and an envelope with a route card. I gave the envelope to Bock and asked him to read the card for me. He put on his spectacles and studied the material by the light of a red-filtered Aldis lamp.

'We are to maintain this heading for one hundred and seven nautical miles to Afyon,' he said, 'then change heading for one hundred and sixty-three miles to Izmir, then again for sixty-eight miles to the island of Arkis in the Aegean Sea. The time en route and fuel consumption are also listed. There is a strip map as well. This is only the first segment.'

'Do we have radio navigation checkpoints?'

'Yes. Afyon is an intersection of two beams. Izmir has a beacon from which you will track outbound to Arkis.'

Behind us, Khadija and her uncle had been talking in Arabic. Their voices had been loud; it seemed obvious they were arguing about something. Finally, she appeared in the doorway.

'My uncle informs me we will be landing at the island,' she said. She didn't say why.

'Okay,' I said. 'How much runway are we going to have?'

'We will land on one of the beaches. There will be five hundred meters of hard packed sand.'

I did the conversion, figured the weight.

'That's just about a thousand feet short with the load we're carrying,' I said.

'You have demonstarted your ability to take off and land within narrow margins,' she replied. 'It is why my uncle has paid you as much as he has.'

'But, *mon dieu!*' Bock exclaimed. 'If there are any obstacles at all, hills, or trees on the approach . . .'

'There are no important obstacles. After we arrive, there will be a

121

brief exchange of cargo. We will not be on the ground long enough to shut off the engines. Once we have left the island, we will fly without interruption for eleven and a half hours. My uncle will give you the segments as we go. He wishes for me to tell you that I have been taught to read the altimeter; also to check the accuracy of your course.'

'Fine,' I said. 'Maybe you'd also like to land the plane.'

She was silent. Whatever had developed between her uncle and her had taken her by surprise and made her angry. I don't even think she heard what I said.

Bock tuned the radio direction finders to the beacons at Esenboga and Cumaovasi in Izmir. By triangulation, he told me when we reached the Afyon intersection. I turned toward Izmir, just over an hour away.

The terrain below us was moonlit and clear. There were scattered pinpricks of light from small farms and villages. The effect was similar to that of flying over the more desolate areas of eastern Montana or one of the Dakotas. I put us on autopilot and studied the map. More than anything else right now, I needed to get a message to Campbell through NATO South.

Khadija had told us we could have free access to the radios. We could listen to the weather reports, the commercial airline chatter, military traffic, whatever we liked. We each had a headset. What we didn't have was a mike. Bock was busily remedying this.

I was so used to having him putter around that I didn't realize at first what he was doing. He popped in and out of the engineer's section, spoke pleasantly to Khadija, said he was having some radio-reception problems, thought there might be a frayed wire or short circuit in his headset. Using a small pocket knife with a screwdriver attachment, he had already taken it apart once and put it back together, but he said it still sounded fuzzy. She asked if she could listen. He said of course. She put the headset on and wrinkled her nose.

'Is there an extra?' she asked.

'No,' he said cheerfully. 'Only two. One for Mateus, and one for me. I will fix it.'

She seemed taken by his charm. She watched him work for a

while, then went aft to visit briefly with her father's men. I glanced through the open door behind us. Sabah was leaning over the navigator's table, writing in his book. When I looked back, Bock tapped my elbow.

On his lap he was holding one of the earpieces from his headset. Wires ran under his knees to the copilot's jack box at his right. He had connected the earpiece to the microphone position. He quietly assured me it would work, and I thought he was right. I had done this trick myself whenever I wanted to record something on my cassette player and didn't have a mike handy. I knew we weren't liable to get much fidelity, but should be able to transmit.

As we passed abeam the Izmir beacon, I tuned the UHF transceiver to guard channel. Then I bent toward the center console, as if to check gauges, and picked up the earpiece. Bock had rigged a trigger wire to activate the transmitter. Khadija was coming back from the cargo section. I had only seconds.

'Papa Wolf to Delta One,' I said. 'Papa Wolf to Delta One. Initial destination Arkis. Repeat, Arkis . . .'

I wanted to go on repeating the message until I was sure one of the CIA or NATO monitors had picked it up, but there was no time. Bock jerked the wires loose from the jack box and concealed the earpiece with his hand as I straightened in my seat.

'Your course now should be one-nine-eight,' Khadija said. she was standing just behind us.

'I'm turning that way,' I said. 'Tell your uncle I've got a problem with his flight plan.'

'The plan was prepared by a pilot,' she said. 'It should be accurate.'

'There's nothing wrong with the accuracy,' I said. 'I'm holding at a thousand feet as ordered, and we're right on course to the island of Arkis. The problem we're going to have lies with the island of Samos. It's in our flight path, dead ahead maybe ten miles.'

She looked puzzled.

'Mademoiselle,' Bock said quietly, 'according to the map, this island of Samos is mountainous and rises over three thousand feet.'

'I will speak to my uncle,' she said.

'Make it fast,' I said. 'Tell him I think we should circle to the west. There's population on Samos. We can clear the mountain all right, but we're still liable to be spotted.'

123

Uncle Sabah approved the deviation from course. Khadija sat at the radio table, reviewing the original flight plan and map.

'Amadi is a fool,' she said finally.

Not to me or to Bock.

To herself.

Chapter Twenty-Three

The island of Arkis was three miles long and a mile wide. The interior was hilly, covered by rocks and stunted trees. Most of the shoreline consisted of low cliffs that had been nibbled away by the water. The island appeared to be uninhabited. To the north, there was a long strip of white sand beach.

I circled once to look things over and check wind direction. We were now at five hundred feet. Through my wing window I could see a cabin cruiser anchored offshore. There were no lights on the cruiser, no lights on the beach. In the brief time it had taken us to detour Samos and fly to Arkis, Sabah's men had opened one of the crates aft and had armed themselves with automatic rifles.

'It is only a precaution,' Khadija assured us. 'My uncle expects no trouble.'

'We're in what amounts to a flying gasoline station here,' I said. 'If we take one slug in the wrong place, we're going to be blown right up Allah's nightshirt.'

'And what is more, mademoiselle,' Bock said, 'there is no safe runout on the beach below. It is blocked by boulder fields at either end. Perhaps you should ask your uncle how essential it is to land in this place, for if it is not absolutely so, I believe it is folly to risk it.'

'He has already assured me there is no choice,' Khadija said. 'You must land.'

I felt my adrenaline kicking up, and the presence of Sabah behind me. I wondered what he would do if I flat refused to take the Gooney down. I remembered how calm he had been when he killed Wyatt, how easy it had been for him to reclaim his knife and wipe it clean on the dead man's shirt. He was a true believer, a fanatical Muslim in this case, who had been given his orders by his brother, Hakim. They were written down in his leather-bound book. The only time he had deviated from them was when we were heading straight for the mountains on Samos. I didn't think there was a chance in the world he would allow any deviation from them now.

'All right,' I said to Khadija. 'Tell everybody back there to get strapped in. You and your uncle too. This one could be rough.'

I glanced at her. I think she was afraid, not so much of the objective hazards we were about to face, but of the gradual unfolding of her father's plan. Whatever it was, it had moved all of us into areas that for her, at least, were unexpected and troubling. I cranked up a smile.

'It's okay,' I said. 'We'll manage.'

'You must,' she said. Then she briefly returned my smile and added, 'We all must.'

I slowed to a hundred knots and turned on the boost pumps. Bock lowered the gear and one-quarter flaps. I wanted to land into the wind as much as possible. I turned a right-hand base leg out over the water, called for flaps to one-half, and started playing my turn onto final.

'A light just flashed from the cruiser,' Bock said.

'There goes another one,' I said. 'On shore, at the close end of the strip.'

'*Merde*,' Bock breathed. 'This beach is short.'

We were on final at two hundred feet. I let the airspeed bleed off to ten knots above stall, pushed the pitch control forward, and called for full flaps. When we reached our touchdown point, I chopped the throttles, pulled back on the control column, and stalled into a slam-down, three-point landing. There was scarcely any bounce, but the sand was very hard-packed and we were racing along it as fast as if it were concrete. I braked the big transport with everything I had. The terrain was skimming by to our left, the water to our right. Ahead of us I could see where the sand ended abruptly in a field of black boulders. If we rammed them, with the fuel load we were carrying we'd go up like a can of napalm.

It was too late to add power and go around. I couldn't turn left, so I turned right, but not all at once. I let the plane drift slightly left, then stood hard on my right brake, swerving us toward the water in a controlled ground loop, praying our gear would hold and our left wing would stay clear of the rocks. When the Gooney started to the right too fast, I gave her a shot of right brake, then let her swing toward the sea again. The force of the turn threw Bock and me leftward against our harnesses. The wing passed over the boulders; the tail swung by. I don't know how much clearance there was. There couldn't have been much. When we finally stopped, the main gear was on the sand, tailwheel in the water, engines ticking over at about half the speed of my pulse. We were facing back the way we had come.

'That's two,' I said.

'Ah, *oui*,' Bock said happily. 'But this time, Mateus, the plane is intact.'

I taxied to the other end of the beach and swung around into takeoff position. Following Khadija's orders, I did not shut down the engines. She and her uncle immediately went aft to supervise a cargo transfer. Bock unsnapped from his harness and stretched.

'I will go and check the fuel bladders,' he said.

As he left the cockpit, I slid my wing window back and poked my head and shoulder out to get a breath of air and see what I could see. I was keeping the engines at a thousand RPM, enough to keep the plugs from fouling and the cylinder heads cool. I had the tailwheel locked and the parking brake set.

The moonlight was bright on the beach. Between the beach and the rising slope of the island – beyond our left wing – there was a margin of driftwood and shrub. I was just about to look away when I saw two figures rise from that area and come toward the plane. One was Dixie. The other was Art Farmer.

They looked as I had remembered them. Dixie wore black pants and a sleeveless jersey. Her face was sharp and thin, right side bandaged now. She carried a rifle in the port arms position. Farmer had on his overalls and a gray sweatshirt. His glasses glowed like phosphorous in the moonlight. He carried an automatic in an open holster at his side. As they walked under the wingtip toward the cargo doors, I could see their hair being whipped by the propwash. I knew if they came on board and saw me, I was a dead man. Sabah had bought my story once. There was no way he was going to buy it again.

With a panicky sense of being trapped in the cockpit, I swung around to look down the long center aisle of the plane. Moonlight

127

spilled in through all the windows. I could see Bock standing by the left-wing emergency exit plug. He was peering outside. Past him, the four Arabs with the automatic rifles were crouched in concealed firing positions on either side of the open cargo doors. Khadija was climbing out. Sabah was about to follow her. He had two rucksacks slung over his shoulder, one large, the other small.

There was going to be trouble. I could feel it building, raising the hair on the back of my neck like an electric charge.

I unsnapped from my harness. I had no weapons. All I could do was watch, and be ready to move if I had to. My best card was to release the brakes, go full power, and take off; but that would mean leaving Khadija on the ground with Farmer. I had the escape hatch in the ceiling. I had Bock. That was it.

I looked through my open window, back past the wing. I wanted to shout to Khadija to get on board, but she couldn't hear me over the noise of the engines – any more than I could hear her now as she began to act as interpreter between her uncle and Farmer.

We were geese on a pond. Farmer could have a dozen people crouched in the brush along the edge of the sand. Whoever was in the cabin cruiser could come in and rake us from that side. When I tried to remember how many people Farmer had had in Piraeus, I couldn't. All I could remember was how they seemed to pour like rats into the hold of the *Lygarius*.

Khadija's uncle put the large rucksack on the ground. Farmer bent down and checked the contents. His back was to me. I could see Dixie looking on. Then Farmer stood up and began to argue with Sabah. It went back and forth. Finally, Sabah folded his arms across his chest, and Farmer waved his hand impatiently toward the brush. When he did, four more people came onto the beach. They were carrying the crate I had first seen in the hold of the freighter. It looked larger than I remembered, and heavy. They carried it with care.

Just before they reached the wing, Farmer motioned for them to set the crate down. Sabah went out to inspect it. He took the small rucksack with him. When Khadija started to follow, he said something to her, and she went back and stood below the cargo doors, next to Farmer. His people had formed a semicircle, facing the plane. They were armed with rifles, which they had taken from their shoulders and held loosely at their sides.

128

When Sabah came back, he seemed satisfied; but Farmer began arguing again. He pointed at the large rucksack, then at the locker, shaking his head, digging the toe of his boot in the sand. Khadija tried to mediate. As she stepped closer to him, I saw him signal to his troops. I shouted to Bock to warn Khadija to get back. When I looked through my window again, Farmer had her by the throat.

He had spun her around, and held her in front of him. He was screaming something as he clawed for his pistol with his free hand. His people had brought their rifles into firing position. As far as I could tell, not one of them got off a shot. They were dropped in their tracks, flopping and spinning, as Sabah's men opened up with the automatic weapons. I advanced the throttles, readying for takeoff. The area around the plane filled with the sound of the engines and the rapid fire and flash and smoke from the guns.

Farmer had his pistol pressed to the side of Khadija's head. He was screaming, his face torn with rage. Sabah, who had started for him, now stood helpless. When the four Arabs started to come out through the cargo doors, he motioned for them to stay where they were. Then, Farmer, using Khadija as a shield, began backing away.

It was at this point that Bock removed the exit plug and eased himself onto the wing. The Arabs saw him. So did I. Farmer didn't.

Moving in a half-crouch, bracing himself against the propwash, he kept pace with Farmer as Farmer backed away parellel to the trailing edge of the wing. All of Farmer's concentration was directed toward the Arabs. The moon was directly overhead: Bock cast no shadow. The noise of the engines gave him the cover he needed.

Farmer had reached the aileron. It was made out of fabric, and there was no way Bock could cross it without punching through. He waited until they were past it. He waited until they had reached the wingtip, which was solid, and then he sprang.

He sprang with both hands extended, going for Farmer's gun. He had the advantage of complete surprise, the disadvantage of Khadija's vulnerability. The force of his jump carried all three of them to the ground, where they thrashed in a tangle of arms and legs. I lost sight of them for a moment, then saw Farmer's wrist locked in Bock's grip, and the muzzle flash of the pistol. Then Khadija was free, running back toward her uncle.

The Arabs took care of her first, hauling and pushing her into the plane. It all happened in the space of a very few frames. Farmer wasn't quite as big as Bock, but he was younger and enraged. He was holding the pistol with both hands, struggling to kick free. In one violent motion, he broke away. They had rolled ahead of the wing and toward the cockpit. I looked down helplessly as Farmer came to his knees and brought the pistol to bear on Bock. The muzzle flashed again as Bock lashed out with a final, desperate kick. Farmer stood up and reared back. He was off balance, still firing the gun, when he stumbled into the field of the spinning prop. I saw his head explode in the moonlight. It exploded into a shower of blood, tissue, and bone. Then his body fell below the arc, and the sand around him began to turn from white to red.

Bock seemed to be all right. He was on his feet, heading for the plane.

The Arabs had gone for the crate.

The cabin cruiser was coming into shore, muzzle flashes winking from its deck.

Chapter Twenty-Four

I had to angle right on takeoff to miss the boulders at the far end of the field. There hadn't been time to close my wing window. The roar of the left engine throbbed and pulsed through me as we lifted off so low the props sucked up spumes of seawater and whirled a white mist past the wings.

The Arabs had gotten the crate on board. The cargo doors were closed. I was alone in the cockpit, holding us about two feet off the water, using the cushion of compressed air between its surface and the wings to keep us airborne until we reached a safe flying speed. I couldn't let go of the yoke long enough to reach down and raise the gear. The lever was locked on the floor between my seat and Bock's. When he finally appeared, he knelt quickly, released the ring catch, and raised it for me. As soon as he did, we lost a lot of drag. I slid my window shut and began to climb. We were out of range of the guns.

'You all right?' I asked.

'I am fine.'

'That was a nice piece of work you did back there.'

Some of Farmer's blood had splattered on his shirt. He looked indignant.

'This man was a *cochon,* to take the woman that way,' he said.

'Could you tell what his beef was with Sabah?'

'I am not sure. The packsack held many kilos of heroin. That much I overheard. Perhaps it was less than what had been promised. Both sides spoke angrily of the Greek. As for the box, I do not know what it contains. They guard it as if it were the holy stone.'

'They laid everything on the line to get it. If I had to guess right now, I'd say it holds something compact and deadly: nerve gas, microbes, fissionable material; something Farmer stole from a U.S. Government depot and was willing to trade for a bundle of dope.

When I talked to Campbell, he said he thought the ante on this trip might have gone up. He sounded more worried than I'm used to hearing him sound. Can you rig things again so I can transmit?'

He shook his head. He was squatting next to me, keeping an eye out aft for anyone who might approach. In the diffused light from the moon, he looked wrung out.

'We took three hits from the cruiser,' he said. 'Two are in the cargo area and have caused no damage. One is near the long-range radios. The bullet was high-powered and the damage there looks extensive.'

He said he would check into this and went aft to get his tools. Moments later, Khadija came into the cockpit. She handed me a flashlight with a red filter, and an envelope that contained another strip map and route card. She also gave me an E-6B computer so I could calculate winddrift. Two of her fingernails were torn. There was an abrasion on her cheek. She looked as if she was still pretty shaky.

'Bock's going to be busy for a while,' I said. 'Have a seat. I could use a hand with the light.'

She eased herself into the copilot's position and held the light for me while I glanced at the route card and map. We were cruising now at a thousand feet. Following the written flight plan, I turned southwest on a heading of 220 degrees. We had a short dogleg to make around the island of Lipsos, then would turn south for three hours over the Aegean and Mediterranean. The segment ended with our coasting out in North Africa between Tobruk, in Libya, and the Egyptian border. The radio navigation beacon frequencies, fuel-consumption figures, and estimated time en route were all neatly laid out. Our final destination was not mentioned.

'I hope this time there are no errors,' Khadija said.

'None that I can see.'

'Has the plane been damaged?'

'Bock's checking that now.'

'My father will pay him well for saving my life. I will see to it.'

'I can't speak for Bock,' I said, 'but I don't think he would want pay for doing that. He lives by a code of honor. He always has.'

'I no longer understand the concept of honor,' she said. 'The world is too complex.'

When I did not reply to this, she leaned her head back on the seat to gaze through the windshield at the night sky. I swung around the island of Lipsos and turned to my next heading. I had just switched over to autopilot when Bock returned to the cockpit.

'The bullet impacted one of the radio junction boxes,' he said. 'We have lost our flux gate compass, our number-two ADF, and the UHF radio.'

The first items didn't matter. The last did. Guard channel on the UHF transceiver was the only link we had to Campbell. There was no radar transponder on board, and, flying at a thousand feet, we were below land-based radar lobes. The Sixth Fleet was somewhere in the Mediterranean, but unless we were intercepted by one of its fighters, we had no way to establish contact.

'We've got backups for the compass and the ADF,' I said, masking my disappointment. 'We can do without the UHF. How's the fuel transferring?'

'Very well,' he said. 'I am going aft where I can lie down for a while. If you need me, please send word and I will come.'

As he started to leave, Khadija reached up and clasped his hand. His face, which had been somber, broke then into a sweet and gentle smile.

'I am very happy,' he said, looking at me, 'that this princess of ours is still alive.'

The engines ran beautifully, in perfect sync. Their power sang through the frame of the aircraft. I tuned in a radio beacon, calculated our wind drift on the E-6B, did my compensations. Then I briefed Khadija on a few simple procedures to follow should something go haywire with the autopilot, and told her I needed to stretch my legs.

I went through the radio and navigation section and on down the narrow aisle between the crates and fuel bladders. Bock was already sound asleep, curled up on the floor in front of the cargo doors. Sabah and his men were eating sandwiches and drinking coffee. They seemed in good spirits, as if they thought the worst of their mission was over. The violent deaths of Farmer and his people did not lie heavily on them, or for that matter on me. My time in Southeast Asia had inured me to combat, armed men set against

133

armed men, one slaughter preventing another. It had been different with the Greek.

The crate with the U.S. Government stencil was strapped securely next to one of the seats. The men nodded pleasantly at me as I walked past them and into the head. They wore their combat fatigues; I wore slacks and a safari shirt. I had a feeling they accepted me.

I used the relief tube, washed my hands and face, opened the vent, and smoked a cigarette. On my way out, Sabah handed me a hamper of food and a thermos, which, he indicated by gesture, Khadija and I should share.

'This man,' he said, struggling for the English and pointing down at Bock. 'Is good?'

'Yes,' I said.

He smiled.

'Is good,' he said. 'This man is good.'

The sandwiches were cold fried mutton in pocket bread. There were green olives from Damascus, which, Khadija said, had been dried of their oil by being soaked in lye. There was goat cheese, pastry, and crisp apples with yellow skin. We were cruising at 1,720 RPM. Below us, the rippled surface of the Aegean reflected the light of the moon. There was a sense of shelter in the cockpit, as if Khadija and I were alone in the plane.

'You don't know what it is we're carrying back there, do you?' I said.

'No. I do not.'

'You must be curious. It almost cost you your life.'

'My uncle does not confide in me. In our society, women do not occupy the same level as men.'

'Who's Amadi?' I said.

She looked at me. I thought her eyes had darkened at the mention of the name.

'He is a pilot,' she said. 'Just as you.'

'One of your father's men?'

'Yes.'

'I get the feeling you don't like him much.'

'It was once my father's intention that I should be Amadi's wife.'

'You disagreed?'

134

'Yes. Not at first, but later as I came to know Amadi better. He is an arrogant man. When he was with me, he was cruel. When I told my father this, he would not believe it. He treats Amadi like a son. It was my uncle who finally intervened. He said I should not be forced into a relationship that caused me so much unhappiness.'

'If your uncle cares that much for you, why did he let you come with him on Turkey?'

'He needed me to speak for him. There was no one else he could trust.'

'Look,' I said. 'I get paid to fly the airplane. With the money you mentioned that first morning at the hotel, I know your father's got some kind of high-risk mission in mind. I don't know what it is, and I don't particularly care. But that crate back there worries me. I'd like to know what's in it. I'd like to know why we're carrying enough Av-gas to fly clear across Libya when Colonel Qaddafi is a friend of your father's and we could easily land at Tobruk and refuel. I'm not looking for trouble. I just get nervous when I'm carrying unidentified contraband that some people are willing to kill for and others don't want to touch.'

'It would be better for you not to question these things.'

'Probably so, but I don't work that way. Maybe I would if I had one hundred percent confidence in the people who were running the show; but your Uncle Sabah damn near got us killed back there. He skates about three feet closer to the edge than I'm willing to go. Unless I've read you wrong, you think he does too.'

'He is like an extension of my father. When you see him act, you see the results of my father's will. Even if I wished to intervene for you, there is no possible way that I could.'

'All you've got to do is ask him what we're carrying.'

'I have. He will not tell me.'

'Okay then, try asking the men.'

'I do not believe they know.'

I looked at her. She brushed back her hair, touched the abrasion on her cheek. She pretended to be preoccupied.

'All right,' I said. 'Forget it.'

'It would be better,' she said, 'if we could.'

'Have you been to Singapore?' I said.

'No. Why do you ask?'

'I'd like to take you there sometime.'

'Oh?' she said 'Why?'

'Because it's a nice place to be.'

'Would you fly me there?'

'Sure,' I said. 'It would be just the two of us in a classy plane.'

'Would we have champagne?'

'Do you like champagne?'

'On occasion.'

'We'd have at least two magnums,' I said.

'In that case,' she said, 'if you really were to invite me, I believe I would accept.'

'You'd have to ask your father first.'

She smiled.

'And my uncle,' she said.

'But not Amadi?'

'No,' she said. 'Not him.'

Shortly after midnight, we passed the Sitia radio beacon, thirty-four miles to our right on the island of Crete. Khadija slept on the copilot's seat with her head pillowed on her hand. Below us, the Mediterranean stretched away in a sheet of moon-bright swells. At one-thirty, Bock came forward, yawning and stretching. He told me to engage the engine boost pumps while he shunted two more fuel bladders into the system.

'She sleeps,' he said quietly, looking down at Khadija.

'She decided to give me the final route card and map just before she dropped off,' I said. 'We're scheduled to fly due south over Libya, then due east into Sudan. Each leg runs over six hundred miles.'

'And the final destination?'

'Somewhere in the Nubian Desert, near the Red Sea south of Egypt.'

Bock raised his brows. Although Khadija appeared to be sleeping soundly, neither one of us would risk speaking freely. I shrugged. Bock's guess was as good as mine as to what we would find at the end of the road.

'We'll be under two hundred feet when we fly over the coast,' I said. 'That should keep us under Egyptian radar. I've tuned El Adem as our radio fix.'

'Do the Libyans expect us?'

'Apparently so. We're authorized to fly over, but not to land.'

'And the Sudanese?'

'We'll sneak in on the deck there too. They're not all that happy with Colonel Qaddafi, especially after last year's raid on Khartoum.'

We were approaching the coast of North Africa. I could see the running lights and silhouettes of the coastal traders, and the dim glow from Tobruk and El Bardia.

'Dog's Wells,' I heard Bock murmur.

'What's that?' I said.

'Bir Hacheim. It is to the west of Tobruk. Some call it Bir Hakeim, which means "Old Man's Wells" in Arabic. In the Legion, we call it Bir Hacheim, which means "Dog's Wells." The 13th DBLE fought there in 1942. We held Rommel for nearly three weeks. We stopped him from going east to Cairo. It is almost as honored as the stand at Camerone.'

'How old were you then?'

'Twenty. I had already been with the underground.'

'I envy your having had a decent war to fight.'

'There are those who will say there are no decent wars, Mateuse. But I am glad I lived when I did and have done the things I have.'

We talked for a while, then he went to sleep some more. Khadija had wakened, and watched him go.

'He tries to hide what he is feeling,' she said, 'but there are times when he cannot.'

'I'm not sure I know what you mean,' I said.

'You are not aware of his condition?'

'No,' I said. 'What condition?'

She went into the engineer's section and came back with her clipboard. She had put the critical document on top. It was a long telex addressed to Pazar. I skipped over most of it. The final paragraph was what she wanted me to see.

**MEDECIN DIAGNOSTIC/HOPITAL DU
SACRE-COEUR/ROUEN**

**MALADE MONSIEUR
VANDERWALD/HONFLEUR**
L'APPAREIL LYMPHATIQUE CANCEREUX

PRONOSTIC AU PLUS GRAVE

'He is dying,' Khadija said. 'The report was sent by one of Mahmet's agents in Paris. The Dutchman has said nothing about this, but I believe you should know.'

Chapter Twenty-Five

At eleven o'clock that morning, with all six fuel bladders empty and both wing tanks low, we were circling the desert outpost of Zahida Al Hakim. From altitude, it appeared to be an abandoned World War II airbase. There were a half-dozen rectangular wood-frame buildings with corrugated metal roofs, sections of which had either collapsed or been blown away by the desert winds. Sand had drifted against the structures, sometimes as high as the eaves. A landing area ran parallel to the buildings, on an east-west line. The surrounding terrain, as far as I could see in all directions, was a wasteland of stippled dunes broken occasionally by a dry wadi or field of flint-colored stone.

Khadija told me to make one right-hand and two lefthand orbits over the field: an identification pattern, she said, that had been prearranged by her father. She and Sabah were at their places in the radio-navigation section. Bock was in the copilot's seat.

'This time the landing area is large, Mateus,' he said. 'Big enough for a 747.' He had taken time to shave, had changed into a fresh white shirt. His color had improved under the sting of his cologne.

As I completed the second turn to the left, two figures appeared on the desert below. They arranged an orange Day-Glo panel into a triangle pointing west. We landed without incident, taxiing to that end of the runway. It was only after touchdown that we were able to see the rest of Hakim's encampment: a number of tents and large camouflage nets which had been invisible from the air. These had been erected beyond the original buildings on the north side of the field.

Armed men in khaki surrounded the C-47 as I shut down the engines. One called out several words in Arabic to Khadija, who answered through the open wing window at my side. I had to bend forward to give her room. As I did, I could feel the firm press of her body as she leaned across me.

'The one I have talked to is Amadi,' she said when she was through.

'His given name is Tawfiq. He will be in charge of you.'

The heat in the cockpit was already stifling.

'I didn't come here to work for Amadi,' I said.

'He serves as my father's lieutenant,' she replied. 'He can be ill-tempered, and is jealous of his privilege. You must do as he says. It is my father's wish.'

'You'll have to tell your father I came here to work for him. I won't take orders from anyone else.'

I was snapping out the words. I'd built up an ill temper of my own from having spent too many hours at the controls of the Gooney, watching the desert slide by a thousand feet below, listening to the monotonous dits and dahs of the identifiers pulsing in my headset, trying to reconcile myself to the fact of what was happening to Bock, the incomprehensible multiplication of cells that would hollow him out until it reached something vital and he would die. It was a scurvy, rotten form of death – worse, in my mind, than any smash up or bullet in the brain.

While I set the parking brakes and impatiently flipped off switches, Bock turned to Khadija and gestured at me.

'Mateus is tired,' he said. 'Before you require him to do anything else, he must be allowed to sleep.'

'My father will understand,' Khadija said.

'I don't like this man Amadi,' I said. 'I'm warning you now if he starts pulling rank on me, we're going to have trouble.'

'I should not have told you what I did about my relationship with him,' Khadija replied. 'I have spoken too freely. Please forget what I have said.'

When I did not answer, she put her hand on my shoulder.

'I ask you,' she said, 'to do this for me.'

Amadi, who wore an aviator's cap and tinted glasses, looked to be in his early thirties. He was a trim, sinewy man of average height, with pronounced cheekbones and a pencil-thin goatee. His skin tones were darker than Khadija's, eyes black and constantly shifting, teeth imperfect behind a smile that slid quickly toward an expression of contempt, Khadija introduced us as soon as Bock and I deplaned.

Several of Hakim's men were starting to erect a camouflage net over the C-47. Others were offloading the cargo we had brought from

140

Turkey. The crate we had picked up on the island of Arkis was already gone. So was Sabah. We stood in the shadow of the left wing, out of the scorching sun.

'There is immediate work for the mechanic,' Amadi said, His accents were slurred when he spoke English, and he had to grope for the words. From the moment our eyes met, I sensed in him a bedrock hatred of Bock and me, of all we represented: the alien cultures, the infidel West. It was the look of prejudice, ugly and irremediable.

Fifty yards distant from the C-47, beyond the landing area, two big camouflage nets bulked above the sand. Bock got his tools and followed Amadi in that direction. I got our bags and followed Khadija toward the woodframe buildings I had seen from the air. There were six in all. They paralleled the field in a double row, three on a side. Even close up, they appeared to be derelict, but there were air conditioners in several of the windows, and I could hear the muted throb of a diesel generator. The door to one of the middle buildings was padlocked. An Arab guard squatted nearby, cradling an automatic rifle in his lap. He smiled at Khadija as we passed.

'Some of my father's men are beginning their second year in this camp,' she said. 'They are dedicated to him and to his cause.'

We didn't have far to walk, but I could feel our pace slowed by the driving heat of the sun. There was no breeze; the air was dry. Highlights of red gleamed in Khadija's hair.

'How long have you been here?' I asked her.

'Only since the first of June. Friends met me in Benghazi and arranged for me to fly in a light plane to the Sudanese border. My uncle met me there and we came the rest of the way together, crossing the desert by jeep at night. Three weeks ago, this time also with my father's men, we returned the same way. They did not want to risk flying. It was long and tiring.'

We passed the last of the buildings and came into an area of tents. There were a dozen in all. They were constructed of canvas and had been randomly pitched. Each was about nine feet by twelve, with sides that rolled up, and overhead flies the same tan color as the sand. Khadija showed me to one that was somewhat removed from the others. It had two cots, and a box for a table. There were two cups, a washbasin and water pitcher, two blankets, a couple of

141

towels without much nap, a colorless bar of soap. There were no lamps or candles.

'I hope this will be all right for you and the Dutchman,' she said.

'It's fine.'

'Only three of the original buildings are usable,' she said. 'Two are for my father's work. We sleep in the other.'

'I've read that your father is an educated man. Is that true?'

'Yes. He studied in Paris. If he had not been educated, he would not have allowed me to be. There are times, even now, when he regrets that I am.'

'How do you feel about it?'

'When I first went to California, I was very frightened. Everything was so different from what I had been used to. I was sure I would not be accepted; but the Americans were friendly and did everything they could to make me feel at home. I had heard about the place of women in your culture, but I could not at first believe the ease with which they moved – how much independence they had, and how free they were to make their own choices.'

'They've had to work for that,' I said. 'They still are.'

'Yes, of course, this is true. But the difference between being a woman in California and a woman in Damascus is like the difference between two distant planets in the sky. My father had warned me this would be true, but it is one thing to hear something is so and another to experience it.'

'Are you glad you had the chance?'

'I think so. But I have had to pay a price. I am despised by many of my own people who believe I have betrayed them and Islam by adopting some of the attitudes of the West. To them it is an obscenity that I drive a car, that I mingle freely with men, that I do not wear the veil, that I appear on television as a spokesman for my father. They count his lenience toward me as his single and greatest flaw. I feel sorry for him. I know there are decisions regarding me he would dearly like to have back. But it is too late.'

'Would you consider living in the West?'

'I did consider that once. When I was in California, I met a young American. He was the instructor in one of my courses. We saw a great deal of each other, and became very close. We talked of marriage. I wanted very much to marry him, but in the end I could not

142

commit myself to staying in California, nor could he commit himself to leaving California for Damascus.'

'Did your father know about the relationship?'

'No. Only Sabah. I would not have dared tell my father.'

Her voice suddenly sounded shaky. She touched her hands to her temples.

'Are you all right?' I asked.

'Yes,' she said, but I could see a sheen of perspiration on her forehead and I thought she looked wobbly.

'Sit down,' I said. 'I'll get you a drink.'

She sat on the nearest cot, elbows on her knees, head in her hands. The pitcher was made of a porous clay, and the water it held was cool. I poured her a cup, which she quickly drank. Then I soaked one end of a towel and she held it against her forehead.

'You are the one who should mind the heat,' she said.

'Maybe it's not the heat you're minding,' I said. 'You've been through a lot these last few days.'

'No more than you.'

'I'm used to seeing men die. That makes a difference.'

'I do not wish to become used to that.'

'I know.'

She looked at me.

'Have my feelings been so transparent?' she asked.

'Not always. They were when the Swede went down. That was the first time I noticed.'

'And when I told you about the Dutchman?'

'Yes.'

She hesitated for a moment, then asked, 'Why does he call you Mateus?'

'We met in the bar at the Grand Hotel in Tripoli, back in the '50s,' I said. 'I bet him a bottle of Mateus rosé I could beat him at arm wrestling.'

'And did you?'

I smiled.

'No,' I said. 'But the name stuck.'

'Before your wife was killed in the war, did she call you Matt?'

'Yes.'

'I think I would feel awkward calling you that.'

143

'It works pretty well,' I said. 'I'd be happy if you'd try it.'

She looked at me and I felt again as if there were only the two of us, as if the rest of the world had dropped away. The light was more diffused in the tent, and the pupils of her eyes had dilated.

'Thank you, Matt,' she said, 'for being kind to me.'

'My pleasure,' I said.

'When we go to Singapore,' she said, 'where will we stay?'

'At the Raffles Hotel.'

'I think if the world were more perfect than it is,' she said, 'we would be there now.'

'So do I.'

She stood up. I told myself we were just having an idle conversation, that there was no way we could have a relationship, that I was too much older than she, that she was too much wedded to her tribe, that we lacked time and opportunity, that the world was so far from perfect it seemed to spin in an orbit of blood.

'Khadija, listen to me,' I started to say, wanting to tell her that I liked her, that if she needed a friend I was willing to be that friend, that once all this was over – whatever it was – I wanted to see her again on some neutral ground, neither mine nor hers.

But before I could say any of this, Amadi appeared at the door of the tent. He spoke harshly to Khadija in Arabic. She looked at him with indifference, then at me.

'My father wishes to see you now,' she said. 'I will take you to him.'

Chapter Twenty-Six

We followed Amadi back up the sandy path between the double row of buildings. Each building was rectangular in shape, measuring about fifteen feet by thirty. According to Khadija, the three on our left, in the row closest to the landing area, were as abandoned as they looked. The three on our right had been reconstructed by her father's men. The first was the one she and her family used as their quarters. The next was the off-limits hut with the padlock on the door. The guard who had been squatting there the first time we had passed was now gone.

Each of the reconstructed buildings had been camouflaged to appear abandoned from the air. The windows had been painted white with streaks of black, the metal roofs rust-colored; split pieces of wood had been nailed haphazardly across the outsides of the doors.

The third hut on the inside row was the one Hakim used for his office and base of operations. Amadi left us there, continuing on toward the big nets where he had originally gone with Bock. Khadija and I went into the ops shack.

Hakim was a thin, sparse man, with a salt-and-pepper goatee, similar in style to Amadi's but fuller. He wore khakis and a muslin head kerchief that fell below his shoulders and was tied at the brow by a coil of black goat's hair. The last pictures I had seen of him had been file photos, and it seemed to me he had aged noticeably since the time they were taken. There was a slight drop to the left corner of his mouth, as if he might have suffered a stroke, and the muscles in his left forearm appeared to be atrophied.

As we came in, he rose from where he had been sitting, behind a large makeshift desk. The room was about fifteen by twenty, air-conditioned, but not enough to make the transition from outside unpleasant. Topographical sheets and chalk boards, filled with notations in Arabic, covered the walls. The windows were opaque. One end of the building had been partitioned off. The door in the partition was closed.

We stood facing each other in the soft pool of light provided by an overhead lamp that flickered in time with the pulse of the generator. I watched as Khadija went to her father and they embraced, kissing each other on both cheeks.

'Father,' she said, 'this is Colonel Eberhart. Colonel, my father, Dr. Hakim.'

He looked at me for several seconds before he spoke, as if he were phrasing what he wanted to say in Arabic before translating it into English. Khadija watched him with an expression that I thought mingled irritation and affection. The family resemblance between them was clear, particularly through the upper facial structure and the eyes. I could see no obvious resemblance between Hakim and his brother, Sabah, except, perhaps, the proud but unaffected way they carried themselves, as if they knew – and had sensed from birth – that they were something more than ordinary men,

'My brother has told me,' Hakim said, 'that you are a pilot of exceptional skill and that the mechanic who travels with you saved my daughter's life. You are welcome in this camp.'

'Thank you,' I said. 'I came here because I was paid to come. At first I thought the money was good, but then the risks started going up, and now I'm not at all sure. If you're ready to talk business, I'd like to do that.'

He smiled, obviously amused by my direct approach.

'Yes,' he said. 'I am ready to discuss our business with you.'

Khadija spoke to him then in Arabic. He shook his head. She repeated what she had said, this time with more emphasis. He made a brief reply. They went back and forth. His tone never altered; hers rose steadily in pitch. When it became clear I was uncomfortable with this, she looked at me and apologized.

'I am sorry,' she said shortly. 'There are things I must speak with my father about. Because I am merely a woman, I will come back when the two of you have finished.'

She turned on her heel and went out. Hakim watched her go. He looked melancholy, as if he thought something a long time ago had gone awry in the upbringing of his daughter, as if he wished he could enter her brain and alter a few city circuits and by doing that bring her back in line with his notion of what a good Syrian female should be.

'She was educated in your country,' he said.

'Yes, I know. In California.'

'I no longer believe this was wise.'

'We probably disagree about that, but it doesn't matter.'

'She will marry soon. She will have children, and live in Damascus.'

'Whether she likes it or not?'

'She will learn to like it. Her roots are in Islam. The rest has been grafted onto her, and will fall away.'

'For her sake, I hope you're wrong,' I said. 'She's a sensitive, intelligent woman. She could do more for your country than raise a handful of children in Damascus.'

'As you say, Colonel, we do not agree about this; but it does not matter. Please be seated.'

We took our seats facing each other across his desk. The desk was littered with slide rules, protractors, compasses, sheets of graph paper, acetate layovers, and what looked to be technical journals in a variety of languages. The only personal item I could see was a small sepia print in an oval frame of a striking Arab woman about his age, who looked the way Khadija would look thirty years from now.

'I accept the principle set forth by Colonel Qaddafi,' he said, 'that there is a sovereignty of our people, united in Islam. I am dedicated in opposition to the corrupting influences which threaten to destroy the Arab world: the Zionists, Shah Pahlavi, Sadat, Hussein, the Saudi princes – those leaders and factions who have been moti-vated by greed, or cowardice or stupidity, to betray their own people and the tenets of their faith.' He looked at me. 'Have I made this clear?' he said.

'Yes,' I said. 'But I have no interest in your politics – or anyone else's, for that matter.'

'Then,' he said mockingly, 'you are cynical.'

'Call it that if you like. I call it practical. I fly airplanes for pay. The more I get, the better job I do, and the more I'm willing to risk. I assume all the men who hire me have their reasons for doing so. I'm perfectly willing to sit here and listen to your philosophy, but when

147

we get down to our negotiations, your philosophy isn't going to influence me in the least.'

In my role as a mercenary, I knew I had to convince Hakim I was truly a hired gun: a man with no important scruples beyond the dollar amount of a contract and how well I carried it out. I found the role easier to play than I would have believed. There was a time when I couldn't have played it at all.

I let my features settle into an impenetrable expression and fixed on Hakim a steady, almost blank gaze, which I knew I could maintain for as long as I had to. It said I would yield nothing further to him: no more conversation, no sign of interest in anything he might say, nothing whatsoever until he decided to come to the point. For a long moment, he returned my gaze, the dropped corner of his mouth twitching slightly, as if he wanted to remind me that I was at his mercy in this place. Finally, he spoke.

'Two nights from now,' he said, 'we will launch an air strike from this camp against a preselected target. There will be two planes. One will fly escort; the other will deliver the ordinance.'

'What's the target?' I said.

'Does the name Ghurs-Al'Asl mean anything to you?'

'No. Nothing.'

'It is the Arabic word for Honeycomb. The Saudis use it to describe the royal compound on the coast of the Red Sea, north of Jiddah. It was built three years ago by King Khalid at a cost of four hundred and fifty million dollars. It contains several palaces and villas, and a jet port and yacht basin. Many of the pro-Western Saudi princes, including the Seven Sudeiris, will gather there this week to enjoy, out of the public eye, the fruits of their corruption. We will destroy them, and the compound.'

I responded as if I had no interest in this. Campbell had said the stakes might be high. It was hard to imagine how they could be higher. Without the Saudi royal line, a major source of our oil would be pinched off at the pump.

I shifted my weight in my chair.

'What kind of airplanes do you have?' I said.

'F-86 Sabrejet fighters.'

'You've got two of those out there?'

He looked pleased.

'Yes,' he said. 'They are parked under the nets you saw as you came in. Amadi will fly escort. You will make the bombing run.'

'Have you got reconnaissance photographs and current maps of the target area?'

'Yes.'

He got them out of a drawer and spread them in front of me. The photos showed a long spit of land that hooked to the north, forming a natural harbor with the mainland of Saudi Arabia. On the seaward side, a hill rose several hundred feet. The palaces and jet port were on the other side of the hill, facing the harbor. There was a golf course, some tennis courts, a stretch of sandy beach, and a small flotilla of boats. The entire compound was surrounded by a high masonry wall with guard posts every hundred feet or so.

'What's the payload?' I said.

'A single five-hundred pound bomb.'

'Loaded with what?'

'You will be advised of that shortly before you take off.'

'All right,' I said. 'I'll want to study this some more. Right now, here are the problems I see. To avoid radar, we're going to have to cross the Red Sea right on top of the waves. There's no way to navigate an F-86 in the dark with the precision required to locate the target; and even if we managed to do that, dive bombing at night without radar in the cockpit is bound to be inaccurate. Furthermore,' I said, pointing to the top of the hill between the compound and the sea, 'there's an antiaircraft gun emplacement up here with an excellent view seaward and over the grounds. The F-86 was designed a long time ago as a day fighter. You're going to need something much more sophisticated if you want to pull this off.'

Hakim smiled.

'You will have your sophisticated airplane, colonel,' he said. 'Your mechanic is already studying and planning installation procedures for an inertial navigation system and a pullup gauge. The navigation equipment will direct you to a point just out of range of the guns. Once there, you will not have to expose yourself to a dive-bombing run. Using the pull-up gauge, you will toss the bomb into the compound. I assume you are familiar with this maneuver?'

'Yes,' I said. He wanted me to be impressed, and I was. The INS equipment, manufactured by Coyle Enterprises, was the most accurate in the world. It used a precision gyro-stabilized inertial platform and a digital computer to determine the great-circle route between two or more known points fed into its data banks. Properly tuned and programmed, it would be accurate within ten feet. The toss-bombing maneuver itself would depend largely on pilot skill, and explain why Bogan, Lutz, and I had been required at Pazar's airfield to do a low-level loop.

Hakim sat with his elbows on the desk and fingertips together.

'As you see, colonel,' he said, 'though we are called terrorists by your press, we have not all been reduced to throwing hand grenades into school buses.'

Chapter Twenty-Seven

I was reluctant to bring up the business of the payload again, knowing if I showed too much curiosity about that, I might tip my hand to Hakim. As a mercenary, two things would be foremost in my mind: the amount of money I could earn, and my chance for a safe return.

'What's the estimated time in flight?' I asked.

'One hour and a half,' Hakim replied. 'Allowing for the variables of wind and weight, it should approximate forty-five minutes each way.'

'Who's doing the flight planning?'

'Amadi.'

'I'll want to double-check him on everything,' I said. 'He made a mistake when he figured our course from Izmir to Arkis.'

Hakim looked uncomfortable at this. Behind him, the air conditioner hummed quietly, lifting the corner of one of the papers on his desk.

'What time do we launch?' I asked.

'Two o'clock in the morning. The moon will have set by the time you reach the Saudi coast. Amadi will fly your wing. You will be in radio contact on a frequency I will give you before you take off.'

'Okay,' I said. 'For the sake of our discussion, let's assume we've approached the target without intercept, and I've tossed the bomb into the compound. It's not going to take the Saudis very long to react, and scramble their air force. They're outfitted with F-5Es these days. If they spot us, they're going to chew us up.'

'You and Amadi will have the critical advantage of surprise. The Saudis will not expect an attack from Sudan. Their first assumption will be Israel or Egypt. You will return here at low level, rise to a safe altitude over the field, then eject from your aircraft, letting the plane fly straight on into the desert. You will parachute to us and we will travel overland by jeep to Libya.'

'What's my guarantee you won't kill me when I return?'

He looked as if he found the question distasteful.

'As soon as the Saudi compound has been destroyed,' he said, 'my brother and I will be on the radio, taking credit for the attack. We are preparing similar missions in other locations. They too will require the services of a pilot with exceptional skills. Having gone to this much trouble to find you, Colonel Eberhart, please believe me when I say I have no intention of bringing about your death, nor anything to gain by it.'

I leaned back in my chair. His arguments struck me as reasonable. A man who wanted stronger assurances than the ones he had made probably would not be a mercenary in the first place. He was offering me a handsome sum, and when we got to the end game, I'd be at the controls of my own airplane. If I didn't like the idea of punching out here, we both knew I could settle for my front money and take my chances punching out somewhere else. I wanted to ask him if his guarantees extended to Bock, but again was afraid of tipping my hand.

'Khadija mentioned a price,' I said. 'The U.S. equivalent of half a million dollars.'

'Yes,' he said. 'This is our offer.'

'I'll want that much for myself. You'll have to make a separate arrangement with the mechanic.'

'As you wish.'

'How do we verify the deposit?'

'There is high-frequency radio equipment here. We can establish contact through a telephone patch with any bank in the world.'

'I'll want sixty percent of mine up front,' I said.

'No,' he said. 'I will not go above forty.'

'Fifty,' I said. 'I won't haggle for less. I'll be taking my biggest chances after the bomb is delivered. If I don't make it back here, I want to be sure that much is locked up for my son.'

His expression softened at my mention of this.

'Your son's name is Brian?'

'Yes.'

'His condition is described in the papers that have come from Mahmet. I too have children who have been taken in war. I hope you are blessed by Allah with his recovery.'

I thanked him for that. In the moment of silence that followed, I tried to imagine him not as a terrorist, but simply as a man from another culture, coming for a visit to my farm. He would seem out of place there at first, but only for a little while. I could picture us in the late afternoon, walking out to the stream and watching the trout begin to rise. He would have sensible things to say about how the property might be managed. He would look across the rolling hills to the west, which stretched all the way to White Oaks, and would tell me he was reminded of the river valleys in the north and east of Syria. We would behave like two reasonable men who had sired children and suffered loss. I knew we were capable of that, of being civilized. It seemed to me most men were. What I had never been able to figure out was why for so many of us it was so hard.

'Then you are satisfied with our negotiation?' he said.

'I've got a problem with the two planes,' I said. 'Amadi isn't going to be worth much, flying escort in an obsolete fighter. It seems to me by sending up two of us, you run twice the risk something will go wrong.'

He smiled, holding his fingertips together again.

'As you must have your safeguards, colonel,' he said, 'I must have mine. If you were an unscrupulous man, you might decide to jettison the bomb and fly elsewhere. Certainly with a quarter of a million dollars of our money safely in your account, you could be tempted. Amadi's presence on your wing will be one of our assurances that this will not happen.'

'Then why not send Amadi by himself? He'd probably do it for a lot less pay.'

Hakim stood up, ignoring my question.

'Come with me,' he said. 'I will show you the planes.'

The F-86 is a low-wing, single-seat aircraft, with smooth, flowing lines. It is built around its engine, with the air scoop in front and the intake running on a center-line arrangement from front to back. The rudder is high, with two horizontal stabilizers. The wings are swept back at an angle of forty-five degrees. Even on the ground, it is a very alert-looking fighter that earns the tag 'Sabrejet.'

Hakim took me to the plane I would fly. The net it was under was supported by a solid wood framework, buttressed to the north and west against the prevailing winds. Sunlight filtered through, dappling the hard-packed sand. The bow canopy of the fighter was the kind that slid straight back. It was open now. Bock was working in the cockpit. An elderly Arab in white coveralls stood on the wing. As we came in, I was startled to hear him speaking in French.

'*Bonjour*, pilot,' Bock said when he saw me. He had his spectacles on.

'*Bonjour*,' I said. '*Comment allez-vous?*'

'*J'ai de quoi faire.*'

'*Ah, oui.*'

'*Superbement*,' the Arab said, making it clear to me that already he was impressed with the quality of Bock's work.

I walked around the plane. It had been painted in a camouflage pattern of desert tan. There were no identifying roundels. An MD-1 power unit stood on the ground by the left side. The unit was about half the size of a Volkswagen sedan, bright yellow, with thick black cables. The fighter carried two wing tanks and, under the left wing, a pylon with an empty bomb rack.

'It's a very clean-looking plane,' I said.

'Both are equally fine,' Hakim said. 'It was Amadi who arranged their purchase and flew them here. Do you wish to view the other as well?'

'Later,' I said. 'I'm red-eyed tired now. I need to sleep.'

He accepted this, and I walked back to the tent Bock and I would share. It was on a rise of ground, higher than the others, and some distance away. I wondered where Hakim kept his radios; there was no sign anywhere of an antenna. I desperately needed to get word to Campbell. I had no idea if his monitors had received the cryptic message I had sent from the C-47 as we had turned past the Izmir beacon on our way to Arkis. Even if he had, we had been out of touch since, and that seemed a long time and many miles ago.

I stripped to my briefs and lay down on my cot in the intense dry heat of the afternoon. The sides of the tent had been rolled up, but there was no breeze. Just before I fell asleep, I saw two of Hakim's guards, strolling casually through the camp. They did not look as if they expected trouble.

I woke at dusk to the sight of Bock sorting out a hamper of food onto our table. There was dried beef in pocket bread. The beef was tough,

Bock said, and the bread was stale. There were canned ripe olives, zucchini and eggplant, and a tin for each of us of warm condensed goat's milk.

'*Bon appetit*,' he said. 'These are some of the provisions we carried from Turkey.' He looked very tired.

'Leave it to you to find an Arab who speaks French,' I said.

'His name is Ahdel. He has been with the Hakims for many years, and is especially close to Khadija. When her father went to study at the Sorbonne, he took Ahdel with him. It was then that he learned the language.'

I told Bock what I had learned from Hakim. He took one sip of the goat's milk and put it aside.

'Both planes are in excellent condition,' he said. 'According to Ahdel, Amadi bought them from the Pakistani air force, where he once served as an F-86 pilot. It was originally thought he would fly the mission alone. The second plane was brought here to provide the spare parts that might be needed.'

'What made them change the plan?' I asked.

'Amadi concealed the fact, at first, that he has difficulty flying on instruments. As long as he can see a horizon, he is capable; but he cannot keep his concentration in the cockpit. The Pakistanis do very little weather or night flying. It took two years before his squadron commander finally became suspicious. He took Amadi up in a two-seater, and required him to fly under a hood. When Amadi failed to control the aircraft properly, he was grounded. Soon after that, he resigned. Hakim finally learned of this.'

'The toss-bombing maneuver requires a pullup on gauges,' I said. 'You have to cross-check G forces, wing level, and heading. There's no way Amadi could do it if he can't fly instruments.'

'He knows that, but it infuriates him that you have been brought here to take his place. I would not trust him. Ahdel and I did a thorough inspection of each plane. While we did, I had a chance to open the ammunition cans. The ones in Amadi's plane are full: three hundred live rounds for each of the six .50 caliber guns. The ones in the plane you will fly are empty, except for the ballast.'

'Hakim figures that way I won't be tempted to abort the mission.'

'He intends to go further. When I have finished installing the

155

navigation equipment, Ahdel says I will be required to boobytrap your plane.'

'How?'

'He did not say.'

'Did he say anything about the payload?'

'He believes it is some sort of incendiary explosive that will create a firestorm within the Saudi compound.'

'I need to know,' I said. 'What chance do you think we have of getting into the locked hut?'

'The lock itself presents no obstacle. All day I have watched the guards. They walk through the camp and then around the perimeter. Sometimes they circle to the left, sometimes to the right. There seems to be no fixed pattern of time, but they are usually gone from the area of the buildings for fifteen minutes or more.'

'We'll try it tonight,' I said. 'After the camp turns in.'

He closed his eyes, stretched his neck, trying to work out the fatigue.

'They want me to work late,' he said. 'They have set up a computer processor and test unit in Hakim's office.'

'If you feel too tired for that,' I said, 'I'll go to Hakim and tell him you need to rest.'

'I don't think he would listen. The work is complex. There have been other technicians here, but now they are gone. Ahdel is the only one left with enough knowledge to help me. We enjoy each other's company. At least there is that.'

'I think he's wrong about the payload,' I said.

Bock had finished his meal and was polishing a St. Christopher medal on the sleeve of his shirt.

'And what is your guess?' he asked.

'I could be off by a mile,' I said, 'but I think Hakim may have managed to latch on to an atom bomb.'

Chapter Twenty-Eight

Something on Hakim's desk had triggered my hunch, four letters in caps on a card that had been briefly exposed when the breeze from his air conditioner had lifted the corner of one of his papers. The effect had been almost subliminal. The letters, upside down and backward from where I was sitting, appeared and disappeared, like the winking of a light at sea. There was only one way to be sure. When Bock returned at midnight, we put together our plan.

Since dusk the air in the desert had cooled to the point where the light sweaters we wore felt good. We lay on our cots, as if asleep, and spoke quietly. I had left the sidewalls up so we could observe the camp.

'Hakim and his brother are still in their office,' Bock said. 'When I asked Ahdel why they were up so late, he said they were working on the announcement they will make once the raid has been accomplished. The words are very important to Hakim. He believes if he speaks them well, much of the Arab world will support what he has done.'

'What about the guards?'

'There are two. They patrol in the same pattern as before. The rest of the camp is asleep, including Amadi. I am not sure about Khadija. Earlier, I saw her by one of the planes. I have not seen her since. Ahdel says she often walks by herself in the desert at night.'

'Can you get me into that hut?'

'Yes, without question. After the guards have passed, I will open the lock. Once you are in, I will close it again. This way, you will have the time you need.'

'Twenty minutes should do it.'

'Then I will let the guards pass once while you are inside.'

'Do we have a flashlight?'

He said he had brought the one from the C-47. I checked my watch.

157

'We've got fifty hours between now and the scheduled launch,' I said. 'Once we know for sure what the payload is, we're going to have to find a way to get in touch with Campbell. Has Ahdel mentioned where the radios are?'

'Yes. In a small room off Hakim's office. But they are monitored twenty-four hours a day.'

'Can we transmit from one of the Sabrejets?'

'There are no microphones or headsets as yet. The headsets have also been removed from the C-47.'

'Any ideas?'

'I have studied the maps. Two night marches from here, on the border with Egypt, there is a small Sudanese army post.'

'How many miles?'

He shrugged, as if the figure was unimportant.

'Sixty,' he said.

'That's too far.'

'Unless the maps are inaccurate, there is nothing else.'

'What about jeeps? Are they in running order?'

'The distributor caps have been removed. Even if they hadn't, the camp would be on to us as soon as we tried to start one.'

'Or one of the planes.'

'Yes.'

'We'll manage something when the time comes,' I said. 'Right now I want to find out exactly what it is Hakim wants me to toss into the laps of the Saudi royal line.'

We waited until the guards had passed. They came from the area of the buildings and walked close by our tent this time – something they had not done before. We could hear them talking as they went by. I lay motionless, with my eyes closed. Bock pretended to snore. If he had wanted to, he could have reached out and touched them.

As soon as they were out of sight, we dummied our beds to look as if we were still in them, and made our way to the off-limits hut. We kept to the shadows, staying off the central path. The throb of the camp generator covered the noise we made. Bock had brought a set of lock picks and small torsion wrenches from his kit. He carried them in a leather packet about the size of a checkbook. It took him just over a minute to open the padlock. He clapped me on the

158

shoulder as I slipped inside, then closed the door, relocking it behind me.

The room I had entered was pitch dark, and warmer than the outside. I waited a few seconds, then, shielding the red filter with my hand, I switched on the flashlight.

The building had been divided in the same way as Hakim's office except that here the doorway leading through the partition into the smaller room was open. I decided to check there first, and found it was being used as a storage room. There were several Mark-82 five-hundred-pound bomb casings with tailfin assemblies standing along the far wall. The floor was cluttered with empty boxes, and what was left of the crate Art Farmer had delivered on the island of Arkis.

I knelt down and began to examine the broken slats. When I had first glimpsed the crate in the hold of the Lygarius, I had come away with the impression that its top had been stenciled with a U.S. Government code. The stencil hadn't been visible when Sabah's men had lashed the crate to the cargo rings on the C-47, but I was certain it was there, and finally I found it: AFAP/203mm. The first four letters were the same as the ones I had seen on Hakim's desk. They stood for Artillery Fired Atomic Projectile. The 203mm designated the diameter of the shell, one of the largest in the inventory.

I checked my watch. The digits sprang toward me out of the dark – 12:40. I had already been in the building ten minutes. In ten minutes more, Bock would take his chances letting me out. I stumbled back into the larger room. The red beam of the flashlight was all but useless for anything but the closest kind of work. I could feel myself hurrying. There were benches and worktables spaced around the floor, metal cabinets along the wall. I began checking them. I knew I was going to need more time, and I hated the idea of having to stay in this place through a second passing of the guards.

At the end of ten minutes, I found what I was looking for: a metal canister on one of the workbenches near the door leading outside. The canister looked like a large ammo can, with handles at each end. It measured about four feet by one by one, and had been stenciled with the same code: AFAP/203mm. Two latches secured the lid. I unsnapped them and opened it up.

The shell was about eight inches in diameter and twenty-four

159

inches long. It rested on braced supports, its metallic surface gleaming in the dull-red glow of my light. The original fuse had been removed. There was a Mark-904 aerial bomb fuse and a couple of circuit testers on the bench nearby. A yellow-and-purple Atomic Energy Commission decal had been fixed to the inside of the canister lid. Next to it was a roentgen counter film badge in a small plastic holder, and next to that a canvas sleeve with a log book. I had just started reading the entries when I heard a sharp rattling sound at the door.

I slid the book back into its sleeve, closed the canister lid, and eased the snaps shut. The noise I had heard was much too loud for anything Bock would have made. I took two quick steps to the door. I knew I had been in the building for more than twenty minutes. I could hear voices through the wall. They were speaking Arabic. I didn't recognize them, and assumed they belonged to the guards, who must have come back through this part of the camp sooner than Bock expected. Then, as they receded, I heard Sabah's voice, and then Hakim's.

I froze for a heartbeat, snapped off my light, and ran on the tips of my toes for the storage room. There was no time to be careful about tripping or stumbling over anything. They already had the key in the padlock. I ducked out of sight behind the partition seconds before the door opened and the overhead lights in the main room came on.

The two brothers were speaking Arabic in conversational tones. Their voices came from the area of the workbench, and I assumed they were looking at the shell, or maybe getting ready to run some kind of test on the fuse. They hadn't been in the building long before they were confronted by Khadija.

She spoke angrily to them in Arabic. Neither Sabah or Hakim replied. I could hear her footsteps, lighter than theirs, as she came further into the room. There was an extended period of silence. Finally, Hakim said something to her. When she answered, she talked for a long time without pause, obviously upset. I could hear Sabah trying to be conciliatory. She paid no attention. She was pacing the room in sharp, quick steps. Several times she would pick up an object from one of the benches and slam it down. She was just on the other side of the partition now. I could see the slice of her shadow through the open door. I flattened myself against the wall and held my breath. Hakim was trying to reason with her. The more he talked, the angrier she became. Her shadow moved relentlessly as she paced. Her voice hardened, as if for the first time in her life she intended to argue him down.

Finally, she came through the doorway.

The light from the main room fell on the bomb casings that stood along the far wall. It could have been these that attracted her, or simply a need to separate herself from the inflexible presence of the two men. Whatever it was, when she spun on her heel to walk out again, she looked straight at me.

I saw her eyes widen, her lips part as if to cry out in surprise or alarm. She wasn't five feet away from the place where I stood. Her hair was pulled back and disheveled. Her face had a dusty, smudged look; I could see the abrasion on her cheek.

We looked at each other, our eyes locked in surprise and recognition. For an instant, I was sure she would feel required to betray my presence here. Then, her expression returning to one of anger, she went back into the main room.

Ten minutes later, the three of them were gone. When Bock unlocked the door for me and I slipped out into the shadows, my hands were still trembling.

He whistled softly.

'Too close,' he said.

In the tent, I told him what had happened and what I had seen. He lay on his back, holding his hands against his chest as if he were in pain.

'She had me cold,' I said. 'One word to her father, and I was dead.'

'She could still change her mind and tell him, Mateus. We should leave tonight.'

'How far would we get? It's already past one. They'd track us at sunrise and bring us back.'

'Where did they get this weapon?'

'According to the inspection log, it came from an artillery group near Kaiserslautern in West Germany. Farmer and his people must have stolen it from there. That should have been a difficult thing to do, but it probably wasn't. I remember reading a couple of years ago about a German employee who drove off an air base with a

Sidewinder missile in the trunk of his car. We're not as sharp and smart as we used to be.'

'So. They will mount the atomic shell into one of the bomb casings, and use the M-904 fuse as a detonator.'

'I'd say so.'

'What kind of yield will they get?'

'Five kilotons, maybe.'

'And what will that mean?'

'The explosion would be about one-half the size of the one at Hiroshima,' I said.

Chapter Twenty-Nine

When I awoke at dawn, Bock was sitting on the edge of his cot, bent forward, hugging himself.

'What's wrong?' I asked.

'It is nothing,' he said. He could hardly speak.

'Do you have medication?'

'I have run out.'

'There must be some in camp. I'll get Hakim.'

'No, Mateus. Please. Let it pass.'

'Pazar got a copy of your medical records from the hospital in Rouen,' I said. 'Khadija showed them to me.'

He was silent. I went to the cot and sat next to him.

'Don't be so bloody goddam proud,' I said. 'Let me get you some help.'

He shook his head.

'It will pass,' he said. 'It already has.'

'There's nothing wrong between you and Colette, is there?' I said. 'You told me there was because you couldn't stand telling me about the cancer.'

He nodded.

'I don't blame you for that,' I said. 'But I do blame you for suffering pain when there may be no need.'

'It is better now.'

'What have the doctors tried to do for you?'

'Surgery first. Then radiation. I was very ill. My skin became scorched and my hair fell out. When they wanted me to try chemicals, I told them no.'

'How much time do they think you have?'

'Six months. Maybe less.'

Unable to reply, I put my arm around him.

'*C'est la vie, Mateus*,' he said. '*C'est la vie.*'

We had breakfast in the tent before he went off to continue his work with Ahdel. I was sure Khadija would pay me a visit, but the hours passed and she did not. At midmorning, I was summoned by a guard to the operations hut where Amadi was waiting to brief me on the mission. We were alone in the room, facing each other across Hakim's desk. Amadi had his feet up and his tinted glasses on. He never seemed to look at me.

'We expect the wind to be calm,' he said. 'We will take off to the east and assume a heading of zero-eight-four degrees at an altitude of three hundred feet. You will go first. I will take off immediately behind you. I will maintain my position in close formation at your five-o'clock position.'

'What about the mountain range on the coast?' I said.

'They rise to seven thousand feet. We will cross them at seventy-five hundred, descend gradually to the Red Sea, where we will skim the waves. It should take forty minutes from the time we take off to the time you will reach the initial point and will begin the toss-bomb maneuver.'

'What's the distance between my release point and the target?'

'Seventy-three hundred feet.'

'Have you got the coordinates for the inertial navigation system?'

'Yes. They are all here.' He handed me a route card similar to the ones Khadija had given me on the flight from Turkey. 'We will give you your setting for the bomb-release unit just prior to takeoff. For accuracy, we will need current atmospheric conditions over the water.'

'It's been a while since I've flown the Sabrejet,' I said. 'I'll want the checklists and some ground time in the cockpit.'

His lip curled back, as if he thought my wanting to do this was a sign of weakness.

'I have offered to fly the mission alone,' he said. 'Hakim has placed too much value on your skills. I would leave at first light, and drop the bomb from altitude. He is nervous, like an old man.'

'Doing it his way, I'd put the chances for success at about fifty-fifty,' I said. 'Doing it yours, I'd say they were less than half that.'

Before he could reply, the door opened, and Hakim came in. As he did, Amadi took his feet off the desk and gave up his chair. The three of us ran through the mission again, including the bailout at

164

the return. At noon, Amadi left, and Hakim took me into the radio room, where his operator set up a telephone patch with the bank number Campbell had given me in Brussels. The confirmation that a quarter of a million dollars had been deposited to my account was verified in less than a minute – much too quickly, I was sure, for the CIA to trace the transmission.

'We are still negotiating with the Dutchman,' Hakim said. 'I am confident we will reach an agreement before the day is over.'

'That's between the two of you,' I said.

He smiled.

'You do not allow your friendships to interfere with your business, do you?' he said.

'No,' I said. 'I don't.'

He gave me the checklists. I took them out to the plane he had said I was going to fly. The preflight, cockpit, engine-start, taxi, and takeoff checks had been copied faithfully from one of the original F-86F manuals. They were expressed in concise, one-line sentences designed to keep in sequence the numerous inspections and actions required of a pilot to get the fighter into the air.

Several men were working under the net. They paid little attention to me as I walked through my preflight. The airplane was spotless and obviously well maintained. All the accumulators had been charged, the hydraulic reservoirs were full, the internal fuel cells and external tanks topped off.

When I climbed into the cockpit, it felt comfortable and familiar. The years since I had flown the F-86 seemed more like days. Once a pilot is familiar with a particular plane, he doesn't forget. The synapses close, the muscles respond. Teach a kid how to ride a bike when he's six and he'll remember how when he's sixty. The reactions of the machine to the control inputs become ingrained.

Within twenty minutes, I felt confident enough to run through the cockpit check with my eyes closed, finding each instrument, switch, and lever, repeating to myself their separate functions. Within an hour and a half, I had gone through all the emergency procedures, and a complete takeoff and landing sequence.

When I was through with this, I examined the inertial navigation system Bock had installed. He had put the mode-selector and control-display units on the right-hand console. These would allow me to turn the set on, align it with our present position, and punch in up to nine sets of coordinates of latitude and longitude. He had fastened the horizontal situation indicator on the instrument panel in front of me, in place of the fuel-pressure gauge, which I wouldn't need. The HSI would give me heading and track information to whatever set of coordinates I called up. The control-display unit on the console would give me time and distance to each point.

He had mounted the pullup gauge just below the top of the instrument panel sun shroud. The gauge was about the size of a Baby Ben clock, and had two long thin needles: one pointing straight up from the bottom of the case, the other lying left to right across the center. The vertical needle would tell me if my wings were level to a fraction of a degree. The horizontal needle would tell me how many Gs I was pulling in the maneuver. Once on course and at a precise location and airspeed, I would have to rely exclusively on these two needles to pull up into the beginning of what would resemble a loop. At about the forty-five-degree angle into the loop, the bomb I was carrying would release automatically and be tossed by the impetus of the airplane onto the target. The maneuver was very much like the underhanded lob of a softball.

I went through everything once, started from scratch and went through it again. I felt good being near the plane. If you peeled me like an onion, when you got to the nub, you'd find a single-seat, single-engine fighter pilot.

I passed Khadija on my way back to the tent. It was late afternoon. She was coming out of the building she and her family used as their quarters. She had her clipboard in hand. I was carrying a basket of food Ahdel had given me for my supper, and for Bock's. When she saw me, she hesitated for a moment, as if she were going to go back inside the building. Then she closed the door behind her and walked past me without saying a word.

Bock returned to the tent at dusk. He had been working steadily for over ten hours. His hands and his clothes were grease-stained, his eyelids twitching from fatigue; but his spirits were good. He beamed happily as he reached inside his shirt, brought out a bottle of wine, and showed me the label. It was a French red: Pomerol, Château Pétrus.

'No tamarind water or puking goat's milk tonight,' he said. 'This bottle has been given to us by Ahdel, who during his time in France discovered a taste for wine. Do you know, Mateuse, there was a case of this on board the C-47? Khadija arranged it privately with Pazar. She and Ahdel are very close. She keeps it for him near the air conditioner in her room, in a carton she has labeled books. If her father discovered it, Ahdel says he would break the bottles and empty them into the desert.'

I rinsed out the cups while he uncorked the wine. When he sampled it, he closed his eyes and breathed a great sigh of satisfaction.

'Eh, Mateus,' he said. 'We are not here in this unforgivable place. We are in Honfleur, at the brasserie. Colette is behind the bar. All the tables are filled with the villagers. We have watched the sun set. The wind is from the west, and the air is full of salt. The nets are drying along the quay, and we are singing – listen, Mateus – "Pauvre Soldat," "Le Boudin" . . .'

He asked me if I could hear the voices of the singers. I told him yes, and it was true. They were as vivid in my memory as they had been the first time I had heard them years ago in Montmartre, and the last time in Izmir.

'It was your father-in-law who contacted me about this job,' he said. 'Did you know that?'

'No,' I said. 'I thought it was Coyle.'

'I agreed at once. It was like an answer to a prayer. To go out one more time . . .'

'Does Colette know?'

'Yes. About everything. She drove me to Rouen each week for the radiation. She read all the books she could find, she consulted with physicians in Paris. . . . And listen to this, Mateus. When I told her I was going off to work with you, she flew into a rage, and then cried, and then put her arms around me and whispered that she loved me, and *bon voyage*.'

I shook a Samsun out of the pack I had gotten in Turkey and lit up. The air was already turning cool. We'd be putting our sweaters on soon. The cigarette was stale.

'I envy your relationship with Colette,' I said.

'I am older than you,' Bock said. 'Fifteen years? Maybe more. So I will give you advice. Find this Australian of yours. Marry her. At least live with her in the same place. Fight with each other as passionately as you can. Eat, drink, and make love. Do not go on living alone, Mateus. It is not good. Ask Monsieur Cooke. He will tell you the same thing.'

'I'm listening,' I said.

'Her name is Jillion?'

'Yes.'

'Find her,' he said. 'Life does not go on forever.'

He poured more wine into our cups, and we drank slowly.

'Ahdel is already at work on your plane,' he said. 'I will have to assist him after we eat. The bomb will be rigged to explode if you lower your gear once raised after takeoff, or fire your ejection seat. You will not be able to release it except by means of the tossing maneuver. If you try to deviate from the mission, or draw attention to it, Amadi will be just behind you with his machine guns loaded. Hakim is taking no chances.'

I nodded.

'Have you worked out a deal for your money?' I said.

'Yes. I let Hakim believe I was extremely dissatisfied with his terms. I told him my work here was nearly finished and he should authorize full payment for me now. He said he would not do this until he had word that the mission was a success. I said that way there would be nothing to prevent him from killing me once he had no further need for my services. I walked away from him in anger. I did this deliberately, Mateus. Tonight, once the camp is asleep, I am going to leave. This way, he will not be suspicious of you when he discovers I am gone.'

'I've been wracking my brain all day,' I said, 'trying to come up with something better.'

'And you have not?'

'No.'

'Then you must leave with me,' he said. 'There are ways to evade pursuit in the desert, fields of stone where a man can pass without leaving any visible sign. Without you to fly the bomber plane, there will be no mission. Certainly not until they find another pilot. By then, we will have gotten word to your father-in-law.'

'I think they've got their other pilot,' I said. 'I think if I drop out, they'll authorize Amadi to try it his way. They've gone too far to turn back now.'

'What chance of success would Amadi have?'

'I don't know. He'd take off at dawn and fly the horizon. He'd be a hundred percent motivated. I'm not sure he'd make it, but I wouldn't bet against him. All he'd need to do was get lucky.'

'So let him try. Why should you risk your own life any further?'

I was silent.

'Is it for the sake of Khadija?' he said.

'I don't know,' I said. 'Maybe it's just the game. I'm in it now. I'd like to play it out.'

'If the planes were F-5Fs,' he said, 'and I could be in your back seat, I too would stay until the end.'

'I know you would,' I said. 'Have you got some gear together?'

'Yes. I will be traveling light. I am good on a forced march. I will cover at least three miles an hour. I have borrowed the small compass from the C-47. I have figured my route. If you will give me the NATO number to contact when I reach the post, I will commit it to memory.'

'I'll do whatever I can to cover for you,' I said. 'I've got an idea some other people will too. Khadija. Ahdel. Maybe even old Sabah.'

He raised his cup.

'Eh, listen, Mateus,' he said. 'Next week you will meet me in Honfleur. We will eat many splendid crêpes and drink the rosé. Colette will treat us as royalty, which is exactly what we deserve. I am blessed, Mateus, to have such friends as the two of you.'

Twenty minutes later we said our goodbyes and he went back to work, walking by starlight through the compound toward the camouflage nets, his shoulders back, his arms swinging jauntily at his sides.

Chapter Thirty

At nine p.m., Hakim's man Ahdel paid me a visit. He brought a pitcher of fresh water for our tent. He said the water came from a small oasis a mile and a half to the southwest, beyond the parked C-47, across the dunes. Speaking quietly in French, he said Khadija wanted to meet me there.

'*C'est urgent,*' he said. '*Allez-vous partir?*'

'*Oui,*' I said.

'*Ah, bien,*' he said.

I thanked him for bringing the message – and the water, and the wine. He smiled. Many of his teeth were gone, and his smile looked like the keyboard of a concertina. I asked him if I could pay him for his services. He said not until the sun had set and the moon had risen a thousand times.

After he had left, I put on my sweater and walked through the camp. There were more people up and about than there had been this hour the night before. When I reached the C-47, I lit a cigarette, then continued my walk, strolling along the track to the waterhole as if I were simply curious as to where it might lead.

I hadn't tried to talk Bock out of his decision to leave the camp, because I knew he would have to leave eventually, and tonight seemed as good a time as any. Once the mission was launched, he would be in extreme jeopardy. I had seen, in the case of George Wyatt, how swiftly Sabah and his men were prepared to deal with agents under cover. If Amadi and I took off and failed to return, Bock would be left as a scapegoat for Hakim's inevitable rage.

So I was comfortable about Bock's decision to leave; and not so comfortable about my own decision to stay. I remembered Campbell's words to me when I had called him from the pay phone at Serkeli. *This transaction may be even more essential than we thought.* Given Campbell's tendency toward understatement, you

170

multiplied by four and wound up with something like an atom bomb exploding in the belly of one of the oil-rich whales.

I wasn't that up on Middle Eastern politics, but I knew enough to know Saudi Arabia was the closest thing we had to an ally among the important OPEC nations. If Hakim's plan succeeded, the power vacuum in that country would be filled by Islamic nationalists like himself, who carried a virulent hatred of the Western influence in their world. The oil taps would shut down. There would be havoc in the economy.

Those were big stakes, but not enough to keep me here. Something had burned out in me a long time ago when it came to fighting for God and country. I wasn't proud of that, but it was a fact and I had to deal with it. Maybe the generation that was growing up now – Brian's peers – would be able to rebuild the kind of national pride and spirit I had once felt so powerfully. I wished them well.

Meanwhile, if I was going to risk my neck by sticking with the mission all the way through launch, I needed reasons of my own. Campbell Cooke was one. I respected him, and he was counting on me to do a job. I might have walked away from Coyle, but I wouldn't walk away from Campbell.

Brian was another reason, although in his case it would take me a long time to sort out exactly why.

Khadija was another. . . .

She sat near a thornbush at the edge of the waterhole. She wore a blue burnoose with the hood up. The waterhole was the size of a large rain barrel. The water was clear and reflected the stars.

'I was told you wanted to see me,' I said, wondering how she would handle what had happened the night before.

'Yes,' she said.

I sat down not far from where she was and lit the last of my cigarettes. The smoke trailed off on a cool breeze.

'I would have spoken to you earlier,' she said, 'but I have been busy. How did you get into the locked hut?'

'I ordered the Dutchman to pick the lock.'

'Ordered him?'

'He owed me a favor.'

'What right do you think you have to violate my father's security?'

'Your father doesn't always play by the rules,' I said. 'As a

171

mercenary pilot, I've got every right to know the details of the mission I'm being paid to fly. Your father negotiated our deal without telling me what kind of bomb we were going to deliver.'

'And now you know.'

'Yes.'

'I'm surprised you haven't used the knowledge in an attempt to raise your price.'

'I might have done that if you hadn't stumbled onto me when I was in the hut.'

'Do you see it as a trade-off? Your restraint for mine?'

'Yes. I could see it that way.'

She had her knees drawn up under the burnoose, and her arms folded across them. She looked biblical against the backdrop of the desert sky.

'Who are you?' she said.

'You know who I am,' I said.

'Your papers are very convincing, but I no longer believe them.'

'They happen to be true. Have you tried running additional checks?'

'No.'

'The radio equipment your father has is long-range. It should be an easy thing to do.'

'Since our return from Turkey, he will not let me near the radios.'

'When did he tell you about his plan?'

'Yesterday afternoon. I kept after him and after him. Finally, he lost his temper and shouted at me the plane would carry a nuclear bomb and the Saudi princes would be in residence at the compound when it exploded. In our original plan, the compound was to have been empty, and the bomb was to have been small and conventional. I accepted the propaganda value of the raid: that we, that my father, could put together a mission using a sophisticated plane and could reach into the Honeycomb itself. But what he proposes to do now is madness – even beyond the killing of the royal line. If the bomb detonates below ground level, and the winds are from the northwest, the fallout could reach Mecca.'

'Have you told him this?'

'Yes. I have tried to persuade him all day that he should give up his plan. He will not listen.'

172

I finished my cigarette and stood up. The tension of all that had happened was getting to me. I wanted to tell her everything, to openly join forces with her, but I didn't dare risk it. She stood next to me.

'I don't know who you are,' she said. 'But I know you are not like the others. You asked me to call you Matt, and so I will. You are a decent man. You pretend sometimes not to be, but you are. So is the Dutchman –'

'You're wrong,' I said, cutting her off. 'I'm a mercenary who works for pay. One night while we were in Turkey, there were two men tied to chairs in a subcellar at Pazar's villa. Your Uncle Sabah killed one of them with the knife he keeps in the short scabbard at the back of his neck. I killed the other with an automatic pistol. I held the pistol with both hands to steady my aim. My shot took him just below the eye. It blew away part of his skull. Listen to me, dammit,' I said. *'He was tied to a chair.'*

I had taken her by the arm. The hood of the burnoose had fallen back, and her hair spilled free in the starlight. She looked at me, defiant.

'I don't care what you tell me,' she said. 'If you did this thing, you did it because you had to.'

'I did it because somebody was going to have to die that night and I didn't want it to be me. The hell with decency. There's precious little of that in the world.'

'Stop it,' she said. 'You speak profanely, but you yourself are not profane.'

'I'm your father's hired gun, Khadija,' I said. 'Don't make me out to be anything else. If you do you're only going to be hurt.'

'You talk to me as if you think I am weak; but I am not weak. I too have seen my family slaughtered. I have seen them cut down and shattered, and have felt the rain of their blood on my face. I should have told you that yesterday when we spoke in your tent. I should not have left you with the impression I was nothing but a faint-hearted female with milk in her veins who had never faced up to the realities of death.

'Do you think I would not kill, if I truly believed a killing was justified? Or if like you I found myself in a position where I had no choice? Or my anger was such it overwhelmed my reason?

173

'If you believe this, you do not know me. You have taken only part of me and weighed it as the whole. Do you think I am not capable of anger? Of passion? Of rage? Do you think I am blind? Do you think I am not woman enough to know when a man feels something for me, and I for him? These are not things that have to be spoken. They exist and are entire to themselves. When you took my hand in Mahmet's garden, our feelings traveled in silence between us. You could not have disguised them even if you wished. Nor could I.'

'There's nothing possible between the two of us,' I said. 'It would be your American lover all over again: two incompatible worlds; neither of us willing or able to cross over to the other.'

'I know that. I know it even better than you. All that is possible for us is what we have now. Here in this place.'

I looked at her. She stood close to me, her head tipped back, her lips parted slightly, her face framed by her hair.

'I'm still the pilot your father's hired to drop the bomb on the Saudis,' I said. 'I've done nothing to earn your trust, Khadija. Or your love. You're a beautiful woman. You deserve more than me. More than this. Much more.'

'I am not asking for more. I give you my trust freely. And my love.'

'I want to do the same,' I said. 'I want to, but I can't. There's too much at stake. If I commit myself to you now, all the risks will go up.'

'You do not have to commit yourself to me. I am not asking you to do that. I believe you are as much opposed to my father's plan as I. You do not have to tell me this. I know it is true when I look into your eyes, when I see beyond your expression and into your soul. You have fooled the men because they are men and rely more on their heads than their hearts. But I am a woman. You cannot fool me. Not anymore.'

I pulled her to me, burying my hands in her hair. Our first kiss was hard, almost brutal. She stood on her tiptoes, with her arms locked around my neck. I felt the press of her body against the blood pulse of mine. Her scent was that of cloves and warm wool.

We began as two people whose need had been bottled up for much too long. We were awkward with each other and impatient, then gentle and kind. The night breeze was cool, but the sand was still warm, and we let that warmth mingle with our own.

Khadija touched the scars on my back.

I touched the tips of her ears.

We were two doomed lovers, alone in a garden that consisted of a thornbush and a small well.

When it was over, I waited for her to bring up the subject of the mission again.

She did not.

She sat sheltered in my arms. I could feel the strong beating of her heart.

'I'll do what I can to stop your father,' I said. 'I'm not sure there's much I can do.'

Chapter Thirty-One

I knew something was wrong as soon as we returned to the camp. A jeep was parked in front of Hakim's office; a half-dozen men were standing by with automatic rifles. As we approached, Sabah appeared at the doorway and motioned us inside. Hakim was at his desk, his face dark with fury. All I could think was that he had had us followed to the waterhole, that one of his men had reported to him the nature of our meeting there.

'My daughter forgets herself,' he said to me. 'She walks like a courtesan in the desert at night.'

'I am not *just* your daughter,' she said. 'I am *Khadija* – '

'Be silent!' he said.

'No!' she said. 'No! I will not be silent! You were once a good and dedicated Syrian, but you have become irrational with pride. Your plan to murder the Saudi princes is an insanity. You admit even Qaddafi will have nothing to do with it. It is like the murder of the Israelis at the Olympics. It is a cowardly, unforgivable act.'

'*Be silent!*' he said. He had stood up. He was holding his withered arm as if he were in pain. His expression was so savage I thought Khadija would back away; but she did not. She faced her father without flinching, the blue hood of her garment thrown back, her hair falling around her face in thick, auburn waves.

Then Sabah stepped between them, speaking quietly to his brother in Arabic. When he was finished, he and Khadija moved away from the desk and Hakim looked at me.

'The Dutchman has left the camp,' he said curtly. 'What explanation do you have for this?'

'He's been restless lately. He's been having some pain. He's probably out on the desert trying to walk it off.'

'Did you help him plan his escape?'

'I didn't know he was a prisoner.'

176

'You must have been aware he intended to leave.'

'No. He did tell me he had a beef with you over the money. He said he feared for his life once the mission was launched. He saw what your men did to the radicals on Arkis.'

'Tonight, as a precursor to the mission,' Hakim said, 'I put this camp on full alert. I doubled the guards and changed the pattern of their rounds. One of the men must have surprised the Dutchman as he tried to slip through the northern perimeter. We found the guard buried in a shallow grave. His neck was broken and his rifle was missing.'

I looked at him the way I had when we negotiated the deal, trying to reveal nothing; but I could feel my right hand close into a fist. The overhead light in the room dimmed slightly, then brightened again.

'The sand is soft for many miles,' Hakim said. 'The Dutchman has left a clear trail. Amadi has taken three men and a jeep.'

'No . . .' Khadija said. She glanced at me as if I had betrayed her by not telling her of Bock's intention to leave. Hakim looked harshly at his daughter.

'He has taken three men and a jeep,' he repeated, 'with my orders to bring the Dutchman back here alive. Because the Dutchman saved your life, there is a balance to reckon between us. He will have his chance to explain to me why he should not be shot as a traitor.'

'Amadi will never bring him here alive,' Khadija said. 'He hates the Dutchman. He hates the American too, and would willingly kill them both. You know this. You know Amadi's arrogance will never accept your having hired another man to take his place – '

Sabah cut her off. He did it with a single word. She started to reply, then stopped. He spoke again with his brother. Hakim's voice became shrill, but I could tell whatever the issue was between them, he was going to yield. Finally, Sabah indicated to Khadija and me that we should follow him outside. Khadija was crying. She was trying not to, but the tears were visible on her cheeks. Sabah lifted her almost bodily into the back of the jeep that was parked in front of the door. One of the guards climbed in next to her. Sabah waited until he had, then looked at me and motioned to the driver's seat. I got in behind the wheel. The windshield was down. By the time I had the engine started, he was sitting on the passenger seat, pointing across the hood toward the desert to the north.

I slammed the jeep into gear and pulled away. I drove without lights. The camouflage nets loomed up in front of me like giant parachutes billowed with air. I passed them to the right, pressing the accelerator to the floor. The jeep was well muffled and the engine was quiet, but there was a lot of windrush and gear whine. When Khadija leaned forward to talk to her uncle and then to me, she had to shout to be heard.

'He says there are men stationed where the guard was slain. You will see Amadi's track.'

'How much lead time does Amadi have?'

'He left half an hour ago.'

I felt something snap shut inside me. I held the wheel with both hands. Hakim's men appeared suddenly to our left and then disappeared as I cut past them onto the open desert. The land looked like a frozen sea with infinite waves of sand. I could see Bock's footprints now. They were as visible as saucers under the stars, a plodding, resolute line, straddled by the double track of Amadi's jeep.

I wanted to drive as fast as I could. I wanted to catch Amadi and his men before they were able to catch Bock. If I could do that, I would ram them, cut them off, go for the rifle of the guard who sat with Khadija in the back seat. She had asked no questions on our walk back from the waterhole – I had volunteered no information. Whatever curiosity she had about me was apparently unimportant to her now that she had decided I was a person she could trust. I was sure she would do nothing to stop me in a fight with Amadi and his men. I thought she might even help. I thought there was a chance Sabah might help too, but I wouldn't be counting on that. No matter how indebted he might feel toward Bock for having saved his niece's life, his ultimate loyalty, I was sure, would lie with his brother, Hakim.

I leaned forward, the wind tearing my eyes. At first we made good time, but then the sand began to soften and I had to engage the front axle. When I did that, we crawled at a pace not much faster than a man could jog.

You must leave with me, Bock had said. *There are ways to evade pursuit in the desert, fields of stone where a man can pass without leaving any visible sign*. I prayed he would find those fields of stone before he was found by Amadi. *I'll do whatever I can to cover for you*, I had said. But at the time he had slipped away, I had been at the waterhole, with Khadija in my arms.

The landscape bleakened into dunes. We climbed to their summits and raced down. The jeep lurched and swayed. Sabah kept his hands on the dash. I could see him in profile, his white headpiece and beard, the solemn jut of his jaw. The guard sat behind him, with the butt of his rifle resting on the floor. Khadija sat behind me, leaning forward.

'Look!' she said, pointing ahead. 'There is something there!'

The tracks we were following, which had been clear and uninterrupted, dissolved suddenly into a morass of sand. I swerved to the left, taking us too close to the edge of a dune, feeling the sand shear away as I swerved back to the right and picked up the trail again. Khadija looked back.

'The other jeep was mired in that place!' she said. 'The Dutchman will have more time!'

'It may come down to Bock and me against your father's men,' I said. 'If it does, are you with us?' I glanced at her. Her face was so close to mine I could feel the lash of her hair. When she answered, her voice was sharp.

'Yes,' she said. 'I am with you.'

The terrain, which had been rising steadily, ended finally above a broad plateau. As I came over the top of the last of the dunes, I saw Amadi's Jeep.

The sand of the plateau looked phosphorescent under the stars. It stretched away toward a broken field of stone. The jeep was well below us, and a quarter mile ahead. I disengaged our front axle, jamming the accelerator to the floor. We sped down the dune, fishtailing onto the plain. The surface here was hard-packed and fast. The wind tore at our faces; the distance narrowed between us and Amadi. We had closed to three hundred yards when I saw the muzzle flash of a rifle from the area of stone.

Amadi's jeep swerved and braked to a halt. He and his men leaped over the sides and spread out in two directions. I caught up and skidded past them, taking us to the edge of the boulders. Khadija was out even before we had stopped. I saw her run past me, into the field of fire. Sabah had stood and was shouting at Amadi's men. The air was full of the smell of powder, the rattle of automatic weapons, and ricochet. When I jerked my head to look behind me, the guard in the back seat was already gone.

There are times when events take place so quickly they outrun a man's ability to sort them out, to react effectively, to bring them under his control. This was one of those times. I needed a weapon, but there were no weapons at hand. Bock was outflanked and outgunned. Before we could take one of the jeeps and make a run for the army post, we would have to overpower a total of six men. I thought we might have been able to do that if Bock hadn't opened fire from his place of concealment; but he had, and whatever his reason for doing so, the die was cast.

Even as these thoughts were clicking into place, I sprang out of the jeep, ducking and running half crouched, threading my way between the boulders toward the place where I had seen the muzzle flash of Bock's first shot. The boulders were the size of automobiles, jutting at odd angles from the ground. The upper surfaces were bright with starlight, the areas between them mazelike and pooled with shadow.

'Bock!' I shouted. 'I'm in the boulders, heading your way! Khadija's somewhere between us!'

'Go back, pilot!' I heard him shout. 'This is not your fight! Go back and draw your pay from these Syrian dogs!'

I saw him pop up suddenly, fifty yards to my right, sighting down his rifle as he snapped off a shot. One of Amadi's men cried out. The automatic-weapons' fire, which had become sporadic, poured into the field. It came from many points in a semicircle behind us. Bullets whanged off the rocks nearby, sending up a shower of lead fragments and flint. Bock fired back methodically, changing positions each time he did. Another of Amadi's men cried out. Amadi himself had taken the high ground at the far end of the field. I could hear him yelping commands in a high-pitched, feverish voice. He was alone and vulnerable. I knew if I could outflank him and take him from behind I would have a weapon, and Bock and I would have the rest of the Syrians caught in a crossfire. Two of them had already fallen. Discounting Sabah, who as far as I knew was still unarmed, that left three. Those were odds that, given the chance, I was sure we could handle.

My hopes rose as I kept behind the boulders, dodging from one to the next, staying below Amadi's line of sight. I hadn't gone far when Khadija appeared suddenly, rising into the field of fire.

She stood fifteen yards to my right, her figure unmistakable against a sky of white cinders and midnight-blue.

'Khadija!' I shouted. 'Get down!'

'No!' she said. 'They must stop! They must stop!'

Sabah, bellowing from somewhere behind me, gave futile commands to Amadi and his men. Bock shouted his own warning to Khadija. When it was clear she was going to stand her ground even while bullets continued to slap and ping off the rocks around her, he rose from his position deeper in the field, holding his rifle in one hand high over his head, calling for a truce until Khadija's safety could be assured. At once the automatic-weapons fire began to fade away, until there was an interlude of silence except for the isolated sound of the night breeze. Bock continued to stand, holding his rifle over his head. Khadija was moving in his direction. She had almost reached him when shooting erupted again.

It came from Amadi. He was firing full automatic from the high ground at the northern edge of the boulder field. At first, the bullets sprayed harmlessly around Bock's feet. Indignant, the Dutchman looked in Amadi's direction, his great face tilted back, his body erect, his rifle still held like a torch, high in his left hand.

'Bock!' I shouted. 'Take cover! Get down!'

He glanced toward me, then back toward the place where the shots had come. It all happened very fast. There was another burst. This time, the bullets found their mark. He jerked convulsively, dropping the rifle, his hands clasping his chest. Khadija screamed. She was still making her way toward him. So was I. I saw him sway slightly, like a wounded bull. Then he went to his knees. And then he fell.

When I finally reached him, my brain shouting its denial of what had happened, he lay on his back, his head cradled on Khadija's lap. She had opened his sweater, enough to see how hopeless it was, how much of his white shirt had shredded into the wounds of his chest. I crouched beside him, put my hand on his shoulder, swallowing back a boiling rage.

He looked up at me and grinned.

'Eh, Mateus,' he said. '*Mon ami.*'

'Take it easy,' I said. 'We'll get you back to camp.'

He coughed once, glancing down at his riddled chest as if puzzled

181

by how much it hurt. Then he laughed. It wasn't all of his old laugh, but it was most of it.

'Eh, Mateus,' he said, 'I decided to make my stand here. Like Camerone.'

'I figured that's what you must have done.'

'It's not so bad, eh? To die like this? Better than the other.'

'Yes,' I said. 'Much better than that.'

He grinned at me. His eyes had already begun to lose their focus.

'I want some wine,' he said.

I told him I would get some as soon as I could. He seemed pleased by that. He said goodbye to me, and then to Khadija. He called her his princess. He said the three of us would meet again somewhere. Then he looked away.

The breeze had gentled.

I heard him sigh once and then he was still.

Khadija groaned, holding him tightly in her arms. Sabah was standing over us now, gazing down, not at Bock, but at me. I knew that by watching my reaction to the Dutchman's death, he was trying to judge how closely allied we had been, and whether or not I too might turn traitor to his brother's cause.

I knew that was what he was doing, but I didn't give a damn.

I turned away from him and looked off into the night sky, where a constellation of stars gradually took on for me the size and shape of the man Bock had been.

He was standing with his back to the bar in the Legionnaire's Café on the waterfront at Izmir, singing the words of 'Le Boudin' in his clear, powerful voice.

I remembered the words.

We are not going to forget you, they said.

Give us your hand, my comrade.

Give us your hand.

Chapter Thirty-Two

Amadi came toward us from his position. He picked his way among the rocks, his weapon slung over one shoulder. The men who had survived the firefight shouted good-naturedly to him as he came. He answered them in kind, grinning his gap-toothed grin, his aviator's cap pushed back on his head. He was still fifty yards away when Khadija sprang up suddenly, with Bock's rifle in her hands.

Before any of the Arabs could react, she snapped the selector to full automatic and began firing from her hip. Amadi froze for an instant, bullets spanging around him. One clean hit and I knew the mission would be finished: Hakim would have to send me up alone in the F-86. But Khadija was too enraged to steady her aim. The moment, which had been so close at hand, was over in seconds. Amadi dove for cover, disappearing into the shadows behind a boulder. I jumped Khadija and grappled for the gun. She swore savagely, lashing out with her feet. Sabah started for us, then ducked away as the rifle spit fire again. We stumbled against the rocks. I crushed her to me. She was incredibly strong.

'There's no chance now,' I said. 'Give it up.'

'Let go of me!' she hissed. 'I was wrong about you! You are a coward like Amadi!'

'You're outgunned and out of ammo,' I said. 'It's no use . . .'

'And you are no friend of the Dutchman's!' she said. 'Or you would help me avenge his death!'

Sabah came up again. I pinned Khadija's arms while he wrestled the gun away from her. As he did, she spit in his face. He wiped the spittle away with his sleeve and looked at her with a gaze that seemed almost hypnotic. She strained against me until her strength was gone. Then she began to sob in dry, wracking heaves.

I helped her kneel again beside the place where Bock lay. Sabah said something in Arabic. Amadi and his men came up, with their weapons leveled. As they approached, my blood began to boil inside me. I was still crouched next to Khadija. I could feel my leg muscles bunching up, as if something primitive and violent in me was going to react to Amadi's presence, with or without the command of my will. It took everything I had to hold it back. He stood over us, looking down at the woman who had once been chosen to be his bride and who moments ago had come within inches of taking his life.

'When your father learns what you have done here,' he said, 'he will assemble the men and will have you whipped until you are naked in front of them.'

'Why don't you speak your threats in Arabic,' she said. 'So my uncle too will understand them.'

'You are no longer one of us,' he said. 'You have corrupted yourself and made yourself unclean.'

I stood up. The muzzles of three rifles followed me as I did. Amadi was close enough to touch. When he looked at me his expression was one of hatred, but his lips curled back in a grin.

'Did you interfere to protect my life?' he said. 'Or hers?'

'I interfered to protect the mission,' I said.

'Then Hakim will be pleased. We can present him with what's left of the Dutchman's body after we drag it back to camp, behind one of the jeeps.'

'The Dutchman was a friend of mine,' I said. 'He made a mistake going AWOL the way he did, but if you lay a finger on his body, I'll break your neck.'

His face darkened. I could see him weighing the risk of forcing the confrontation between us. Finally he looked once at Sabah, turned silently, and walked away. One of his men went with him to help collect their dead and return to camp. The two others stayed.

'There's a trenching tool in the jeep,' I said to Khadija. 'Tell your uncle I'm going to get it. Bock spent a lot of years in the desert. He'd want to be buried here, in the place where he fell.'

She looked at me, her dark eyes shining. She seemed calmer now.

'I will help you,' she said, 'even if the others will not.'

It was three a.m. when we arrived back at camp. Sabah was taking no chances. He had one of Amadi's men drive. I was ordered to sit on

184

the front passenger seat, with Sabah sitting just behind me. Khadija sat between her uncle and the other guard.

Amadi and Hakim were standing in front of the operations hut as we pulled up. Hakim spoke sharply to Khadija. She did not reply. She got out of the jeep and strode past him, going in the direction of her quarters. He waited until she had slammed the door behind her, then turned to his office and motioned us inside.

'My radio operator has picked up a transmission from a Sudanese patrol plane,' he said. 'They've reported activity on the desert north of here. They may decide to investigate; they may not. In any case, I will take no chance of being discovered. We will launch the mission in one hour.'

The light in the room was dim; the air conditioner was off. I could hear the dull throb of the camp generator, coming like a distant drumbeat through the wall.

'Do you have the atmospheric data over the Red Sea?' I said.

'Yes. Your setting for the bomb release unit is forty-one point eight degrees. You already have your coordinates for the INS.'

'What about the radio frequency?'

'You and Amadi will use two-five-eight point eight on the UHF. I will monitor until you are on the other side of the mountains, and will pick you up again once you have recrossed the mountains on your return.'

Sabah stood with his arms folded across his chest. Amadi lounged against one wall. He looked very sure of himself with his tinted glasses and pencil-thin goatee.

'The plane has been wired to prevent you from ejecting or lowering your gear until after the strike has been accomplished,' he said. 'If you attempt either of these things, the bomb will explode under you. If you go off the radio channel Dr. Hakim has prescribed, or attempt to deviate from the mission, I have my orders to shoot you down.'

'I've got a feeling you'd like that, Tawfiq,' I said.

'If we are suspicious of you now,' Hakim said, 'it is because of the Dutchman's attempt to escape.'

'You had my plane wired before the Dutchman left,' I said. 'You've been suspicious of me from the start. You'd be foolish if you weren't. I don't take it personally.'

185

'Good,' he said. 'The bomb has already been placed on the pylon. In addition to the regular contact fuse, we have added a hydrometric detonator which will go off in water at a depth of thirty feet. The bomb is atomic, with a five kiloton yield.'

He paused, to see how I would react. I looked at him without changing expression.

'I figured that was why you were paying so much,' I replied.

'Please sit down, Colonel,' he said. He seemed relieved. 'The four of us will go over the mission, step by step, one more time.'

An hour later, when we came out of the operations hut, there was feverish activity in the camp. All of the tents had been struck. Several jeeps and troop carriers loaded with equipment were standing by. A dozen of Hakim's men were pulling the camouflage nets away from the F-86s. The sky over the desert was clear, and bright with stars. The air was cool. There was only a slight breeze.

I went to my plane and did a quick preflight. The bomb pylon looked like a small aluminum canoe fixed to the underside of the left wing between the outboard fuel tank and the fuselage. Ejection cartridges inside the pylon would automatically jettison the bomb when the plane pulled up to the angle programmed into the release unit.

The bomb itself hung from a rack below the pylon. It was olive-drab and deceptively mild-looking. From tip to tip, it measured about five feet, and was less than nine inches in diameter. It carried a tailfin assembly with four blades. The 904 fuse, resembling a shiny tiny can, was attached to its nose. The bombrack safety pin had already been pulled, the arming wire installed.

On the F-86, a fold-down panel step at the left wing juncture leads to a higher step and handhold, providing access to the upper wing surface and the cockpit. As I pulled myself up, Ahdel appeared. He said he would be acting as my ground mechanic. The auxiliary power unit was plugged in. He would start it when I gave him the word.

I climbed into the cockpit and removed the canopy and the ejection-seat safety pins. The warning ribbons were inscribed in Pakistani. The only warning I needed to remember was that if I tried to eject from this particular plane before its payload was released, I'd go up on a five-kiloton blast.

I buckled my parachute straps, snugged up my shoulder and lap belts. I had on my slacks and safari shirt, and a pair of desert boots I had borrowed from Sabah. I strapped the kneeboard Amadi had given me to my right leg, route cards and pencil clipped to it. The flight suit he had wanted me to wear had been a size and a half too small.

He was climbing into his plane as I signaled for Ahdel to start the APU and give me power. I would need 28½ volts DC at a minimum of 500 amperes to turn the engine over. The APU would deliver this via a gas-driven generator on the ground.

As the power surged into the aircraft system, I turned the instrument panel and console lights full up and placed the INS mode switch to standby. While the system was warming up, I punched my present position and the initial point into the computer; but instead of the pullup point Hakim had given me, I punched in the coordinates for Sharm El Sheikh, a city located where the southern tip of the Sinai meets the Red Sea. There was an Israeli fighter base there. As far as I knew, they were the closest friendlies. I also knew before I could hope to make contact with them, I would have to get rid of Amadi.

My plan for doing that was already half formed. It changed abruptly when Khadija appeared, intent, I assumed, on saying farewell.

She looked exactly as she had the first time I had seen her at the Merhaba Hotel. She wore her khakis and Wellington boots. Her hair was pulled back. She carried her clipboard in one hand.

Hakim and Sabah watched as she climbed up onto the wing and leaned over the canopy rail. She looked tired in the red glow of the cockpit lights.

'My father wishes to know if everything is in readiness for takeoff,' she said.

'Everything's ready,' I said.

'Is the computer functioning correctly?'

'Yes.'

There were things we both wanted to say, but for a moment there was an awkward silence between us.

'I hope it doesn't go too hard for you,' I said finally.

'My father is angry with me. But he has been angry that way before. It will pass.'

'Good,' I said.

'I am glad to have known you,' she said. 'You and the Dutchman.'

'Maybe we'll meet again somewhere,' I said.

'In Singapore?'

'Singapore would be fine.'

She smiled. Her smile was brief, and reflected the strain she had been under, and the loss of some good things that might have been possible for us in another time or place.

Then she looked at me in her businesslike way and said:

'Your machine guns are armed. I have done this with Ahdel. Go now, with the blessing of Allah.'

Before I could reply, she was gone, swinging down from the wing, walking briskly toward the place where her father and uncle stood waiting.

Amadi's auxiliary power unit had roared into life. I could see his head and shoulders illuminated in the cockpit. He already had his helmet on. I pulled mine on, and plugged in the oxygen hose and radio lead. I switched the UHF channel selectors to 258.8. There was a headset built into the helmet, and a microphone in the oxygen mask.

'How do you receive me?' Amadi asked.

'Loud and clear,' I said.

'Is the navigation system programmed?'

'That's affirmative.'

'Start your engine,' he said.

I rechecked the throttle off, pushed the engine master switch on, held *Start* for a few seconds, then moved to *Battery*. The engine shaft began to revolve. At three percent, I held the throttle outboard to engage the fuel booster pumps and energize the ignition system. The engine rumbled as the fuel in the flame cans torched off. At six percent, I eased the throttle to idle and watched the RPM climb. As it passed twenty-five percent, I signaled for Ahdel to unplug the APU.

In seconds, I had good oil pressure, and an idle RPM of thirty-five percent. I went through the hydraulic flight control and utility system checks, set the altimeter, and switched on the external fuel tanks.

Then I lowered the cockpit lights.

'Ready to taxi,' I said.

'Taxi,' Amadi said.

As I began to move toward the end of the runway, I had one last glimpse of Khadija, standing between Sabah and Hakim. I gave her the thumbs-up sign. She tipped back her head, a strong and proud woman, stretched on a rack between two cultures. I did not believe we would see each other again, not in Singapore, or in Damascus, or at Cedar Run; but I knew I would not forget her and I felt my own sense of loss as I taxied away.

At the edge of the strip, I held the toggle switch forward to slide the canopy closed. I had to duck my head as the low front bow passed over me and snapped into place. When it did, I could feel the change in cockpit pressurization. I went through my run-up checks. All the gauges were green. Amadi's plane was just behind me.

'Ready for takeoff,' I said.

'Go,' he replied.

I put the flaps down, ran the throttle up to one hundred percent, engaged the nosewheel steering, and released brake pressure. The airplane surged forward, pressing me back, screaming as it gathered speed. The dusky runway slipped under me in an accelerating blur as I glanced between it and the airspeed indicator. At 115 knots, I raised the nose; at 130, I was airborne. Gear up at 150; flaps at 160. I held the sleek Sabre on the deck until I had 325 knots indicated. Then I brought the throttle back to eighty percent.

The moon was waning, and low on the horizon. I flew away from it and toward the east, over a bleak landscape where just over two hours ago I had buried the body of a good and decent friend.

Now it's our turn, I thought.

Mon ami.

Chapter Thirty-Three

My fuel flow was just over three thousand pounds per hour. The tanks were feeding properly; all the gauges checked out. I unlocked my shoulder harness and glanced back to locate Amadi. He was in wide trail formation, to my right and rear. My original plan had been to try to outmaneuver him and force him into a low-altitude spin. It was all I had been able to think of before Khadija had stepped up on my wing to tell me my machine guns were armed and I should go with the blessing of God.

In a few scant minutes, the Kassala mountain range rose steeply in front of us.

'Push it up,' I told Amadi.

'I will give the commands,' he replied.

'Suit yourself.'

'Advance throttle to ninety-six percent,' he said.

'Roger.'

'Level out when you reach seventy-five hundred feet. Begin your descent at seventy percent.'

He lagged behind me as I crossed the range. Ahead and below, I could see a few dim lights from the small town of Dunjanab to the south, and the surface of the Red Sea itself, stretching away to the east like a vast, rippled sheet of steel.

Amadi caught up to me and resumed flying in a loose formation at my five-o'clock position.

'Once we reach the water, descend to wavetop height and advance throttle to eighty percent,' he said. 'Have you cross-checked the navigation coordinates?'

'That's affirmative,' I said. 'We're on course.'

'If we are intercepted, I will break off and engage,' he said. 'You will continue on toward the target.'

'The last I heard the Sudanese were flying MIGs,' I said. 'I don't know how good their pilots are.'

'I am not concerned about their pilots,' Amadi said 'We will maintain radio silence now, until we are over the water.'

During our descent from the mountains to the sea, I switched the A-4 gunsight on and dialed the rheostat so I could just make out the reticle projected on my forward windscreen. I would use the pipper in the center of the circle of diamonds to aim with. The arrangement was like the ones on the coin-operated simulators at amusement parks. All you had to do was line things up and pull the trigger. The rest was automatic.

I placed the mode selector from BOMB to GUN.

I charged the guns by flipping a switch that chambered ammunition into each of the six M-3 .50 calibers. The unmistakable *chunks* I could feel through the airframe as I did were solid and reassuring. Ahdel and Khadija had done their work.

The area of coastline we crossed was flat and uninhabited. We came over the water at an altitude of a hundred feet. I eased the F-86 down to twenty, then ten. My airspeed now was 375 knots per hour. This close to the deck, flying by starlight, depth perception was tricky. Even a small pilot error could be fatal. I kept easing down. Amadi had said to skim the waves. Okay, I thought. Right now they looked as if they were coming into the cockpit. The clearance between the water and the bomb hanging off my left wing couldn't have been more than a foot.

I didn't dare turn my head. I adjusted the right-side canopy mirror by feel to the place where I thought Amadi should be. When I gave it a quick glance, he showed up, a dark shape high on the glass, his image wobbling from the engine vibration. He was holding at an altitude of about thirty feet, well off to the side so my jet wash wouldn't tip him up or slam him into the water.

'You're too low,' he said.

'Come on down, Tawfiq,' I said. 'The water's fine.'

He was silent. I wanted to taunt him some more. I felt an almost overpowering hatred for him. I wanted him to pay with his own agony for what he had done to Bock. I think if I had had him on the ground right then, I would have cut him apart, piece by piece, and would have taken a long time doing it.

No, Virginia, I thought. There isn't any Santa Claus.

I put my thumb on the speed-brake switch on my throttle. I knew if I activated it, two hydraulically powered panels would pop open, one on either side of the fuselage, and the plane would undergo a rapid deceleration. Flying at altitude, the braking maneuver wasn't dangerous. Flying a few feet off the deck it was.

I remembered the peculiarities of the F-86 when the speed brakes were applied. The two panels on this particular jet were located aft of the center of gravity. When they popped out, the nose would rise, and I would have to correct the trim. If I overcorrected, I would run the risk of putting the plane into a pilot-induced oscillation, thereby snagging the water, or pitching in.

So my stick input was going to have to be steady and sure. If it was, and I yanked the throttle back about ten percent, I'd lose fifty knots of airspeed in the blink of an eye.

By feel I reached down to the gun panel, raised the red plastic guard, and flipped the master gun switch up. Now the trigger on the stick grip would electronically fire all six guns, with a quarter-inch movement of my index finger.

I checked Amadi in the rear-view mirror one last time.

Okay, pal, I thought. Do it right.

Keeping my eyes glued to the dim sea-sky horizon in front of me, I took a deep breath, thumbed back the speed-brake switch, and reduced throttle. There was a terrific roar as the panels extended suddenly into the slip-stream. The deceleration was instantaneous. It hurled me forward into the harness. I çaught the peripheral shadow of Amadi's fighter streaking past. He was in front of me now, high and to my right. I had braked so quickly he had no time to react.

I slammed the throttle to full power, thumbing the boards in, yanking the stick back and to the right. In a blinding flash of motion, my plane flicked up. A carrier wave came through my headset as Amadi pressed his transmit button. Nothing else came over. He was in too much trouble to talk.

I closed instantly to two hundred feet. Just before the gunsight pipper zeroed in on Amadi's jet, I began firing. I had six guns, and each one of them poured out six hundred rounds per minute. They made a lot of noise. The slugs slammed into Amadi's left wing, then into the wing root, then back along the fuselage as I slid into his six-o'clock position and bore-sighted the slugs through his exhaust pipe into an engine that was turning fifteen thousand RPMs.

I was being buffeted by his jet wash, but I didn't care. Even after his engine began to disintegrate, I kept hammering away. His high-pressure lines, ripped apart by flying shrapnel, began spraying fuel and hydraulic fluid into the mangled flame cans, where temperatures would be running just under two thousand degrees. A lick of flame came out the exhaust, then a great gush. I pulled violently to the left to avoid sucking debris into my air scoop. The other plane was finished. Flame poured from the left wing and tailpipe.

He was arcing almost straight up, losing airspeed as his engine flamed out and his fighter began breaking up. He had blown the canopy, but it was too late for him to eject. The F-86 exploded at the top of the arc. There was a bright fireball, a kaleidoscope of burning metal against the night sky, a falling trail of sparks.

'You son of a bitch!' I yelled into my mask. *'That's for Bock!'*

Chapter Thirty-Four

The fuel in my two drop tanks was gone; I pickled them off to reduce drag. As I climbed to altitude, I turned northwest over the Red Sea, keeping the throttle at one hundred percent. To prevent the five-hundred-pounder from releasing automatically when my angle of climb passed 41.8 degrees, I kept the mode selector on GUN and the master switch off. Now that Amadi was skragged, I wasn't ginned up over the mission any more. All I wanted to do was toss the bomb into a piece of desert somewhere, get on the ground, and go home.

At 35,000 feet, I throttled back to eighty-five percent and figured the burn rate for my remaining fuel. By flying at altitude and holding down my speed, it looked as if I would have just over an hour before the engine flamed out. That wasn't a lot of time.

From my vantage point seven miles above the earth, dawn had already broken and visibility in all directions ran 250 miles. To my right, the sun was an immense, blinding globe on the eastern horizon of Saudi Arabia. To my left, the Nile cut a green ribbon through Egypt and into Sudan. Five hundred miles to the north – dead ahead and not yet visible – lay Sharm El Sheikh at the southern tip of the Sinai. The search radar from the Israeli fighter base located there would pick me up soon as an unidentified bogie on their screens. Maybe they already had.

I shrugged my shoulders and heaved one of my patented Eberhart sighs. I wanted to be optimistic, but the more I thought about my situation, the less hopeful it seemed. I had become what amounted to a nuclear time bomb, flying in an unmarked plane into the middle of some of the most contested real estate in the world.

I rechecked the gauges and trimmed the F-86 for level flight. Then I switched to 243.0 megacycles on the UHF: the guard channel monitored by military and civilian air-craft all over the world. I was out of range of the U.S. Sixth Fleet in the Med. All I could hope was that some friendly pair of ears would relay my message to the Navy command net that could then patch me in with Campbell.

My hand was shaky as I pressed the transmit button on the throttle. I decided to preface my message with the international distress call to assure priority.

'Mayday, Mayday, Mayday. This is Papa Wolf on guard channel, repeat, Papa Wolf trying to reach Delta One. Any station reading Papa Wolf please give me a call.'

There was a pause of several seconds, as if all the air-borne pilots and ground controllers who had picked up my unusual message were sitting around waiting for somebody else to answer. I was about to transmit again when a deep voice came through my headset. The signal was very strong, which meant whoever was doing the transmitting was close. He spoke in measured tones, obviously uncomfortable with English, pronouncing his w's as r's. His call sign was Dukhan Leader, which indicated to me he was airborne and probably commanding a flight of interceptors scrambled from an adjacent country when my blip had appeared on one of their ground radar scopes. He told me to identify myself.

'Dukhan Leader,' I replied, 'this is Papa Wolf. I'm in an F-86F at thirty-five thousand heading three-three-five degrees. I require immediate contact with any American station that can relay a message for me.'

I glanced to the rear and low on both sides. Four black dots were climbing toward my position from the right. I could see their contrails, and guessed from the direction of their approach they were Saudis.

They were coming up fast.

'We know your position, Papa Wolf,' the flight commander said, 'state the nature of your emergency and your intentions.'

'Dukhan Leader, I've got four airplanes approaching at five o'clock low,' I said. 'Is that you and your flight?'

'Affirmative, Wolf. We will be joining up with you. This is not a hot pass. We repeat, this is not a hot pass.'

'I intend to stay in neutral airspace over international water,' I said. 'I am not an aggressor. I will make no attempt to evade.'

The commander broke his flight into two elements: one fighter on either side of me, the other two high and upsun as reserves in case of

195

trouble. The planes were English Lightnings, armed with Firestreak homing missiles and twin Aden .30mm cannons. As the lead ship joined up on my right wing, I could see the green-and-white roundel of the Saudi air force, with the crossed swords and palm tree.

'You are armed, Papa Wolf, and have no identification markings,' the lead pilot said. 'If you deviate from your present course or approach Saudi airspace, I have orders to shoot you down.'

Before I could reply, another voice sounded in my headset.

'Papa Wolf, this is Aswan Red One. You are threatening Egyptian territory. You will vacate immediately or we will open fire.'

I glanced to my left. Four more interceptors were boring in, two high and two low. As soon as the Egyptian commander had delivered his warning to me, he engaged his Saudi counterpart in a rapid-fire exchange of Arabic. When it was over, the Saudi flight pulled discreetly high and to my right. In something of a panic now, I hit the transmit button.

'Aswan Red One, this is Papa Wolf. I say again. This is a Mayday situation. Repeat, Mayday, Mayday. I require immediate contact with any American station for a relay to my command center. I am not violating your territory intentionally; I am not an aggressor. Repeat, this is a Mayday situation. I need to contact Delta One, Delta One.'

'Papa Wolf,' another voice broke in, 'this is Kelim Control. Do you read?'

'Roger, Kelim Control, Go ahead.'

'You are approaching Israeli-controlled air space. You are denied entry. Acknowledge, over.'

'Kelim Control, this is Papa Wolf. I am an American pilot with a priority-one emergency. I urgently request that you contact the Sixth Fleet for a patch with Delta One, over.'

'Papa Wolf, this is Kelim Control. We say again. You are not permitted to enter into Israeli-controlled airspace.'

I felt a pounding of rage.

'Listen to me, goddammit!' I said. 'I've got a highly explosive bomb under my left wing and just about forty minutes of fuel remaining! If somebody doesn't patch me in to Delta One, I'm going to dump this son of a bitch from altitude! Do you copy?'

There was a period of silence. I could see Aswan Red One hanging

196

off my wing, studying the five-hundred-pounder nestled in its rack under the pylon. The Egyptians were flying MIG 23 Flogger B models with Apex air-to-air missiles. There was enough firepower around me to start the next war. I punched the transmit button again and kicked up my decibles.

'Kelim Control, this is Papa Wolf,' I said. 'Did you copy my request for a patch to Delta One, over.'

'Stand by, Papa Wolf. This is Kelim Control. We're working on your patch.'

The next voice that sounded was far away, but clear, authoritative, and with enough of a Southern accent to be unmistakably U.S.

'Attention all aircraft in the northern Red Sea area,' it said. 'This is Dixie Station Commandar, United States Sixth Fleet, assuming control of Papa Wolf. Repeat. This is Dixie Station to all interceptors. We are assuming control of Wolf. Acknowledge, Aswan Red One . . .'

The Egyptian and Saudi flight leaders acknowledged the transmission, but continued to maintain positions flanking me to my left and right. The Israeli control center at Sharm El Sheikh advised the Sixth Fleet commander they were receiving instructions now over a secure land line. Then the American came on again.

'Papa Wolf, how to you read Dixie Station, over?'

'You're coming up loud and clear, Dixie. Do you have contact with Delta One?'

'That's affirmative, Wolf. We want to clear guard channel and go to three-four-zero point zero, acknowledge.'

'Roger, three-four-zero point-zero.'

I switched to the new frequency – along with everyone else in the area who had been monitoring our exchange. Then Campbell came on. There may have been a time in my life when I was happier to hear someone's voice, but if so I don't remember when.

'Papa Wolf, this is Delta One,' he said calmly. 'How do you read?'

'There's some background clutter,' I said, 'but I can copy.'

'We're familiar with your payload. Repeat, we are familiar with your payload. Do you have fuel enough to reach the Israelis at Sharm El Sheikh?'

'I'm not sure,' I said. 'In any case, I can't land until I get rid of the bomb. It's been rigged to explode if I lower the gear or fire the ejection seat.'

He was silent for a moment. Then he crackled on again.

'Do you know what type of fuse you're carrying?'

'It's a Mark 904 with a standard arming wire. There's also a hydrometric detonator.'

'Papa Wolf, this is Kelim Control. We understand your situation and are cooperating with Delta One to help resolve it. Can you give us the setting on the detonator?'

'I'll need authorization before I can reply,' I said.

Campbell broke in. Speaking rapidly and succinctly, he said he had received my message out of Izmir and had tracked me as far as the island of Arkis. There he had picked up the survivors of the fire fight, on board the cabin cruiser Farmer had used. They had told him, finally, what kind of bomb I would be carrying. They didn't know what the target would be. Campbell's best guess had been Jerusalem or Tel Aviv. He had brought the Israelis in at once. It had taken only minutes for Mossad, their intelligence arm, to brief Kelim Control in the southern Sinai.

'Tell Kelim whatever they want to know,' he said. 'We're on board a helicopter and heading your way, but we won't be able to reach you inside the time frame. Meanwhile, maintain your present heading and set your throttle for maximum endurance.'

'Roger, Delta One,' I said. 'I'm at those settings now.'

'The Sudanese report a shootdown off their coast north of Dunjunab. Was the casualty part of your flight?'

'That's correct,' I said. 'The casualty was a bad guy.'

'We acknowledge that,' Campbell said. 'Can you give us the coordinates of the launch site?'

I hesitated, thinking of Khadija and how vulnerable she would be in any assault on the camp. When it became clear Amadi and I were not going to return, I knew she and her people would make a run for Libya. At least that way she would have a chance.

'That's negative on the launch site,' I said. 'Stand by One. Kelim Control, do you read Papa Wolf?'

'We read you, Wolf.'

'The setting on the underwater detonator is thirty feet. We're talking about a pretty big bang here. Can't you just give me a piece of desert where I can dump this thing off?'

'You are still denied permission to enter our airspace,' Kelim replied. 'Stand by for instructions.'

'Matt, this is Delta One,' Campbell said. 'We're negotiating right now with both Egypt and Saudi Arabia. They're convening their heads of state. As soon as something breaks, we'll let you know. The Israelis are opposed to a land drop. They think you can handle it another way.'

'That's swell,' I said. 'However we handle it, we're going to have to do it in a hurry.'

He asked me to give him my estimated time for remaining in the air.

'Thirty minutes,' I said.

And we were counting.

Chapter Thirty-Five

Sunlight was flooding the cockpit. I caught a glimpse of white under the gunsight. Somebody had folded an envelope and tucked it there. My name was printed across its surface in strong block letters. When I opened it, I found Bock's St. Christopher medal and a brief message:

> **Mateus**
>   **If things do not work out for me, please get
> this to Colette.**
>   **Au revoir, Mon Ami**

I closed the medal in my hand, felt a wave of emotion that gave way finally to laughter.

Dutchman, I thought, you'd have bloody well loved this. Tooling along up here with less than thirty minutes' worth of fuel while seven miles below the heads of three states that have never been able to agree on anything are trying to decide who should receive the five-kiloton blast. The Egyptians will suggest the bomb be dropped on Saudi Arabia. The Saudis will point to the Israelis. The Israelis will point to the Red Sea. It's going to be the old game of hot potato and musical chairs.

Oh yes, I want to go through the door.

But after you, Alphonse.

I remembered how Campbell had laughed when the two of us had been locked up and left for dead in the boatswain's store of the *Lygarius*. I laughed that way now. Maybe, like Campbell, it was the only way I could think of to get the tension out.

'Papa Wolf, this is Kelim Control, do you copy, over?'

'Roger, Kelim.'

'We are hooked into a computer and will need data from you. We understand the bomb fuse is a Mark 904 with a standard arming wire?'

'That's correct.'

'Can you give us a close estimate on the safe separation time?'

'I'd say thirty to forty seconds.'

'Copy that. Stand by, Wolf.'

Safe separation time was the span in seconds from the moment the bomb was released to the moment the fuse was armed. While the bomb was mounted on the aircraft, a thin wire prevented the small wind-driven propeller on the nose of the fuse from revolving. When the bomb was released – either conventionally or by means of the tossing maneuver – the wire pulled free, thereby allowing the fuse propeller to revolve in the wind. After a preset number of revolutions a plunger would close, completing the fuse circuit and allowing the contact fuse to detonate the bomb when it impacted the ground.

I was trying to decide why the Israelis wanted the fuse information when Kelim came back on the air.

'We're sending a commando group in two patrol boats to a zone of open water ten miles due south of the Sinai, Wolf. They are equipped with nets and pontoons and will establish a target for you spanning an area approximately eighty by two hundred and thirty feet. We think you should be able to come in very low at minimum speed and jettison the bomb safely into the water. We'll give you the precise coordinates as soon as the target is in place –'

'You don't understand,' I said. 'The plane I'm flying has been boobytrapped. I can't jettison the bomb from the cockpit. If I try to do that, it's going to explode. Ditto if I lower the gear or try to eject. The only way I can get it off the pylon is to do a pitch-up. The bomb is set to release automatically at forty-one point eight degrees.'

I was told to stand by again. The clock on the instrument panel said I had twenty minutes left. I wasn't laughing anymore. Things were getting dicey as hell. I could see the Egyptian fighters flying in close formation to my left, the Saudis to my right. They had more fuel than I did, and a lot more firepower. As long as I maintained a straight and level course toward the Sinai, it looked as if I was going to be all right. Any departure from that and they had their orders to shoot me down, bomb or no bomb.

I started considering the trigonometry that would be required if I agreed to try the Israeli solution. The setting dialed into the release mechanism was fixed. That could only be changed when the plane was on the ground. Other factors were variable: the initial point where I would begin my pitch-up, the entry speed into the maneuver, and the number of Gs I would pull. Hakim's mission had called for a four-G pitch up, entered at exactly four hundred knots. Allowing for pertinent atmospheric conditions, the bomb would lob the calculated distance from release point to impact.

But it was one thing when the target consisted of a large compound like the Honeycomb; another when it measured a scant 80 by 230 feet. I would have to come in on the water with just enough speed to reach the required angle without stalling, then toss the bomb close enough to reach the nets before the safe separation time was up: thirty to forty seconds. If the bomb was in the air longer than that it would be armed and would explode on impact. If I missed the nets altogether, the bomb would detonate seconds later at a depth of thirty feet. Either way, I would go up with the mushroom cloud.

The hell with it. I needed exactly what I had told them I needed from the start: a couple of hundred square miles of sand where I could dump the bomb from altitude, get down, and go home.

I pressed the mike button and got hold of Campbell.

'Listen,' I said. 'We're out of time on this. If I could pickle the bomb off, the Israeli plan would be fine; but I can't. All I can do is toss it. Before I do that, I'm going to need an empty place for a drop zone, and somebody's going to have to call these interceptors off.'

When Campbell came on, he sounded tense.

'The Egyptians and Israelis are adamant,' he said. 'They refuse to authorize a nuclear explosion over any land area they control. The Saudis are willing to consider the possibility, but before they make a decision they want further reassurance the bomb isn't even more destructive than we say it is.'

'How long is it going to take for you to get them their reassurance?'

'Matt, we're doing all we can. Don't tie me up on this. I'll get back to you as soon as I have something.'

'Papa Wolf, this is Kelim Control. We have a computer readout for a low-speed, soft toss into the nets. Are you ready to copy, over?'

Reluctantly, I took the pencil from my kneeboard and told Kelim to go ahead.

202

He gave me the data. They had calculated my gross weight on approach to the target at 12,850 pounds and assumed a two-G pullup from sea level with 150 knots indicated at a release point of 41.8 degrees. My release altitude would be 1,800 feet, toss distance 3,006 feet, time of flight 16.8 seconds.

'Are you allowing for air density and temperature?'

'That's affirmative. We'll update the weather input as we go.'

'What's the entry speed into the pullup?'

'Two hundred and five knots.'

'Can your radar tell me when I'm exactly three thousand six feet from the nets?'

'We're cooperating on that with an Egyptian patrol boat in the area. Their call sign is Blue Water One. They're of the Nyrat class, with excellent shipboard missile-tracking radar. They'll give you a countdown through your approach to your precise pullup point.'

I wasn't sold. Not even a little. One glitch in the computer input and all bets would be off. I wanted time to think, but there wasn't any. Kelim fed me the coordinates for the initial point, and I punched them into the INS, along with the location of the nets. I had less than sixty miles to go. I called Campbell again.

'What do the Saudis say?' I asked.

'They've authorized one drop zone, three hundred miles east of your position –'

'Jesus Christ!' I shouted. 'I'm down to four hundred pounds of fuel! If I'm lucky, I've got about ten fucking minutes in the air!'

'Are you willing to try for the nets?'

'What happens if I'm not?'

'We're afraid there's going to be an incident,' Campbell said.

'You mean these interceptors are going to blow my ass off, don't you?'

He was silent. Two of the Egyptian fighters had already dropped back into my five-o'clock position. I felt like a mouse crawling down the barrel of an elephant gun. Give me the chance to do it over, I thought, and I'd say the hell with the Saudi royal line and tuck this bomb right in their knickers.

'All three countries are willing to let you try for the nets,' Campbell said.

'You're talking eighty by two hundred and thirty feet!' I said.

203

'You've hit smaller targets, using the same technique.'

'*One* time!' I said. 'That was a gun emplacement on the Trail in Laos. And if you've seen the report you'll know I had to make *two* passes!'

I released the transmit button and began to swear. What they were asking me to do was like trying to score a basket, underhanded, from the far end of the court. If I missed, the game was over.

The Saudi flight commander had pulled up along my right side and was peering in at me as if he was curious to know what I was going to do.

I was still looking for options when my engine flamed out.

According to the gauges, I had over three hundred pounds of fuel left, but when I went through the restart procedure, nothing happened. The noise in the cockpit diminished as the engine continued to unwind. In a few brief moments, the F-86 converted from a jet-powered airplane to a glider, I did some fast calculations. At an altitude of seven miles, a glide ratio of 13 to 1, holding 185 knots of airspeed, I would have a range of eighty-six miles.

According to the INS, I was now exactly fifty-two miles out from the nets.

Chapter Thirty-Six

I contacted Kelim Control, explained the flameout situation, and established my glide. As I did, I saw my fighter escorts extend their speed brakes and throttle back. Everything geared down then to a sort of tumbling slow motion while I tried to compute my chances of tossing the bomb with nothing more than glide speed. Numbers swirled giddily in my brain. My pencil seemed to float in my hand. An almost fatal interlude passed before I realized I was losing oxygen.

My cabin pressurization depended on the engine. When the engine flamed out, the pressure had begun to lower from eight thousand feet to my current altitude of over thirty thousand feet.

I glanced at my oxygen gauge. It read zero.

Abruptly, I put the F-86 into a sharp descent. The Egyptian flight commander came through my headset, demanding to know what was wrong. I told him, grunting out the explanation, continuing to hold the plane in its dive. There was a jumble of radio traffic. Then a familiar voice crackled in my ear.

'Matt, this is Campbell. Is there a bail-out bottle on your chute?'

'No, negative.'

'You've got to stick with it then. Get below twenty thousand.'

'I'm trying to, but I'm fuzzing out.'

I felt giddy and euphoric. Nothing mattered anymore. Campbell screamed in my ear.

'Stick with it, mister! Get it down!'

I tried to keep my eyes pegged on the altimeter. The numbers wandered and blurred, then sharpened again. When they showed eighteen thousand, I could feel my brain beginning to clear. I came out of the dive with 380 knots indicated. The interceptors had followed me down. I reestablished my glide path and checked the INS. I was now forty-three miles out from the nets.

'Papa Wolf, this is Kelim Control. Are you breathing easier?'

'Roger that,' I said.

'Are you ready to give the nets a try?'

'If I understand what you've been telling me, it looks like that's all I've got.'

'Good,' Kelim replied. 'We're running the problem through our computer again, this time using zero thrust on your airplane. Stand by.'

I could see the coast of Sinai, dead ahead, and the specks of the two patrol boats. The air overhead was streaked with the contrails of fighters orbiting: still too far away to be sure, but probably Israelis, scrambled to see to it I did not enter their airspace.

'Papa Wolf, this is Kelim. We have the revised data.'

The cockpit was getting warm. Sweat was stinging my eyes.

'Go ahead, Kelim,' I said.

'Your toss distance is now three-zero-eight-nine, your pullup speed two-three-zero knots, you release altitude one-five-five-zero feet, do you copy, over.'

'I copy,' I said. Then the Egyptian boat with the radar picked up.

'This is Blue Water One to Wolf. We have you on missile track. You are just over four minutes from pullup. We will begin your countdown at two minutes. Please acknowledge, over.'

'That's affirmative, Blue Water One. Is the target area clear?'

'Wolf, this is Kelim Control. The nets are in place and the patrol boats are pulling away. Six of our commandoes are staying in the water with the pontoons to keep them from fouling up. Otherwise, the target area will be clear.'

For me, it was a big 'otherwise'; six good men bobbing in a small patch of the Red Sea, gambling their collective lives that when I finally tossed the bomb, I wouldn't miss. If I needed any more determination to give it my best shot, their presence in the target area gave it to me.

Blue Water One continued the count. I eased the nose down to gain airspeed. I wanted to level on the water five hundred feet short of the pullup point, with an indicated speed of 235.

At altitude, I had felt as if I were gliding at a slow, almost sluggish rate of speed. Now, as I came down over the water, it felt as if my engine had kicked in again. I was racing toward the nets, having

206

long since reached the point of no return. The interceptors peeled away from me on either side. I moved the mode selector from GUN to BOMB and flicked the master switch on. Blue Water One continued the count. When I leveled on the deck, my shadow skimmed to my left, a sleek, rippling silhouette.

Two seconds from pullup, my airspeed was 238. When Blue Water One gave me the final word, I had 232. Since flameout, I had been operating on battery power only, with most of my gauges out.

I pulled back on the stick and held two Gs by the manual G-meter on the panel. I kept my peripheral vision on the horizon to be sure my wings stayed level. As the F-86 pitched up and came through 41.8 degrees, I heard the sound of the cartridges firing and felt the airplane become lighter as the bomb left the pylon and began its long arc toward the nets.

From then on, it was Katy bar the door.

I jammed the stick forward to zero G, banked right to avoid the target area, and let the plane rise as far as it could. At two thousand feet, I trimmed the nose down and rolled level. Ducking my head, I raised the right armrest on the ejection seat and blew the canopy. I heard a loud bang and then a roar. The canopy disappeared from around my head. The wind blast in the open area was terrific – like a firestorm of a five-kiloton bomb.

I slid my feet back from the rudder pedals into the stirrups that were attached to the seat, put my head back against the head rest, squeezed the trigger that had been exposed by the upraised armrest. My last view in the cockpit was of the airspeed indicator quivering at ninety-five knots.

I felt rather than heard the explosive charge under me, driving the seat up the rails and into the clear sky. Punching out at this slow speed, the ejection sequence was easy. I didn't tumble, and had plenty of time to undo my lap belt and push away from the seat itself.

I stabilized myself in the air, face down, reached for my rip cord and pulled it. The pilot chute sprang out, pulling the main chute after it. I heard a *whumping* sound, and felt a strong jerk against my harness.

Everything's Jake, I thought. My risers are clear, no tears in the silk, and that bloody bomb didn't go off.

I looked around from my place in the sky. To the east, I could see the F-86 just nosing over into its final dive. To the north, the two patrol boats were streaking through the water, one going in the direction of the nets, the other heading for the place where I would splash down.

I grinned.

Then I began to laugh.

'Hey, Bock!' I shouted, as if he were hanging from his own chute, drifting down beside me toward the hospitable sea.

'We made it!' I yelled at him. 'By God, we made it!'

Chapter Thirty-Seven

That night, I was sitting in the main salon of the *Cri du Coeur* as she cruised from the island of Malta, north toward Sicily. Campbell was in the salon with me. So was R. J. Coyle.

After a debriefing with the Israelis, Campbell and I had hopped a military transport from Sharm El Sheikh to the RAF base at Malta. Coyle had been waiting for us there. We had had our cocktails and supper on board the yacht as she put out from the harbor. Now we were having brandy and cigars.

The sliding windows of the salon were open; the air was tart and cool. There were fresh tulips in the crystal vase. We sat under the glow of an overhead lamp that swayed gently with the motion of the boat. Coyle looked tanned and fit in his blue blazer and clean white ducks. Campbell looked drawn with fatigue. I held my brandy without tasting it.

'This was an excellent piece of work,' Coyle said. 'Truly it was. I'm not that easily impressed, but I'll tell you quite honestly this time I am.'

'It was close,' Campbell said. 'According to the men in the water, the bomb landed just twenty feet short of the far end of the nets.'

'You didn't tell me that,' I said.

He smiled tiredly.

'I didn't want you to worry,' he said.

'I had the shakes for a while after the patrol boat picked me up,' I said, 'but I'm fine now.'

'Then I can tell you the rest. The Sudanese Air Force finally located and destroyed the camp that was used as the launch site. They caught Hakim's convoy in the desert and strafed it. According to the initial reports, there were no survivors.'

I was silent. Initial reports had a way of turning out wrong. Until I knew for a certainty that Khadija had died, I would go on believing

209

she was alive. There had been too much death on this one, too many good people who wouldn't be coming back. Khadija and I hadn't loved each other; there had been no time for that, no way under the circumstances we could have discovered whether or not our feelings could go that deep. Operating on little more than instincts I will always believe are essentially female, she had made a determination that I was a man she could trust; and once she had made that determination, she had never looked back. The stand she had taken against her family had been based on principle and had required a standard of courage as high as any I knew. By arming my plane, she had done everything she could to help abort her father's irrational plan. Yet in the end, she had remained at his side.

Campbell knew why I had withheld the location of the launch site. At Sharm El Sheikh, I had told him everything.

'When you made your feelings clear about Khadija,' he said now, 'I thought it was better not to tell you about the strafing. At least not until you had time to rest.'

'I appreciate the consideration,' I said, looking pointedly at Coyle. 'I slept for six hours on the plane. I'm ready to hear everything now.'

I watched as a brief smile crossed Coyle's delicate features. His hand was steady as he poured himself another brandy. When he was through, he raised the snifter thoughtfully and looked at Campbell.

'I predicted this would happen,' he said.

'I don't know where I stand in the IQ sweepstakes,' I said. 'But I'm no dunce. Unless I've forgotten how to count, our friend Mahmet Pazar diverted a grand total of *one* of your INS systems from the warehouse at Esenboga and sold it to Hakim. That doesn't strike me as a serious threat to your reputation in the international market-place as a reliable company. It also doesn't strike me as justification for hiring a mercenary pilot at two grand a day plus expenses.'

Coyle sipped his brandy. The yacht made its steady headway under a clear night sky and through light swells. Campbell shifted his angular frame uncomfortably, as if the salon, which was quite large, had suddenly gotten too small for him.

'You're getting into an area that's very sensitive,' he said. 'It might be better for all of us if you would agree to let it go.'

'No,' I said. 'I won't agree to that. I lost one good friend on this one, and if it's true there were no survivors in the Sudan, I lost another.

I'm up to here with bullshit and hidden agendas. If Bob Coyle wants to run them by me, that's his business. But by God, Campbell, I expect a whole lot more from you.'

Campbell stood up. I had never talked to him this way before. He was angry, but I could see he was worried too – and that whatever his concern was, it went beyond anything personal that might lie between us.

'For the last several years,' he said, 'the Agency has been torn apart, by the press, by the Congress, by the radicals, even by some of our own . . . it's gotten to the point where we can hardly function at all. Our budgets have been slashed. Our charter has been amended. The names and locations of our agents are published in the paper. We're the laughingstock of the world. *Yes*, we've made our mistakes. There isn't an agency of any government that hasn't. But we are in the middle of a very dirty, very deadly game here, with our survival as a free people at stake. The communists and the fanatics don't give a damn about playing by the rules. They play to win. We've got classified material in our files right now that would scare John Q. Citizen out of his undershorts if he had access to it. I'm not talking about infringements on his liberty. I'm talking about what the Russians are prepared to do in the Persian Gulf, in Africa, in South America, in the Indian Ocean. I'm talking about the economic evisceration of this country: not war, Matt – that may come too – but *economics*.'

He bent toward me, blue eyes intense.

'Where do you think we would be tonight,' he said, 'if Hakim's strike on the Honeycomb had succeeded? Do you have any idea how quickly Saudi Arabia would have been taken over by forces hostile to us? Do you know the Russians are already in South Yemen, getting ready to build pens for their atomic subs? Do you know where we would be *without* Saudi oil? Dammit, Matt, I don't have to tell you any of this. You already know it. We've been holding our breath waiting for the first terrorist group to get hold of a nuclear device and use it against a critical target. How many times have you heard people say, "It won't happen"? Well, this time it almost did; and sooner or later it almost certainly will. The only way we have of stopping it is with a strong intelligence net and the ability to conduct clandestine operations when they are, without any question, in the interest of national security.'

'I don't have any trouble with what you're saying,' I replied. 'What I don't understand is where Bob Coyle fits in.'

'He's what we call in the trade a deep pocket. When we need more money than we've got in the budget, we go to him.'

'Are you telling me a private U.S. citizen is bankrolling covert operations for a government agency?'

'Yes. That's exactly what I'm telling you.'

'Well, I'm going to have just one *hell* of a lot of trouble with that,' I said.

'Do you have trouble with the fact that just before World War II, Roosevelt and Churchill operated a complex intelligence network without the knowledge or approval of the Congress or Parliament? And that if they hadn't done that, we probably would have lost the war?'

'Of course I'm aware of that,' I said. 'But Roosevelt and Churchill were heads of state.'

'So is the current President.'

I looked up in disbelief, at Coyle and then at my father-in-law.

'The arrangement is closely held,' Campbell said. 'If it became public, the President would face impeachment.'

'Then why is he risking it?'

'I think I can answer that,' Coyle said. 'He knows we are moving through very dangerous times, and he believes in Campbell's integrity.'

'If I had known this was the answer to my original question,' I said, 'I wouldn't have asked it.'

'I'm glad you did,' Campbell said. 'We've never kept much from each other. I haven't enjoyed keeping this.'

'Did you know from the start that Farmer had a nuclear device in that crate on board the freighter?'

'No,' Campbell said. 'But we had our suspicions.'

I looked at Coyle.

'What's in this arrangement for you?' I asked.

He smiled.

'I'm a patriot, Matthew,' he said. 'I'm also very practical. When the country is threatened, my business is threatened. Campbell and I, as you know, are very old friends. When he needed financing for this sort of thing, it was quite natural that he came to me.'

No, I thought. There's got to be more. With you, there always is.

I léft the salon shortly after that, and went onto the afterdeck of the *Cri du Coeur*. Coyle's consort, Dominique, was there. She stood leaning against the wall, looking out past the wake, back toward Malta. Her hair was wavy and auburn, the way Khadija's had been.

'*Bon soir, colonel!*' she said happily.

'*Bon soir, madame,*' I replied.

'Is it true you must leave us in Sardinia?'

'Yes,' I said. 'There's an air base there. I'll catch a hop to Zurich.'

'To visit with your son?'

'Yes.'

'Robert speaks so highly of him. He says young Brian has great courage, and will one day be whole again.'

'I pray for that,' I said.

'You must come visit us in Paris,' she said. 'We will be there again in late summer.'

'I'll be on my farm in Virginia by then,' I said. 'But I appreciate the invitation. Maybe some other time.'

'I have been practicing my piano every day since you left,' she said. 'Do you remember the Chopin?'

'Yes,' I said. 'You played it well.'

She smiled.

'I will go and play it now,' she said. 'Before I sleep.'

I stood alone at the rail for a moment. Then Maul came out to join me. He had on a pair of white tennis shorts and a blue short-sleeved shirt with a gold ship's wheel stitched over the pocket. His legs were knobby with muscle, thatched with hair, and slightly bowed. His sneakers were the old-fashioned kind – no racing stripes or super soles. They squeaked like a couple of mice as he came onto the deck.

'Hear you had some action,' he said.

'We could have used you,' I said. 'We got flanked by some bad guys on the desert. One more gun would have made the difference.'

'This Dutch guy you were with – he was good material?'

'The best.'

Maul nodded.

'I lost most of an A-team once in the Highlands near Pleiku,' he

213

said. 'They say you get over it.'

'No,' I said. 'You bury it. But it's always there.'

'Yeah, right,' Maul said.

The yacht rolled on a swell. I heard his stomach rumble. He looked down, annoyed.

'I'm going to the galley,' he said, 'to eat some red meat. You hungry?'

'No thanks,' I said. 'If you're up for a drink when you get through, I could go for that.'

'You're on,' he said.

After he left, I stood on the afterdeck, listening to the steady throb of the engines and the distant sound of Dominique playing the Chopin. I could feel Bock's St. Christopher medal in my shirt pocket, a reminder that after Zurich I would be going to Honfleur, where I would have to tell Colette that the man she loved had died.

What would I say about that? I wondered. What would Bock have said?

I knew, of course.

His words would have been the same as the words of Mermoz.

It's worth it.

It's worth the final smashup.

**TODAY IN PAPERBACK.
TOMORROW IN THE PAPERS.**

THE LAST DAYS OF AMERICA

PAUL E. ERDMAN

In 1976 Paul E. Erdman wrote THE CRASH OF '79. Now he predicts THE LAST DAYS OF AMERICA.

A multi-million dollar missile deal is about to collapse. And in America, in 1985, the company must survive.

No matter what the cost.

And suddenly, the life of Frank Rogers, President of the Missile Development Corporation, has a very low price tag.

The events Erdman writes about read like newspaper headlines.

So if you want to read tomorrow's news, read THE LAST DAYS OF AMERICA today.

ADVENTURE THRILLER   0 7221 3350 2   £1.95

Tiger Hunt!
JADE TIGER
Craig Thomas

The bait: a defecting Chinese agent selling secrets.
The trail: every bolt-hole and hide-out from Hong
Kong to Berlin.
The quarry: JADE TIGER
JADE TIGER, the thrilling new masterpiece from
Craig Thomas, finds espionage veteran Kenneth
Aubrey facing his toughest assignment yet. In six
months he could crack the Chinese defector. But he
doesn't have months, he has weeks. Two weeks
before the Berlin Wall is bulldozed into history. Two
weeks to discover the truth behind the network of
misinformation coming his way . . .
JADE TIGER is the story of a race against time, a
chase across three continents. Ranging from the
heart of Communist China to the Australian
Outback. JADE TIGER is classic thriller writing of
the highest order.

ADVENTURE/THRILLER   0 7221 8451 4   £2.25

Don't miss Craig Thomas' other bestsellers:
FIREFOX
SNOW FALCON
RAT TRAP
WOLFSBANE
SEA LEOPARD
also available in Sphere books.

CLIVE CUSSLER
NIGHT PROBE!

May 1914. Two top diplomats hurry home by sea
and rail, each carrying a document of world-
changing importance. Then the liner *Empress of
Ireland* is sunk in a collision, and the 'Manhattan-
Line' express plunges from a shattered bridge –
both dragging their VIP passengers to watery
oblivion. *Tragic coincidence – or conspiracy*?

Three-quarters of a century later a chance
revelation re-opens the question. In the energy-
starved, fear-torn 1980s, those long-lost papers
could destroy whole nations – and Dirk Pitt, the
man who raised the *Titanic*, confronts his biggest
challenge yet. Racing against time, against the
hired killers of enemies and allies alike – and the
horrors of the sea bed – he launches his
revolutionary deep-sea search craft in the hunt for
the documents. 'Night Probe' has begun . . .

ADVENTURE/THRILLER   0 7221 2746 4   **£1.95**

A SELECTION OF BESTSELLERS FROM SPHERE

FICTION

THE MOGHUL	Thomas Hoover	£2.50 ☐
FAR FROM THE SEA	Evan Hunter	£1.75 ☐
A VIEW FROM THE SQUARE	John Trenhaile	£1.95 ☐
THE VEGAS LEGACY	Ovid Demaris	£2.50 ☐
BODIES AND SOULS	Nancy Thayer	£1.95 ☐

FILM & TV TIE-INS

SUPERGIRL	Norma Fox Mazer	£1.75 ☐
INDIANA JONES AND THE TEMPLE OF DOOM	James Kahn	£1.75 ☐
THE IRISH R.M.	E. E. Somerville and Martin Ross	£1.95 ☐
THEY CALL ME BOOBER FRAGGLE	Michaela Muntean	£1.50 ☐
MINDER	Anthony Masters	£1.50 ☐

NON-FICTION

2 PARA FALKLANDS	Major-General John Frost C.B., D.S.O., M.C.	£1.95 ☐
RUNNING FOR FITNESS	Sebastian and Peter Coe	£2.95 ☐
THE FRUIT AND NUT BOOK	Helena Radecka	£6.95 ☐
THE LAST LION	William Manchester	£5.95 ☐
THE ROLLING STONES	Robert Palmer	£7.95 ☐

All Sphere books are available at your local bookshop or newsagent, or can be ordered direct from the publisher. Just tick the titles you want and fill in the form below.

Name _____

Address _____

_____

Write to Sphere Books, Cash Sales Department, P.O. Box 11, Falmouth, Cornwall TR10 9EN

Please enclose a cheque or postal order to the value of the cover price plus:

UK: 45p for the first book, 20p for the second book and 14p for each additional book ordered to a maximum charge of £1.63.

OVERSEAS: 75p for the first book plus 21p per copy for each additional book.

BFPO & EIRE: 45p for the first book, 20p for the second book plus 14p per copy for the next 7 books, thereafter 8p per book.

Sphere Books reserve the right to show new retail prices on covers which may differ from those previously advertised in the text or elsewhere, and to increase postal rates in accordance with the PO.